TARZAN
THE EPIC ADVENTURES

TARZAN
THE EPIC ADVENTURES

R. A. SALVATORE

BASED ON THE TELEPLAY BY BURTON ARMUS

Inspired by **The Return of Tarzan** and **Tarzan at the Earth's Core**
by Edgar Rice Burroughs

A DEL REY® BOOK

BALLANTINE BOOKS · NEW YORK

A Del Rey® Book
Published by Ballantine Books
Copyright © 1996 by EDGAR RICE BURROUGHS, INC.

Trademark TARZAN® Owned by EDGAR RICE BURROUGHS, INC. and
Used by Permission.

All rights reserved under International and Pan-American
Copyright Conventions. Published in the United States by
Ballantine Books, a division of Random House, Inc., New York,
and simultaneously in Canada by Random House of Canada
Limited, Toronto.

http://www.randomhouse.com

Library of Congress Catalog Card Number: 96-96542

ISBN: 0-345-40810-1

Manufactured in the United States of America
First Edition: October 1996
10 9 8 7 6 5 4 3 2 1

To Burton Armus, who did the difficult work.

To Steve Saffel, for thinking of me for this project.

And to Edgar Rice Burroughs, of course.

I humbly stand on the back of a giant.

TARZAN
THE EPIC ADVENTURES

PROLOGUE

He walked across the rolling countryside, the smell of vineyards thick and sweet in his nostrils. He avoided those places, though, the cultivated lands, moving to the forested hillside where there were no houses apparent, where no man had made a claim. This was his place, a place free of the imposed rules of civilization, a place that followed the natural order, simple rules of survival and respect that he could understand.

The air was warm, the breeze gentle, and he heard the sound of a spring stream, bouncing down along the rocks of the hillside.

He made for it, wanting to witness the simple beauty, wanting to see the sparkles of the sun and better hear the song of the dancing water as it thinned and leaped across the stones. He moved around a patch of trees, through some brush and over an outcropping of bare stone. And then he stopped, stunned and dismayed.

The way was blocked by a high fence, a wall of wooden

pickets tied so closely together that he could hardly see the flickers of sunlight dappling the stream beyond them.

It seemed such an odd place for a fence; he couldn't understand who had put it there, or why anyone would want to so block out one of Nature's most graceful creations. The eight-foot-high fence assaulted his sensibilities and seemed to insult the entire hill, but in truth it wasn't much of a barrier to the athletic man. He crouched, his strong leg muscles bunching and tightening, and then he sprang high, catching the top of the pickets and, with an easy pull, maneuvering himself right over them. He landed on the uneven ground on the other side in a graceful and perfectly balanced crouch, his legs absorbing the impact.

The dogs were on him in an instant, fur ruffled, teeth bared. Big dogs, wearing chain collars. Muscled and angry dogs, animals trained by men to kill.

The man locked them with his stare and set his posture accordingly. He showed no fear, for he had none, though the three formidable dogs could easily kill any human.

But they would not attack, he knew, for he would not give them any reason to. Everything about him, his posture, his movements, his stare, even his smell, was unthreatening, and soon enough the dogs stopped growling and began sniffing him curiously, their tails wagging.

He had a way with animals.

But not so much with people, and the next one to greet him, a sour-looking old man with a very big breach-loading shotgun, would be a bigger problem. He knew it immediately as the fellow stepped into view. He studied the old man intently, noted the tension pulling at the many wrinkles, the dull glaze of the eyes, the crooked posture.

The old man yelled at him in French. He understood, but was too amused by this whole unpredictable scenario to immediately respond.

"You speak English, then?" the old man asked in a stilted accent.

He nodded.

"You are on my property," the old man said, motioning at him with the gun barrel. "Unless you are a fool, back over the fence you go!"

"I want to see the stream," he replied. His tone was perfectly calm and steady, a quiet, unthreatening rationale. "I want to feel its chilled waters against my hand, and watch the sun sparkling in tune to its dance."

"It is my stream!" the old man shouted.

The younger man shook his head. "You cannot own—" he started to say, but the look of the old man, eyes growing wide with outrage, stopped him short, warned him that he was in very real danger.

He saw the flash of the muzzle, heard the tremendous thunder as the weapon overwhelmed the sound of Nature's stream. He felt the sudden, burning impact, the explosion of pain and shock.

Tarzan sat up straight in his bed, drenched in sweat. He recalled every moment of the dream, every sight, sound, and smell, for this was not the first night in which he had met the crusty old man with the anger and gun. That old man of his dreams represented the epitome of the people of this world he had somehow stumbled into, the world of society, of civilization, of laws that moved farther and farther from the simple logic of Nature.

These people craved ownership of everything, of gems and

false money; not only of foodstuffs, but of the right to produce the food and hold everyone else hostage for it. Most of all, they craved ownership of land, and to Tarzan that seemed the most perverted thought of all. These barriers they built, fences and walls and hedgerows too thick to pass through, cut up the land into parcels, prevented a man from walking and experiencing the true glory of the world. Who was that old man in the dream to claim ownership of a stream, of that which could not be owned? How, after all, had the man gained ownership of such a parcel? Through what authority? The authority of other men, of a government created by other men?

Tarzan shook his head, unable to comprehend the logic behind it all. What value was a piece of paper scribbled with words claiming ownership? Certainly he had had no say in the transaction. Nor, likely, had any of his ancestors. So where had it begun, by whose authority?

Tarzan rolled to a sitting position at the side of his soft bed—one he had never found comfortable—and dropped his face in his hands. He was out of place here, bound by rules that made no sense to one who had grown up in the free wilds of Africa. The masking clothes, the masking smells of perfume, the masking chatter of incessant conversation—all of it asked him to be someone he was not.

Tarzan looked out the window of his bedroom—and thankfully that window faced away from the great city of Paris, whose skyline assaulted his sensibilities almost as much as the fence blocking the stream. The grounds of the villa, the estate of his friend Paul D'Arnot, were neat and cultivated, with aesthetically pleasing gardens and sculptures. By the measures of society, Tarzan had a fine life here, a life of comfort and luxury, of good wine and well-bred company.

By his measure, every fence, every wall, every hedgerow, formed a jail cell. He liked many of these people, Paul D'Arnot perhaps most of all, but the basic tenets that formed their society brought to him the dreams of the old man with the shotgun.

It was time to go home.

CHAPTER 1

The night air was filled with the scent of spring, the renewal of life, and a gentle rain brushed the budding leaves and flowers and tickled the thickening grass. It gathered in puddles on the paved roadway, creating a spiraling dance of countless rings, waves intersecting waves, bouncing about in rhythmic patterns.

Tarzan watched those rings as he glided past, his steps silent as those of a hunting cat, graceful as the antelope. He pulled his cloak back, that he might feel the rain gently brushing his skin, and his breathing was deep and exaggerated, basking in the smells of spring, an aroma that even the smells of the nearby city could not fully defeat.

He could not hold his solemn mood, though, despite the rings, despite the scents, for he heard the noise of the revelers, the unmistakable chatter of society, and he was reminded that he was far, far from home.

Trance broken, Tarzan continued his walk toward the vast and sprawling estate surrounded by the sweet smell of vineyards. He knew that this villa was the envy of the region, and that this region, the quiet outskirts of Paris, was the envy of many people all over the civilized world.

He simply didn't understand the sentiment. To him the villa, with its stucco walls and solid roof, was more a barrier than a shelter, a place to hide from the sun and stars, and he couldn't understand why any man would wish to shield himself from those delights. He didn't dwell on that thought, though, for it was not his place to judge. He was different; they, these men and women he had come to know as friends, were different from him.

"*Pas plus tard,*" he said quietly. "Not much longer."

So entranced was he with the thought of going home that he was caught by surprise—a rare occurrence indeed!— when a hand landed firmly on his shoulder.

He spun immediately, dropping to a crouch, graceful, cat-like, ready to defend. His sudden, fluid movement startled the man who had touched him.

"*Pardon, monsieur,*" said the man, a gendarme, as he pulled his hand away and cautiously backed a step. "I did not mean to surprise you, but it is very late. Do you have business here?"

"Of course," he replied, relaxing and straightening, dropping his hands to his sides, palms up, in an unthreatening display. "I am staying there," he explained, pointing to the magnificent villa, "at the D'Arnot residence."

The gendarme eyed him curiously, even unconsciously moved his hand closer to the pistol holstered on his hip, a movement the wary Tarzan marked well. If, for some inexplicable reason, the gendarme went for the gun, he would catch the man's hand before it fully closed on the pistol. A shift in weight would pin the gendarme's hand to his hip, a subtle twist of his wrist would take the gun away. It was a simple move, really, one that these people, grown soft from city life, would stare at in amazement, a maneuver for which the vast majority of them would have no defense. But what then? the stranger in this world had to wonder. What might he do with a gendarme's pistol?

"Monsieur D'Arnot?" the gendarme asked, his voice thick with skepticism. "I know Monsieur D'Arnot. Who are you, sir?"

The stranger didn't blink, didn't flinch, at the gendarme's accusing tone, his sparkling eyes staring intently into those of the policeman.

"Tarzan," he replied. *"Je suis Jean Tarzan."*

The gendarme swallowed hard; he had heard the name.

The music, the laughter, the cheers and disappointed groans, assaulted Tarzan as he neared the door to D'Arnot's villa. The house was transformed this night, as it was once every month, into a casino. Paul D'Arnot was Tarzan's friend, as he seemed to be friend to everyone in Paris. More than that, D'Arnot was Tarzan's mentor in his introduction to society, and truly the man who had lived the majority of his life in the jungle could not have asked for a better instructor. For though he played by society's rules, D'Arnot was, Tarzan believed, of temperament similar to his own, a man of high standards and moral character, though those morals often turned on precepts foreign to Tarzan.

Tarzan's smile widened as he considered the dapper D'Arnot, a man he could not help but love, despite their obvious differences. Bolstered by that thought, he pushed open the door, handed his cloak to the attendant standing nearby, and walked into the light and the tumult.

He spotted D'Arnot almost immediately, a cane hooked over his arm, his dimpled smile, as usual, ear-to-ear. Paul D'Arnot was not a big man, standing just a few inches over five feet and weighing at least fifty pounds less than Tarzan's more than two-hundred-pound frame. His hair was yellow, but paling toward white, and longer than the cuts worn by most of the other gentlemen, though not nearly as long as Tarzan's thick and wavy brown hair. D'Arnot was closer to fifty than to forty, and his face showed the weathering of those years. But his smile and his eyes certainly did not. For all his exposure to society, Paul D'Arnot retained the enthusiasm and lust for life of a young man. Perhaps that was why Tarzan so loved his company.

In this room, Paul D'Arnot provided an oasis for him, a fact driven home clearly to Tarzan as he moved across the crowded floor and felt the curious gazes following his every step. He carried himself differently than these people, and not just because he was taller than most, or that he was lacking the softness a life of luxury had placed upon the bodies of the gentlemen. His ponytail certainly stood out in a room where most of the men wore their hair shortly and neatly cropped, but it was more the intensity of Tarzan's gaze, his darting, alert eyes, and the sheer grace of his stride, the natural perfection of his posture, his muscles moving in perfect fluidity, that set him apart.

He walked by one group of ladies who stared openly, even turning their heads to regard him from every possible angle as he passed. "A monkey," he heard a man standing with one of the women whisper, and that only made Tarzan smile all the more, for he, unlike the speaker, did not consider the words an insult.

"Ah, Jean!" D'Arnot exclaimed when he spotted Tarzan. He extended his hand for a warm shake and patted Tarzan on the shoulder. "I thought you would stay out all the night."

Tarzan didn't reply, but his look showed that to be a desirable suggestion.

"No matter," D'Arnot continued, "we will play until the dawn!"

Tarzan's smirk turned into a frown.

D'Arnot, hardly surprised, merely nodded in the direction of the ladies, who were still staring at Tarzan, to the obvious dismay of the impatient gentlemen standing near to them. "Much better than the jungle, eh, *mon ami*?"

"Different, D'Arnot," Tarzan replied, clearing his throat. "But sometimes very much the same."

D'Arnot gave a chuckle and offered a salute to the ladies, who finally turned away. "You fight civilization and your rightful title of Lord Greystoke with the tenacity of the wild animals you left behind in Africa," he said. "Why not just accept your position, *mon ami,* and marry the woman you love?"

It was a question that D'Arnot asked of Tarzan every day, and one that never failed to give the strong man pause. "There is always the possibility that you are right," he admitted.

"You see?" D'Arnot pressed.

"I do miss Jane," Tarzan said with all sincerity. "But I did right in telling her to go on with her life, for it is the life that she needs. She was raised in your society, a world too different from my own. I am not the right choice for her."

"Presumption," D'Arnot put in without hesitation. It was rare that he got Jean Tarzan to admit so much, so openly, and he sensed that the stubborn man might be vulnerable. D'Arnot wanted nothing more than for his dear friend to accept and enjoy this new and, in D'Arnot's estimation, far better life. "Have you bothered to inquire of Jane how she feels about it?"

Tarzan gave a great and tired sigh, his expression showing D'Arnot clearly that he had again reached a dead end for his hopeful reasoning.

"Ah, but you can take the man out of the jungle," D'Arnot replied with a sigh of his own.

Nikolas Rokoff's attempt to be charming ended abruptly as his companion, who was laughing and shaking with exaggerated movements over Rokoff's last witticism, splashed him with red wine.

The lady tittered and glided away, sweeping down the stairs of the balcony to the main floor of the ballroom, leaving Nikolas Rokoff red on his shirt and red in the face. His huge companion, Alexis Paulvitch, clumsily moved at him with a handkerchief, spouting apologies, and spilling even more wine with every jerky movement.

"Back! Back!" Rokoff growled at him, and though Paulvitch was easily a hundred pounds heavier than Rokoff and looked as if he could break Rokoff in two, there could be no doubt as to who dominated this relationship. Paulvitch was a massive man, thick-limbed and round in the torso, and with hardly any neck to speak of. Even his head, with light hair that was no more than tiny stubble, seemed to bulge with muscle. He looked out of sorts in his light gray suit, a gentleman's wrapping on a street brawler's frame. Rokoff, by comparison, was trim and quite dapper in his darker suit, a garment of perfect cut for his tall frame and solid shoulders. His hair was brown and neatly trimmed, and he fit well into the society crowd. Except for his eyes; those who looked closer at Nikolas Rokoff recognized an intensity in his dark eyes that hinted at danger. Most of D'Arnot's guests were jovial sorts, fortunate people living in luxury, but Rokoff's eyes seemed more the orbs of one who felt as if he had not gotten his due in life.

"I did not mean . . ." Alexis Paulvitch stuttered. He moved for Rokoff again with the handkerchief and got promptly slapped away.

"Back," Rokoff said again, this time in low and calm threatening tones, and Paulvitch, like a beaten dog, slid away.

"You make of me a spectacle," Rokoff fumed, slapping futilely at the prominent stain. "How am I to conduct my business . . ."

Paulvitch paid no attention to Rokoff's typical tirade, his thoughts arrested by the sight of the pair entering the villa, an older gentleman with a beautiful young woman on his arm. The man's once-black hair was turning to gray, the skin about his handsome face was beginning to sag, but he held himself with perfect posture and did not appear decrepit in any way. The woman alongside him stole glances from every man she passed, and with good reason. Her dark brown hair was done up fashionably, tied in back with gem-studded ribbons that matched her lavender gown. Her bright eyes, normally light blue in hue, now seemed to reflect the color of that gown, and her smile was truly brilliant and truly infectious. Her features were classic French, angular yet gentle, and her skin was smooth and light golden, accented beautifully by a white silken scarf she wore draped over one shoulder.

Paulvitch dared to interrupt Rokoff, who was looking down again and patting his shirt, by dropping his huge hand on Rokoff's shoulder.

Rokoff glared up at him.

"Collette de Coude and her father have just arrived," Paulvitch explained, somewhat frantically.

Rokoff quieted immediately, his hungry gaze snapping down to the lower floor and locking on the pair. "Then it will be tonight," he said.

"You are sure that Count de Coude has it?"

Rokoff's glare fell over him once more. "If I were not sure, would I continue this foolish game?" he asked, his tone showing that he was fighting hard to control his anger. "And would I keep you beside me?"

Paulvitch focused his gaze on Collette de Coude and worked hard to ignore Rokoff. Every word Rokoff spoke to him was filled with disdain and contempt, though he could have lifted him up and squeezed the life out of him with hardly an effort.

But that Alexis Paulvitch would not do. Like the powerful dogs kept by the gentlemen back in their homeland of Russia, Paulvitch was the servant, and Nikolas Rokoff, the son of the tsar, the unquestionable master.

She wore too much of the fashionable face paint, and her scent came from a pretty bottle, but Tarzan could see the bone structure under that paint, and the light in her eyes was surely real. Also, he could smell her—not the perfume, but the woman—and the scent was far from unpleasant. She was beautiful, undeniably so, and Tarzan could only imagine how much more beautiful she would appear were she not trapped in this supposed "fashion."

Her escort was an elderly man, sharply dressed and holding himself so straight that his posture would rate an eleven on a scale of ten. Still, what he lacked in fluidity, he more than made up for with elegance, and his smile, unlike those of so many of D'Arnot's guests, seemed genuine.

"*Bon soir, Henri!*" D'Arnot exclaimed when he noticed the duo. "*Comment allez-vous?*"

"*Tres bien, merci, Paul,*" the man responded kindly, sharing a warm smile and handshake with D'Arnot.

D'Arnot took the young woman's hand and kissed it, then turned to Tarzan. "Allow me to present Count Henri de Coude," he said, "and his charming daughter Collette."

The count gave a slight bow and extended his hand to Tarzan. The older man's grip was strong and sure, and Tarzan nodded his approval.

"Jean Tarzan," D'Arnot introduced him, and it was apparent by the brightening expression on Collette de Coude's face that she had heard the name before.

"My pleasure," Tarzan said to Count de Coude, eyeing his daughter all the while.

"But it is mine," Count de Coude said emphatically. "I have been looking forward to meeting you, sir. Paul has told me so much of your most fascinating past."

Collette gave a slight nod of assent, and a somewhat naughty smirk that caught Tarzan off guard. He was used to the titters and even leers of these society women, but somehow it was more intriguing, and more surprising, coming from this young woman. She offered him her hand, and he took it and brought it to his lips gently, his eyes locking with hers.

"I am a collector of African artifacts," Count de Coude went on, speaking to Tarzan. "A hobby I do hope to expand into a business venture in the very near future. Perhaps you and I might discuss this at length at a more convenient hour."

Tarzan gave a polite nod, though in truth he had no desire to be part of any business venture.

"Collette, *ma petite*," Count de Coude said, clearing his throat and exchanging a grin with D'Arnot, for it was obvious that there was some tingling electricity between the two younger people, "do show Monsieur Tarzan my latest acquisition."

Still locking Tarzan with her stare, Collette demurely slid the silken scarf from her delicate shoulders.

"I know very little about business," Tarzan began, a bit embarrassed by Collette's bold movement and trying hard not to be obvious. "And . . ." The word was lost in his throat, and no others could get past the lump that suddenly material- ized there. Collette's bare neck and shoulders were certainly beautifully formed, and the low cut of her dress invited any man's imagination, but Tarzan was not looking at her at all, not at her body, not at her sparkling eyes, but only at the six- sided amulet hanging about her neck, crystalline and glis- tening as if with an inner light of its own.

"A unique piece, is it not?" Count de Coude said proudly.

"How did you come by this particular amulet?" Tarzan

asked, and the sudden seriousness, even urgency, of his tone gave Count de Coude pause. He and Collette exchanged curious looks.

"Do you know it?" the older gentleman asked.

"I have knowledge of it, yes," Tarzan admitted, and again the count and his daughter looked at each other with surprise.

"Tell me, then," Count de Coude said. "You must tell me! What is its value?"

Tarzan shook his head. "Your meaning of 'value' and my own are not the same, I fear."

"Monetary value?" The count pressed. "Estimate a monetary value for it."

"Impossible," Tarzan replied. "It is impossible to place a monetary value on such a treasure. It can be considered priceless, in ways that you cannot imagine."

Count de Coude gave a chuckle. "Tell me, Paul, does your friend always speak in so cryptic a manner?" he said to D'Arnot, his tone less serious, for he was perceptive enough to understand that he would get little more information from Jean Tarzan at this time.

"Enough of business," Collette declared, taking her father's cue. She moved over and hooked her arm about Tarzan's. "I will take custody of this mysterious man while you two make your usual donations to the card game."

"Ah, but Jean," D'Arnot protested, "will you not be joining us?"

Tarzan's look was purely incredulous; D'Arnot had known him for a long time, and never once had he shown any interest in such games.

"Of course he will not," Collette announced. "Monsieur

Tarzan is much too civilized for a game of cards. Roulette is the better choice for him."

Tarzan's expression didn't change, but it shifted from D'Arnot to Collette.

She, however, wasn't waiting for his assent. She tugged him along on her merry way.

"Perhaps you should never have educated her, Henri," D'Arnot said with a chuckle when the young couple had moved off.

"She is her mother's child," Count de Coude replied affectionately. "With a spirit that will not be held back."

"She does not know a woman's place," D'Arnot said, obviously kidding.

"Ah, but she does, I fear," Henri replied without hesitation. "And that place is not what you or I, or so many others, might believe it to be."

D'Arnot gave a laugh. He adored young Collette de Coude, particularly her irreverence toward society's attitudes. Intelligent and opinionated, and always willing to say what was on her mind, she was, by his estimation, many times more intriguing and interesting than the vast majority of society's women, who had been trained in their proper place. "Jean will find this night most interesting," he remarked, and Henri joined him in his laughter.

The two men walked off the other way, turning their attention to the strategies they would employ in their high-stakes card game.

Not far away, another pair of men observed the exchange, but they were not laughing.

"She is wearing the amulet," Paulvitch blurted, then looked around nervously to make sure that no one nearby had heard.

"De Coude is a fool," Rokoff replied, too intent on Collette's pendant to take note of Paulvitch's potential slip—a fact that made Paulvitch sigh with sincere relief. "He has no idea of its value or he would protect it with his very life. Who is this man with Collette? A bodyguard?"

"His name is Jean Tarzan, a guest of Paul D'Arnot's," Paulvitch replied. "They say he was found in the jungles of Africa. Does he mean anything to you?"

Rokoff spun on him with such intensity that the big man backed off a step. "Any man who entertains my fiancée means something to me, you fool!" Rokoff growled. He was also thinking that Tarzan's knowledge of Africa might prove a dangerous thing, for if he recognized that amulet and alerted Count de Coude to its significance . . .

Paulvitch held up his huge hands in a placating manner, trying to defuse Rokoff. "But Nikolas," he blabbered, "the engagement has been canceled."

"It is not canceled until I say it is canceled," Rokoff countered. "And that, my stupid friend, will not happen as long as Collette de Coude wears the amulet. Watch them, and closely. I have other business to attend to. Hear their conversation, and if any mention is made of the amulet, alert me immediately." He spun on his heel and walked away, assuming an innocent smile as soon as he mingled among the other guests.

Paulvitch puffed and sighed, then made his covert way on the trail of Tarzan and Collette.

———

The spinning wheel was far from mesmerizing, as were the hands of the croupier, though the man's gestures were obviously designed to confuse the gamblers. Tarzan, though, kept his focus true to the wheel, measuring its spin and the gradually decreasing rotation of the ball.

"The numbers pay thirty-five to one," Collette explained. "Black or red pay even." She moved her pointing finger to the various boxes as she spoke, but that, too, could not distract Tarzan. "Then there are boxes and lines," she continued, "and other bets at different odds."

Collette paused, studied the intent gaze of Tarzan's handsome face, and realized that he was hardly listening to her. "You know this already, don't you?" she asked, giving his arm a shake.

"Know what?" Tarzan asked coyly.

"Of the game," Collette answered with a huff. "Of all the games. You know, though you may pretend otherwise."

"I know that this wheel is designed so that he"—he pointed to the croupier—"will win more than those who come to play against him."

"He is the house," Collette explained. "The house will usually make money. Otherwise, why would anyone ever set up a casino?"

"He will make money?" Tarzan echoed.

Collette nodded.

"From those who play," Tarzan reasoned, his tone showing that the simple logic was reason enough not to play against the house.

"You miss the point," Collette replied, stomping her foot in exasperation. "Yes, you will lose. Many times, you will lose. But you might win, and win big."

"But you must first have the money to lose."

"Of course."

Tarzan shrugged. "Then it seems to me that if you have a great deal of money, you can win a lot more of the same."

"That is gambling," said Collette.

Tarzan nodded, feigning interest. "And when would you stop?"

"When you lose enough—" She stopped as she considered her own words, the blatant illogic of gambling against the odds.

"Then why start?" Tarzan asked, too innocently.

Collette's eyes narrowed as she considered his superior pose. "Do you not gamble?" she asked. "Have you never?"

"For food," Tarzan admitted. "For life. For money? No. Money meant neither in the jungle."

"But you are no longer in the jungle," Collette reasoned. "Perhaps it is time that you were taught the pleasures of society." Smiling widely, so full of excitement, she handed him a couple of chips. "Play," she instructed. "I doubt that you will be disappointed."

Tarzan believed differently, but he took the chips out of politeness, then sent his focus back to the wheel. The speed had lessened considerably, making it easier to decipher.

Collette placed her chips on number twenty-six, an obvious mistake to perceptive Tarzan.

"Thirty," he corrected, putting down the chips she had given him.

"Twenty-six is my favorite number," she explained.

"Your age?" Tarzan asked, but he recanted immediately, remembering that he had been taught it was not polite to inquire of a woman about her age.

Collette only laughed, though, too intelligent to be insulted by such petty things.

"Thirty will win," Tarzan insisted.

Before Collette could begin to argue, the wheel slowed and the bouncing ball skipped from place to place before settling in the thirty slot. Collette watched wide-eyed as the croupier swept in the losing chips, hers included, and paid off Tarzan's bet. Then, with a burst of laughter and exuberance, she leaped up and gave Tarzan a kiss on the cheek. "Are you psychic?" she asked. "Will you next be shackled upside down in a tank of water, to escape certain drowning with the aid of your mystic powers?"

Tarzan's expression was purely incredulous.

"I have heard of such things," Collette declared. "There is a man in America who claims such extraordinary abilities. Do you have a sixth sense?"

"On special occasions only," Tarzan replied dryly.

Collette let it go at that. "Back to roulette," she said. She started to move away from Tarzan, but reversed herself and gave him another peck on the cheek. "Your presence here has not only affected every woman in the room, but has affected my luck with this wheel. I can feel it—"

Her conversation ended abruptly as Nikolas Rokoff grabbed her by the arm and spun her about to face him. Collette's smile disappeared immediately, especially when she regarded the hulking Paulvitch, hovering behind Nikolas.

"You look very lovely tonight," Rokoff said, his grasp turning gentle. Then he let go of Collette altogether and shifted his hand to stroke the amulet, a movement that Tarzan did not miss.

"Very unique," Rokoff said, his eyes shining as he regarded the pendant. "Like you, my dear."

Collette slid back a step, her expression sour, lips tight, as though she could find no response to the man's sudden appearance. Rokoff didn't pursue her, but rather turned his attention to Tarzan.

"I am Nikolas Rokoff," he said, not bothering to extend his hand. "Collette will be spending the rest of the evening with me."

Tarzan studied Collette's expression, noting that she was glancing about and suddenly uncomfortable, her smile having vanished. She obviously did not want to cause a scene, though, in the house of her friend.

"You are presuming far too much, Nikolas," she said quietly.

"Presuming?" Rokoff scoffed, moving closer to her. "There is our betrothal and other personal matters which we must discuss, my dear."

"You may have proposed marriage and a merger of our families as part of your African venture with my father," Collette scolded, her voice rising, "but you cannot command my affections. There is not, and never has been, any betrothal."

Tarzan was glad to see Collette back on firm footing, glad to see that she had overcome her initial uneasiness at the sight of the man. There was something special about Collette de Coude, he suspected, something strong and true.

His attention was caught, then, by the look that Rokoff gave him, an expression that the man from the African jungle had seen before, but on humans only and never on animals. It was an expression wrought of anger and embarrassment.

Rokoff put his lips near to Collette's ear. "You are dishonoring me by speaking of this matter in front of strangers," the Russian said quietly.

"*Au contraire,*" Collette replied, and she shifted away. "Monsieur Tarzan is not a stranger."

"To me, he is," said Rokoff. "We will talk further, but in private." Again he grabbed Collette by the arm, and none too gently. Collette protested, but Rokoff ignored her and started pulling her away.

He hadn't gone a step before an impossibly strong, paralyzing grip latched onto his forearm, squeezing so tightly, and at just the right pressure points, that Rokoff could not even keep his fingers clenched. He looked at Tarzan, outraged and threatening, but Tarzan only squeezed harder, practically bringing Rokoff to his knees.

Paulvitch was in between them in an instant, reaching for Tarzan, but quicker than he could react, Tarzan's free hand snapped in between his reaching arms to clasp firmly onto his throat. Paulvitch slapped at Tarzan's forearm, grabbed his wrist and tried to twist it away with all of his considerable strength.

But Tarzan's muscles were locked and Paulvitch couldn't budge him.

Tarzan did let go of Rokoff then, sending him stumbling back a couple of steps. "Do you know who I am?" Rokoff protested.

"I believe you said that your name was Rokoff," Tarzan replied calmly. Paulvitch slipped down to one knee, his pudgy face turning a delicate shade of blue. Mercifully, Tarzan let him go. He fell to all fours, sputtering.

"Nikolas Rokoff!" Rokoff barked importantly. "Does the name mean nothing to you?"

Tarzan shook his head.

"Son of the Tsar of Russia!" Rokoff roared.

"Then I would presume you to be a gentleman," Tarzan replied calmly. He let his gaze drift from Rokoff to Paulvitch, the big man still down, on one knee now, and gasping for breath. With a smile to Rokoff, Tarzan offered Collette his arm and began to lead her away, the pair pointedly turning their backs on the fuming Russians.

Rokoff trembled with rage. He looked to Paulvitch, and the big man, embarrassed by the ease with which he had been humbled, needed little prodding. Up went Paulvitch with a bearlike roar, charging at the back of the departing Tarzan.

At that last moment Tarzan simply stepped aside, dragging one foot so that Paulvitch tripped headlong, stumbling awkwardly to crash into and overturn a poker table, sending cards and chips flying everywhere. Cries of surprise mingled with gasps of astonishment and sheer disgust, and with more than a few amused titters, particularly from the younger ladies. Count de Coude and Paul D'Arnot came rushing over.

"*Arrêtez!*" Count de Coude said firmly to Rokoff. "This is a social gathering I invited you to, and not some waterfront bar. You and your man are embarrassing me with you conduct!"

"That man is drunk!" Rokoff retorted, pointing at Tarzan. "He offended me. He created this disturbance."

"I believe that the word across the channel is 'poppycock,' " D'Arnot interjected. "Jean Tarzan has never been drunk or offensive in his life!"

"Well, never drunk," Tarzan whispered. Collette giggled and stepped on his foot.

"Never, until now, then!" said Rokoff.

"It was you who provoked this incident, Nikolas," Collette interjected. "You and your bully. And not the first time you two have behaved so badly, I am sure!"

Rokoff started to reply, but Count de Coude, with his perfectly straight back and squared shoulders, stepped between him and Collette. "You were invited here as my guests," he scolded, "and your behavior is offensive and detestable." The count turned to D'Arnot. "You have my apologies, monsieur."

D'Arnot nodded his acceptance; not that he had ever blamed the good man.

"How dare you chastise me?" Rokoff exploded. "I am your future son-in-law."

Count de Coude's expression did not show any agreement with that remark.

"Are you prepared to lose your business ties with my father?" Rokoff argued, straightening his back and lifting his chin in an arrogant pose.

"Do you wish to sever the arrangement?" De Coude replied coolly.

"If it becomes a point of issue."

"If that is the price I must pay to keep my daughter and my self-respect, then so be it," the count replied. "We have nothing further to discuss, Monsieur Rokoff. I am confident that your carriage is waiting."

Rokoff met the count's indifferent look with an outright glare, a threatening look that he shifted over Tarzan. "You will regret your interference in my affairs," he said as a pair of butlers bracketed him and led him away.

"I regret ever having met you," Tarzan answered.

CHAPTER 2

D'Arnot's hard shoes clicked on the wet pavement, the rhythm intermittently broken by the tapping tip of his cane, but Tarzan, stepping in a toe-heel manner, made hardly a sound as the pair walked along a Paris street very late that same night. The rain had stopped, its remnants shining in evenly spaced pools under the light of weak streetlamps. The casino had ended earlier than usual this night because of the disturbance with the Russian men, an incident that had shaken D'Arnot more than Tarzan. The perceptive Tarzan could see it in every twitch of D'Arnot's furrowed brow, and he was relieved when his friend finally expressed his turmoil.

"You have made a very dangerous enemy in Nikolas Rokoff," D'Arnot remarked, his tone grave.

"His threats are meaningless to me," Tarzan replied.

"Take him at his word," D'Arnot warned. "He is not a man to be so easily dismissed.

"I do not understand how Henri could have made this

marriage arrangement with him," D'Arnot went on. "Rokoff's only desire is the De Coude wealth and the power that comes with it. He never cared for Collette, and she is certainly deserving of someone better."

"Is he not the son of Russia's tsar, as he claimed?" Tarzan asked, trying to sound interested, though he found the whole subject of Nikolas Rokoff tiring. To Tarzan, Rokoff seemed the epitome of societal intrigue, a game in which the man of the jungle had no interest. He agreed wholeheartedly with D'Arnot's estimation of Collette, though. She was far above the likes of Nikolas Rokoff. "As such, why would he need the De Coude fortune?"

"The situation is much more complicated than that," D'Arnot tried to explain. "It may be decades before Rokoff receives the spoils of his heritage, if ever. And he has never been regarded as a patient man. He craves a way in which he might come to power sooner, and he'll use Collette de Coude, or whatever means he can find, to achieve that end."

That notion struck a chord in Tarzan, sent his thoughts spiraling in another, very important, direction. "He must not have the amulet," he replied.

D'Arnot stopped in his tracks and stared curiously. "What amulet?"

"The one Collette was wearing tonight. The six-sided crystal."

"But why?" D'Arnot asked. "It is merely a relic of Africa; a lovely item, I would agree, but it is of no great value to anyone but a collector, such as Henri."

"There you are wrong, my friend," Tarzan replied. "It is of *great* value."

D'Arnot eyed him for a long while, but did not press the

point. Tarzan obviously knew something important concerning that amulet, and D'Arnot was confident that he would tell him in his own time. One simply did not press Jean Tarzan.

D'Arnot led on then, walking quietly, giving Tarzan his space. The streets grew darker, for the lamps were more widely spaced, and several were not burning. If he had not been so absorbed by Tarzan's last words, D'Arnot would have seen the movements to the side sooner.

He was surprised indeed when half a dozen ruffians stepped out of the shadows to block his path. D'Arnot started to protest, but his words fell away as he considered the men and, more particularly, their weapons. Two carried clubs, two wielded pipes, another held a blackjack, and the last, the closest, swung a length of chain easily at his side.

Tarzan pulled D'Arnot by the collar, leaping defensively in front of the smaller man even as the chain-wielder began his attack. The thug came at the pair in a straightforward manner, swinging the chain up over his shoulder and down at Tarzan's head.

"Second mistake," Tarzan muttered, crooking his right arm at the elbow and raising it up high to block. The man's first mistake, by Tarzan's estimation, was the fact that he had the chain tied about his wrist and could not easily let go of it. That point was driven home by Tarzan as the chain wrapped harmlessly about his own forearm. He turned his arm in and down, reached it behind the man's extended arm and caught the chain firmly in his grasp, then, with a simple twist and downward pull, sent the man spinning a half circle, off balance, and pulled him low to the side.

The second ruffian came in hard in the wake of the first,

but Tarzan stepped ahead boldly with his left foot, planting it securely, and knifed his left arm out, brushing it against the attacker's recoiled arms. The man tried to swing his club anyway, but Tarzan easily turned the blow up high. Then he used the thug's own momentum as a weapon, pushing the man out and into a tumble over his extended and braced knee.

On came two more, with the remaining two charging hard at D'Arnot. Holding fast to the chain, its owner still attached to the other end, Tarzan looped his arm and yanked out to the right, pulling the caught man into a half flip that ended when his own comrade connected with the blackjack. The man's breath came out in a rush, and he cried out again as Tarzan flipped him back the other way, this time squarely in the path of a swinging pipe.

D'Arnot met the charge of the remaining two bravely, whipping his sturdy cane in a wide-arcing swing that knocked the closest thug aside. The second man rushed right in on the other's heels, though, too quickly for D'Arnot to execute an effective backhand. The gentleman did manage to get his arm up high enough to partially deflect the oncoming blow, and then he and the charging ruffian went flying backward and to the ground in a tumble.

Tarzan heard D'Arnot's gasp, but his own situation would not allow for a break. He let go of the chain and shoved the battered thug out hard, right into the legs of the man with the pipe. In the same fluid movement, Tarzan half turned, reaching out with perfect timing to catch another attacker's club in mid-swing. A subtle twist, over and down, defeated the man's momentum, and Tarzan yanked the club straight away, pulling it from the man's grasp. Then Tarzan stepped forward forcefully, stabbing straight ahead with the club, jabbing the man right in the chest. He fell away with a gasp, but the man Tarzan had flipped over his outstretched knee was back into it now, leaping onto Tarzan's back and wrapping him in a tight bear hug.

On came the pipe-wielder, and though Tarzan, with a spinning forearm block, managed to turn the weapon harmlessly low, the man dipped his shoulder and barreled in.

Amazingly, Tarzan held them there, both of them, one man squeezing and twisting and trying to jerk him side to side, the other scraping his feet against the slick pavement, trying to move Tarzan backward.

He wouldn't budge, not an inch, but he felt the chain slap about his ankle and lock fast. As the man pulled up to the side, Tarzan realized that his hold was lost. He went with the flow then, diving into a somersault, bringing the man holding him from behind right over to cushion his own heavy landing on the hard pavement.

Three were down in a heap. The fourth, the man with the chain, stood over them, trying to line up Tarzan for a clean hit.

All of them froze then, suddenly, as a woman on a nearby balcony let out a scream. That pause gave Tarzan the split second he needed to seek out his friend, poor D'Arnot, and the sight was not encouraging. One thug held Paul in a rear stranglehold, while the other pounded away at his exposed midsection with a club.

The sight sent a burst of sheer rage coursing through Tarzan's veins, sent his sensibilities careening back to his first home, the jungle, where the primary instincts overruled reason. Suddenly everything seemed to be moving in slow motion, the men grabbing at him, the man above him swinging the chain, smiling evilly as he at last found an opening.

Tarzan issued a roar so fierce, so primal, so intense, that the man hesitated, and Tarzan braced one foot under him and somehow, impossibly, drove up to a standing position, taking both grappling thugs with him. Tarzan seemed huge then, as though his rage had swelled his powerful body. A sudden uplift of his arm sent one assailant flying. He snapped that same arm back over his shoulder, grabbing the man on his back by the coat while at the same time catching the flying end of the chain with his other hand.

Again came that terrorizing yell as Tarzan pulled his arm over his shoulder, yanking the thug from his back and sending him flying away into the darkness.

The chain-wielder, apparently not stupid enough to repeat his mistakes, slipped the other end of the chain from his wrist and ran off, and Tarzan didn't pursue, but rather turned and went to D'Arnot. He slammed the man clubbing his friend in the back, catching him by the collar and the belt, heaving him right over D'Arnot and his own comrade and over a wrought-iron fence behind them, to crash into a pile of boxes on the other side.

Tarzan kept coming forward, snapping out his hand to grasp the hand that was strangling D'Arnot. He deftly hooked his thumb under the thumb of the ruffian and twisted it backward to break the hold. The ruffian responded by shoving D'Arnot forward, into Tarzan. But Tarzan was too quick and agile for that predictable maneuver, catching his friend with his free hand and guiding him easily to the ground.

On came the ruffian, launching a heavy punch with his free

hand. Again Tarzan was too quick, easily catching the fist and twisting his hand, slipping his thumb right into the crease of the fist to put that hand in a similar lock as the other. The ruffian let out a howl, twisted, and jerked wildly, but futilely.

Tarzan squared up to the man, holding both his arms extended, twisting the thumbs back over the man's hands. Tarzan tucked his legs under him then, taking the man's hands down with his fall. He turned his hands under those of the ruffian, palms up, as he landed, and the sudden, violent force broke both of the man's thumbs. Tarzan was back up in an instant, finished with the man and turning to D'Arnot's aid.

The ruffian tucked his broken hands into his belly and shuffled away, groaning, calling pitifully for his friends.

"Are you all right, my friend?" Tarzan asked, helping D'Arnot to his feet.

"Behind you!" D'Arnot warned.

Tarzan spun about, amazed to witness one of the thugs coming in for more.

"And up there!" D'Arnot added, pointing to a balcony three stories up, where another one of the men had run and now stood, poised to throw a knife.

Tarzan yelled and slapped the charging ruffian aside, then ran for the lowest railing of the wrought-iron balconies.

The man up above threw the knife, but Tarzan skittered too quickly and the weapon bounced harmlessly on the pavement. The thrower cursed and stamped his foot.

He should have been running instead, as he realized only an instant later. Tarzan hit the railing at full speed, shifting his momentum from forward to up. Hand over hand, foot over foot, he scaled the balconies as fast as he had crossed the level pavement.

"Of the apes," D'Arnot muttered in disbelief, for no human should have been able to climb so quickly, so gracefully.

Before the ruffian had moved two steps back from the railing, Tarzan was over it and beside him, catching him by the collar and swinging him out to hang over the three-story drop.

"Tarzan, no!" D'Arnot cried.

With one arm extended, Tarzan held his squirming captive. The man pleaded for his life, but Tarzan, locked in the mindset of the jungle, hardly heard the words. Gradually he relaxed, coming back to his sensibilities, though his corded muscles held firm, and he eyed the man directly.

He noticed that the man looked right past him, though he tried to hide it, and Tarzan was sharp enough to understand what that might mean.

He spun and tugged with all his strength, yanking the man back in over the railing and launching him across the balcony to slam into his comrade, who had been trying to sneak up on Tarzan. The momentum from the great throw carried both of them crashing through a window, tumbling into one of the flats.

A woman began screaming immediately, a man began cursing, and both the thugs came out fast and hard, fleeing for their lives at the wrong end of a swinging broomstick.

Tarzan went over the railing and leaped across the way, catching a gutter support and swinging right about it. As he came around, he launched himself back the other way—where he caught a balcony support more than a story down, to swing about that and go back the other way again, landing in a crouch lightly on the pavement just a few feet from his shaken friend. He scooped up D'Arnot's dropped cane and brought it up with him as he rose to his full height, handing it over. "Are you all right?" he asked again.

"I'm fine, *mon ami*," D'Arnot replied, brushing himself off. "We are a tough team to beat, eh?"

Tarzan smiled and nodded, and a calm came over him. He didn't seem so huge now, so imposing. He was Jean Tarzan again, Lord Greystoke, a gentleman.

The change was too subtle to be caught by a pair of witnesses concealed behind a curtained window farther down the street.

"Whatever you paid them, it was too much!" Rokoff fumed.

Paulvitch had no answers for his master. They had witnessed enough of the fight to see their hired thugs routed. "I would have gone myself, but you—"

"Enough!" Rokoff snapped at him, refusing to take any of the blame for the disaster. "And enough of this Tarzan. Kill him. And do it yourself. I will go and get the amulet."

Paulvitch's bald head bobbed eagerly at the end of his thick neck. He pushed the curtain aside and peered down the dark, rain-soaked street, watching the two forms recede into the darkness.

Tarzan tried hard to keep his smile concealed, biting back his amusement as he regarded D'Arnot's puffy strut.

"Size and weapons are secondary," the small man was saying, and it seemed to Tarzan that his friend was rehearsing the reenactment he would offer for the other gentlemen, and particularly for the ladies. "My agility and quickness are what's important."

Tarzan stared straight ahead, chewing his lip. D'Arnot's recollections receded, Tarzan's thoughts looking past the fight, past the casino and gambling, and back to a world more sincere. There were no enemies in the jungle, just creatures competing honestly for food and for life. No ruffians in the shadows. The pleasures taken were simpler, and, to Tarzan's thinking, far more satisfying: the sweetness of fruit found and picked, the warmth of the westering sun, the startling horizon, acacia trees cutting dark, stark shadows at sunset.

"Mon ami?" D'Arnot said, and when Tarzan came out of his trance and looked at his friend, he realized that it was not the first time D'Arnot had called to him.

"Where are you, my friend?" the Frenchman asked.

Tarzan's smile was one of the purest contentment.

"Ah," D'Arnot sighed, guessing Tarzan's thoughts.

"It is time, D'Arnot," Tarzan said quietly, his eyes still seeing things far, far away. "It's time for me to go home."

"I can tell when you're thinking of Africa," D'Arnot replied. "But it was only a street fight . . ."

"The fight was unimportant," Tarzan put in.

"You must give yourself a chance," D'Arnot pressed, stopping and grabbing Tarzan by the elbow. "You have wealth and title. You could have Jane. It could be a good life, *mon ami.*"

"If I were truly Lord Greystoke and not who I am," Tarzan replied evenly. "I am Tarzan, not Jean Tarzan. Just Tarzan, son of Kala the ape." He gave a snicker and looked all around at their city surroundings. "You can see that I don't belong here. I belong in the jungle."

"Is that why you gave up the woman you love?" D'Arnot asked quietly, meaning no offense.

"This is Jane's home," Tarzan replied. "Her place. She does not belong in the jungle and could never be happy there."

They started walking again, side by side, though it seemed to both of them that they were suddenly worlds apart.

"You are as a brother to me," D'Arnot said at length. "You know?"

Tarzan didn't have to respond, and D'Arnot knew that he felt the same way.

"I can only try and understand your needs," D'Arnot went on thoughtfully, head down as he carefully considered each word. "Though I admit that sometimes they seem beyond comprehension. You do look at the world differently than any man that I have ever known, but that, I believe, can be your strength in this situation. For though I have infinite trust in your instincts, there are times when I must dispute your decisions. You judge too quickly, my friend. You have seen so little of what this world might offer. I believe in you; I believe you can conquer civilization as you conquered the jungle. Then you might learn to truly enjoy all that this world of mine offers." He looked up as he finished, to judge what effect his little speech might have had on his headstrong friend, only to find that he had been talking to himself. Tarzan was nowhere to be seen.

D'Arnot gave a small, resigned laugh. "Ah, but you would not have listened anyhow," he admitted.

CHAPTER 3

He was greeted by the roars and growls, the sharp shrieks of the spider monkeys and the occasional trumpet of the massive elephants. And every call sounded as the sweetest music in all the world to Tarzan as he stood outside the wall of the Paris Zoo. He closed his eyes and basked in the sounds and the scents. These perfumed people of civilization always complained about that natural odor, for they were so accustomed to masking their own smells, and so convinced that those smells were foul.

To Tarzan, who had not been so brainwashed, the aromas emanating from the zoo carried with them images of home, of freedom, of truth. Even more importantly, those aromas carried information. To those who understood, like Tarzan, like the animals themselves, like the skilled hunters of the Waziri and Kikuyu tribes of Tarzan's homeland, the scents of animals were at least as informative as the sights and sounds around them. An animal's scent told of its emotions, of fright, of hunger, of pain, and by paying attention to the spoor on the wind, by using the higher senses like those of the various animals around him, Tarzan could elevate his own awareness.

These people of Paris, of all civilization, had lost that truth, had dulled their own perceptiveness, trapping themselves within their societal tenets. That was why Collette de Coude, and the croupier, for that matter, had been so amazed by his understanding of the roulette wheel.

His prediction of the ball's placement had not been a trick of magic. Nor had it been accomplished via any psychic powers, but rather by simple, careful observation.

It is difficult, Tarzan supposed, to be observant of one's surroundings when one is too busy worrying about one's own appearance.

He wouldn't judge them harshly, though, especially not Collette de Coude. She was a person of spirit, Tarzan reflected, one who, under different circumstances, might have thrived in the jungle.

The excited howl of a monkey brought him from his reflections. He breathed deeply, basking in the smells, garnering information, and then he considered the high wall. To most of the city people, that eight-foot barrier would appear unclimbable, a sheer and smooth obstacle, but to Tarzan every crack and indentation showed as clearly as a staircase. He was up and over in a matter of seconds, landing lightly on the other side, bending his knees at just the right moment when he landed, to absorb the shock of the drop.

He relaxed at once, sniffing the air again, delighting in a world without pretense, a world where words could not twist feelings. Perhaps that was it, Tarzan mused as he walked past the cages, pausing in front of each to greet the animals contained within. Perhaps that was the cause of all this perversive civilization.

Words. Words that disguised truth; words that bent reality to fit the speaker's viewpoint. The language here in the zoo was simpler and more direct. And more important. Animals did not "speak" for the sake of hearing their own voice, but only to convey information.

Tarzan knew a few humans who could take such a lesson.

He winced when he passed the lion cage, noting the ragged manes of the two males and the lethargic manner in which they paced. Male lions were thought by the Europeans to be lazy. Females did all the hunting, according to the conventional wisdom, while the males lay around sleeping all the day and all the night.

Tarzan nearly laughed aloud at that thought. These scholars observed wild lions only during the daylight hours, when the pride, particularly the males, did indeed settle down to conserve their energy. Would that he could take all of these "scholars" into the jungle one night and let them witness the sheer power of a hunting lion, male or female. When—If—the scholars ever found their voices again, they would speak differently, and with a good deal more respect!

A lion's resonating growl, that low, throaty roar that carried for miles and miles, the ultimate word in the jungle, followed Tarzan as he moved to the next cage in line. He paused and considered that sound, and thought of a common phrase. These civilized people were always worried about who would get "the last word."

"The lion," he said aloud. "Always the lion."

Except in here, he mused. While Tarzan loved the zoo's residents, he hated their home.

A large rhinoceros was resting in the next cage. Its horn was nearly worn away, no more than a bump, seeming little like the magnificent spear a wild rhino might carry. In the jungle, rhinos sharpened their horns on the soft bark of trees. Here in the zoo, they continued their ritual sharpening, but against the stone walls, so their horns fast wore away. The sight broke Tarzan's heart.

"Someday you will be free," he said to the forlorn-looking animal. "Believe that." The rhino made no response and Tarzan walked on. "Believe that," he said again, but he did not have faith in his own words. These animals, after only a short time in the zoo, lost their wilderness edge. Released back into the jungle, most of them would be dead in a very short time.

Tarzan wondered if that might be his own fate. Had his days in England and Paris taken the wilderness edge from him? He shook his head, dismissing the thought. Worrying over the notion was moot, because he meant to go home in any case.

Soon after, Tarzan came to his favorite enclosure: the chimpanzee pen. He crouched in front of the cage, lifting his palm to place it against the bars. The chimps hopped about excitedly, calling to each other. Their scent revealed their excitement, and their trepidation.

Tarzan answered those fears with sounds and nonverbal signals, reminding them that he was no threat, but a friend. The largest male—Tarzan had named him Papa—came to the front of the cage and put his palm against Tarzan's, their bond renewed.

"I am going home, Papa," Tarzan said quietly, reaching in to stroke the head of the chimp.

The ape looked up at him with understanding. The actual

language was lost on Papa, of course, but the inflections of Tarzan's voice and subtle movements were not.

"I wish I could take you with me," Tarzan went on. "All of you." He looked around at the rows of too-small cages. "All of them."

Tarzan put his head down and blew a deep sigh, remembering a less-than-cordial discussion he had become engaged in with one of the younger zoo attendants, concerning the accommodations. "They do not understand, Papa," he said to the ape. " 'A life of luxury for them,' these people insist," he went on, imitating the voice and thick accent of the zoo attendant. " 'No predators, and all the food they could want. What life could be better?' "

Papa bobbed his head excitedly, hopped up and did a complete spin, coming back in a crouch in the exact same spot.

"They do not understand," Tarzan said again, and then he carried on the line of thinking, musing privately. These people were so caught up in their pursuit of luxury, so enamored of the ideas of servants and ease, that they had lost their understanding that niceties are nothing if they are not earned; that relaxation, to be truly enjoyed, must come after accomplishment. "A life of luxury for them," the attendant had said concerning the animals, and Tarzan knew that the young man, in his ignorance, believed it, because he, like so many others in society, lived in the hopes that the roulette wheel would one day stop on his number, and that the payoff would allow him to relax for the rest of his life. A poor notion of happiness, Tarzan understood, and he looked deeply into Papa's black eyes and felt sincere sympathy for the chimp. Given the choice, Papa, and all of these animals, would opt for the hardships of the jungle.

Their lives would likely be longer in here, their physical health certainly better. No longer did they have to crouch in fear when they heard the roar of the lion. Yet it was a passion-less existence. Those moments of terror in the jungle made the moments of ease so much the sweeter. The triumph of victory over a rival, of finding water in the seasonal drought, of escaping the hunting pack, gave meaning to their lives, gave passion to their hearts.

Tarzan thought of the ladies at D'Arnot's house, their lusting eyes as they had watched him pass. Such sexual chal-lenge was the only pursuit, the only passion, left to so many of them, a game that all of them played continually, and usually to disastrous consequence. So much of their identities—the conquest for the men, the allure for the ladies—had become enwrapped in that game, and defined by that game.

Even in that, perhaps the most powerful instinct for man and animal alike, the truth had been twisted.

"They do not understand, Papa," Tarzan said one more time, and then he went quiet, in word and in thought, savoring the moment with his hand, touching the rough yet gentle palm of the great chimp.

Papa's widening eyes were Tarzan's first sign of danger. He spun about, rising tall and rolling onto the balls of his feet. He saw the hulking form standing in the shadows to the side of the cage, arm uplifted toward him. Spin continuing, Tarzan jerked his head to the side, purely on instinct, just as the pistol the man was holding flashed.

Tarzan felt warm blood spilling down from his forehead. All the world was spinning, spinning. He continued his turn because he could not stop, or maybe he was not turn-ing. Maybe the world was spinning—he could not be sure.

And then the ground came rushing up suddenly to swallow him.

Collette de Coude sat at her vanity, brushing her long brown hair and replaying the evening in her mind. This was her favorite spot for contemplation, and she had gone right to it upon her arrival home; she hadn't even bothered to change out of her evening gown. Even Rokoff's rudeness could not steal the pleasure from this night—this night she had met Jean Tarzan. He was handsome, to be sure, so tall and broad-shouldered, and with that thick ponytail bouncing about his shoulders, and those intense gray eyes, lightly shaded in green. But Collette's fascination with Tarzan went far beyond his physical appearance. There were plenty of handsome men traveling in her father's society circles, but they were all so . . .

Collette paused in her brushing to search for the right word. "Boring," she said after a while, and then she smiled widely and went back to work on her hair. Yes, boring was a good word, she thought. All of them pursued the same things: power and money. And they only did so for the women their gains would bring them, any woman, all the women.

But not Jean Tarzan. Collette knew that from their discussion at the roulette wheel, and from the look in his eyes. He did not leer at her physical attributes as most men did; he had looked her in the eye, in the heart, in the soul. His perspective on life, so unusual and refreshing to her, made him all the more attractive. She knew of his past and tried to conjure an image of it—Tarzan running through the tall grasses of the

Serengeti, his muscles interacting in a graceful, sinewy harmony. Running . . . naked.

Collette blushed and giggled, and quickly draped animal skins on her imaginary jungle man. Not too many skins, though, for she didn't want to hide that perfection of form, the interplay of hardened muscle.

"What do you find so amusing?" came her father's voice behind her.

Collette turned about, giggling still.

"Thinking of Monsieur Tarzan?" Henri de Coude asked slyly. He knew his daughter well.

"He is an interesting man," Collette admitted.

"Am I to lose my daughter, then, to the wilds of Africa?"

Collette smiled all the wider when she considered the various interpretations of that statement, and Henri did, too, as the double meaning of his words sank in.

"He is a handsome man," Henri agreed. "And Paul speaks of him with the highest respect."

Collette brought her finger up to her chin and chewed her bottom lip in a pensive pose. "A question," she said.

"Yes," her father prompted.

"No, no," she explained. "I mean that Monsieur Tarzan is a question."

Her father looked at her quizzically. "You mean that he is puzzling?"

"No," she replied. "A question. That is the word. Monsieur Tarzan, by his mere presence, poses questions about the way we look at our world. Our perceptions appear almost stilted against his simple logic."

"The world is a wide place," her father, who had traveled extensively, agreed. "And we would all be fools to think that all people think as we think, or behave as we behave."

"I doubt that many see the world as Monsieur Tarzan sees it," Collette said.

"Touché," Henri agreed. "You get to sleep now," he said, moving over to kiss Collette's forehead. "Perhaps your dreams will shed new insight into this mysterious Monsieur Tarzan."

Collette was sure that she was blushing.

"Pleasant dreams, I am sure," her father added, for he liked seeing his daughter so obviously flustered. It reminded him of those times, not so long ago, but seeming like a hundred years, when Collette the teenager had just begun to notice boys. He gave her face a gentle stroke, then left the room. Though he was charmed by Collette's attitude, Henri de Coude wasn't sure how he felt about her obvious attraction to the mysterious Jean Tarzan. He wasn't overly worried, though, for he and his late wife had raised their daughter well, and he trusted implicitly in her judgment.

And he did enjoy the almost-little-girlish look on her face.

That look remained as Collette went back to her brushing, rolling out the silken hair over one shoulder, holding it in one hand and gently brushing with the other. She was staring into the mirror, but she wasn't seeing her reflection. She was viewing the Serengeti, the swaying grasses, the running man . . .

A long while later Collette pulled herself up from the vanity, drifting toward her wardrobe, unsnapping and unzipping her lavender gown as she went. She opened the door and took out her nightgown, then turned back to her vanity table.

Never noticing the booted feet below the wall of hanging clothes.

"Do you always spend so long preparing yourself for bed?"

The question came from behind her, a voice that she knew and that sent a cold shiver down her spine. She turned her head to the side and saw, in the mirror of the vanity, the strong face of Nikolas Rokoff, the black hair short and tightly cropped, the dark eyes as intense as Tarzan's, perhaps, but for very different reasons.

Rokoff stepped right up behind her and put a finger to pursed lips, then reached around Collette with his other hand, brushing her neck and fingering the amulet, which she still wore. "It is so beautiful, as are you," he whispered.

Collette was about to scream, but Rokoff's other hand, now holding a thick cloth, snapped about her face and clamped over her mouth. She struggled for a few moments, but her efforts quickly became halfhearted as a strange and powerful aroma filled her nostrils.

She peered over the fringe of the cloth, into the mirror, to see Rokoff's face again, his visage set in frightful determination. Then he seemed far away, surrounded by a dark fog that was closing, closing, over him and over her, over all the world.

The hulking form moved over the prone form of Tarzan. He kicked at the limp body, then raised his pistol again, just to be sure.

Papa's arm slipped out through the bars of the cage, the chimp's hand grabbing the large man's wrist. The man regarded the ape incredulously—Papa was, at best, one-third his size. But he didn't understand the strength of animals. He pulled back against the ape's grip, thinking to extract his arm, thinking, with some amusement, that he might slam the beast against its cage bars at the same time.

But it was the man who was yanked, and with apparent ease, to slam against the bars. His elbow hit the cage hard; the pistol went flying into the darkness.

He managed to wriggle himself free of Papa's grip, and, with one final look to the limp form, decided that his job was done and stumbled away.

CHAPTER 4

Everything was blurred and colorless, images without meaning. His thoughts spun and spun as he desperately tried to find a focus, as he tried to hold on to some image or some memory.

A flash, sharp and distinct; the warning cry of a chimpanzee.

His eyes popped open, his muscles tensing for a spring. But then, suddenly, he calmed.

He was not at the zoo, but in a room. A room familiar and comfortable, and without danger.

Tarzan relaxed even more when he saw D'Arnot and Henri de Coude standing vigil, each holding a glass of wine. D'Arnot's face brightened, though his smile was surely strained, when he noted Tarzan's open eyes.

"Well, you're alive, and you just proved it," D'Arnot said, trying to be lighthearted.

Again Tarzan noted some strain in the man's voice, some deep worry.

"Now you can explain why you were almost dead," D'Arnot

went on. "You've been unconscious for the better part of a day, *mon ami*."

"I saw a flash," Tarzan answered, propping himself on his elbows and moving to sit up. "That's all."

"You were shot," D'Arnot explained, moving beside his friend. "But there is no trace of your assailant—unless, of course, one of the chimps held the pistol they found at the zoo."

Tarzan managed to sit up; D'Arnot plopped down on the divan beside him. "The bullet grazed your head," he said, and then he caught Tarzan as the big man reeled. "Are you listening?"

Tarzan righted himself and with a deep sigh, found his center of balance. "Barely," he replied.

"Barely is enough to hear bad news," D'Arnot said grimly.

Tarzan straightened and eyed his friend directly. Measuring the mood of the pair—considering that he was alive and apparently on his way to full recovery—led his thoughts down the path of several disastrous possibilities, and when Count de Coude stepped over to interrupt, one path in particular came to him with crystalline clarity.

"I am sorry for what happened to you, Monsieur Tarzan," the older gentleman said sincerely. "I believe that I am the cause of it. We have both been ambushed by the same man."

"You *know* who shot me?" Tarzan asked imperatively, for of course, considering the events at the casino and the fight in the street shortly afterward, he had some very definite suspects.

"Nikolas Rokoff," Count de Coude answered without hesitation. "Or one of his lackeys. It was he who broke into my home last night. Of that, I have no doubt."

"The amulet," Tarzan stated. "He took the amulet your daughter was wearing."

"But if that were all . . ." Count de Coude replied, his voice faltering as he turned away.

"He took Collette, Tarzan," D'Arnot quietly explained. "We believe that he and Henri's daughter are already on their way to Africa."

"If Rokoff has the amulet, and he knows of its worth, then he is," Tarzan replied.

Count de Coude turned on him sharply, sensing that he knew something more about all of this, something important. Paul D'Arnot had already informed him of the cryptic warnings Tarzan had offered concerning the amulet. "Will you help me get her back?" the count implored.

"Of course," Tarzan replied. His gaze drifted away from De Coude, apparently staring off into nothing as he considered all that he knew about that amulet—a legend in his homeland—and all the terrible possibilities raised by its appearance. "I have to," he finished, and it seemed to both De Coude and D'Arnot that he was speaking of something entirely different, of something larger even than the kidnapping of Collette.

The mere possibility that anyone could believe that *any-thing* was more important than the kidnapping of Collette at first offended De Coude, but not D'Arnot. D'Arnot knew Tarzan well enough to understand the gravity of the situation, and he began to wonder then just how important that amulet might be.

He lifted the pistol from the crate as gently as if it was a new-born baby, cradling it in his arms, his eyes glowing. Up it came and he swung it about, feeling the light weight and superior balance. Then, embarrassed when he noted the looks the others were giving him, Rokoff placed the weapon back into the crate and slammed the lid tight, noting its lettering:

A. ZEK IMPORTS

MOROCCO, NORTH AFRICA

CHINA-GLASSWARE — USE NO HOOKS

Rokoff nodded to one of the workers, who immediately came over and began driving nails to secure the lid. Then Rokoff motioned to Paulvitch and the two men walked off to the side, alone.

"These are the latest models," Rokoff explained. "Automatic pistols manufactured in America."

"Achmet Zek has some very valuable items here," Paulvitch replied.

Rokoff gave a wry smile. "The weapons will also serve us," he said, and started away, Paulvitch obediently falling into line behind him. Moving around several piles of stacked crates, they came in sight of one of their henchmen, the man standing behind Collette de Coude, holding her arms firmly behind her back.

"Be sure your man does not damage her—in any way," Rokoff said sternly to Paulvitch when he noticed how tightly the man was gripping Collette, and the hungry expression on his face. "She could have additional value to me."

"Don't worry," Paulvitch assured him. The big man dared a grin when he saw that Rokoff wasn't looking at him. He detected more than a hope for monetary value in Rokoff's tone. His master was cold and calculating, a man who would murder his own brother or father if he could profit from the act, but Collette had indeed touched some nerve within that monster. And though Rokoff would deny it with all his words, and had probably convinced himself that she meant nothing to him, the subtle undertones of his voice betrayed his heart. Even more telling, Paulvitch knew, was the fact that Rokoff had Collette completely under his power and yet he had not taken advantage of her.

"Don't worry," Paulvitch said again, soothingly. "The guards do what they're told, and no more than that."

Rokoff turned to him, and Paulvitch feared that perhaps he had been too condescending. "But so far, not very efficiently, right, Alexis?" Rokoff snapped.

The big man reddened with frustration. He fell silently back into step again as his master moved to Collette and the guard. "I think we should worry more about Achmet Zek than Collette de Coude," he offered defensively, wanting to change the subject. "Zek is not to be trusted."

"Why?" Rokoff replied with a dismissive chuckle. "Because he is greedy? If he was not deceptive and dishonest, I would not be able to buy him with words and weapons." He turned on Paulvitch, stopping the big man's progress, his expression resembling something akin to the disappointment of a dog trainer when his student cannot grasp the simplest of concepts. Up snapped his hand, in front of Paulvitch's pudgy face, the crystal amulet dangling on its chain from his fingers. "Achmet Zek told us where to find this," Rokoff said. "And he knows much more. I do not doubt that Achmet Zek has his own agenda." Rokoff snickered again and dropped his hand, then turned and started away.

"Just as I do," he added under his breath.

"But when we return to Africa, he won't need us any-more," Paulvitch reasoned as he shuffled to catch up. "He could kill us and take the amulet."

"He could," Rokoff admitted, his casual tone showing that he wasn't very concerned. "But he will not—not while he can use us. And we will allow him to believe that he can use us for as long as we need him."

Paulvitch was again beginning to protest, but that last statement satisfied him, convinced him that Rokoff did indeed understand the dangers of dealing with one as ruth-less as Achmet Zek, and was apparently making provisions to divorce himself from the man.

They reached Collette's side then, Rokoff moving immedi-ately to stroke her delicate face. With that typical indomi-table spirit, Collette tore her arm free of the ruffian's grasp and slapped Rokoff's hand away. He moved as if to strike her, but held back, snarling.

Collette remained undeterred. "Take me home!" she screamed in Rokoff's face. "Take me home now!"

Rokoff backed away a step, his snarl transforming into a wicked grin. He was in control here. "You are home, my dear," he said calmly, moving his hand, now that Paulvitch's bully had regained control of Collette, back to stroke her cheek. "You are in the company of your future husband. There is some business that I must handle in Africa, and then, perhaps, we shall be married."

"Never," Collette spat, twisting both to get free of the ruf-fian and to get out of Rokoff's reach. "I'll never marry you. I'd rather be dead!"

Rokoff scoffed at the notion. "I haven't offered you that

option," he said. "Though you might beg for it. Your other alternatives, I fear, are far less desirable."

Again the woman tugged free of Paulvitch's man, even going so far as to half turn and slap the lackey across the face, and to stomp on his foot for good measure. Then she came for Rokoff viciously, hands extended as if they were claws. She never got near him, though, for Paulvitch stepped between them, sweeping one powerful arm across to get Collette's scratching hands down and to put her off balance, then grabbing her shoulder and spinning her about, quickly wrapping her in a powerful bear hug. Paulvitch lifted her right off her feet, swinging her back and forth to keep her from finding any firm balance as he moved her back to her place.

Rokoff wasn't even watching. Laughing, he turned about and simply walked away.

From the window of the train he watched the world flying past him. Flying in an uncontrollable blur, and to Tarzan that image seemed appropriate.

He knew, vaguely, the legend of the six-sided amulet, and the stories of the Temple of the Ancients, and though the particulars escaped him, the overriding sense of danger did not. Every one of the legends he had heard concerning the temple were spoken of in hushed, fearful tones, and never in the dark of night.

And often by jungle tribesmen, warriors all, who were not easily scared.

"We will be in Marseilles this evening," Paul D'Arnot said as he rejoined Tarzan in the car, taking a seat opposite his friend.

"I must stop Rokoff," Tarzan said grimly.

"Collette is in great danger," D'Arnot remarked, and he watched Tarzan's reaction closely. The man from the jungle nodded, but there was a faraway look in his eye, again making it appear as though Collette's fate was not the only thing worrying him.

"I do not understand," D'Arnot said sharply.

Tarzan blinked and stared directly at him, surprised by the sudden change of tone.

"What is this amulet that it has you so worried?" D'Arnot asked bluntly. "It's just a piece of crystal. Would you value that above the life of Collette de Coude?"

"Of course not," Tarzan was quick to reply. "But, indeed, as you said, you do not understand. This amulet is reputed to be a key."

"To . . ."

Tarzan shook his head. "All I know is that if Rokoff is allowed to use it, then many people, perhaps all the world, will likely be in great danger," he explained.

D'Arnot's expression revealed his skepticism.

"Do not underestimate the power of such a gem," Tarzan warned.

"I have seen many more expensive, many larger, many finer," D'Arnot pointed out.

Tarzan sat back in his seat, his gaze going back to the countryside that continued to hurtle past his window. Paul D'Arnot, like his fellow gentlemen of the civilized world, was a man of logic and science. Tarzan would not devalue the power of those two disciplines, but it seemed to him that society was embracing them at a severe cost: a blindness to anything that did not fit into their scheme of things. D'Arnot would not be able to appreciate that which his science could not explain. He and his fellows would likely dismiss any of the old legends as mere superstition, just as the medical doctors of the day dismissed the herbal healing skills of the jungle tribesmen—despite the very real anecdotal evidence that the salves and potions often worked.

"I can give you no specifics," Tarzan said evasively. "That single crystal could bring war, famine, or plague—dangers such as Africa, as all the world, has never seen."

Now D'Arnot fell back in his seat. War was a concept that he most certainly could appreciate; there always seemed to be one or another going on someplace. The United States couldn't seem to keep its army out of the Caribbean, and tensions in all of Europe were high. He gave a derisive snicker as he considered the truth that many of history's battles had been fought over something as petty as a piece of jewelry.

"Then I must go with you, *mon ami,*" he said at length. "If this amulet is so important, then we must find it—*and* Collette."

"I hope she will still be alive," Tarzan said, his voice fading away, his gaze lingering on the countryside.

D'Arnot, who had seen Tarzan's exchanges with the enchanting Lady de Coude, believed him, and allowed him his privacy. D'Arnot, too, looked out the window, noting the rolling farmlands of southern France. He recognized one distant farm, a landmark for train travelers, and knew that they were getting close.

The train arrived in Marseilles right on schedule, soon after sunset. D'Arnot wanted to go and secure a hotel room, but at Tarzan's insistence, they went right to the docks and began their search.

"I have contacts here," D'Arnot explained, working hard to keep up with the impatient Tarzan. "Perhaps I can learn of Rokoff while I book us passage to Mombasa."

Tarzan stopped short and looked hard at his friend. "Us?"

"I said that I would go with you," D'Arnot protested immediately, recognizing that doubting stare. "All the way."

Tarzan thought about it for just a moment, then smiled and motioned for D'Arnot to be on his way.

"Will you accompany me to the tavern where many of the ship captains spend their nights?" D'Arnot asked. "Who knows what information we might discover there?"

"I am not accustomed to spying," Tarzan replied. "Scouting, not spying."

"Is there a difference?"

"You search the secrets of men; I search the secrets of shadows," Tarzan said, his alert gaze darting from ships to piled crates to warehouses. He jerked suddenly, startled.

"What do you know?"

Tarzan held up a hand, begging silence. After a moment he relaxed somewhat. "Make your inquiries and secure our passage," he said, and before D'Arnot could press the point, he sprinted away, blending effortlessly with the night.

"So good to know that we are working in harmony," D'Arnot said dryly. "One hand coordinating its movements with the other, of course." He held up his hand as he spoke, and looked from it to the shadows wherein Tarzan had disappeared. "Not that my hand has any idea of what Tarzan's hand might be doing," he remarked with a great sigh.

———

Tarzan moved silently away from his friend, using the shadows for cover. He found a good hiding place, dark and quiet, then stood perfectly still, cocked his head and listened.

The sound came again, a low growling, a noise wrought more of frustration than anger, a noise well known by the man who had come out of the jungle into the civilized world. He moved down an alley, its left wall comprised of more piles of crates, its right the unremarkable wood of an old warehouse. Woven within the smell of the sea was another scent, a familiar scent. He came around the building; the scene, though it was not unexpected, disheartened him.

A black leopard, a large male weighing well over two hundred pounds, crouched in a cage that was barely as large as the average Paris outhouse. Tarzan closed his eyes, all other problems vanishing in the face of this insult, this tragedy. He moved to the cage and squatted in front of the bars.

The leopard's ears went back, lip curling away to reveal fangs still white. That would change, Tarzan knew. Those beautiful incisors would soon go yellow, would probably rot and fall out.

Like the spirit of the cat.

Tarzan grasped the bars, never taking his gaze off the great cat, locking stares and telling the creature with his expression and his scent that he was no enemy. The ears came up; the snarling visage flattened to calm. Tarzan reached forward to gently touch the leopard's chin, and the animal, desperate, nuzzled his hand.

"Is this your cage?" Tarzan asked suddenly, not of the cat, but of the man he sensed behind him.

"Neither the enclosure nor the animal," came the reply in

a perfect British accent, one that Tarzan, Lord Greystoke, knew well. He pulled the leopard's ear, then stood upright, turning about—and was somewhat surprised to find that the man watching him was black-skinned, an African, though he was dressed in a suit customary of British society.

"He should be free," Tarzan said.

"So should we all," replied the stranger, extending his hand. "I am Joshua Mugambi."

Tarzan accepted the shake, felt strength and sincerity in the man's grasp. "My name is Jean Tarzan," he said.

"I thought he would tear your hand away," Joshua remarked, looking past Tarzan to the cage.

Tarzan smiled. "I have a way with animals," he explained.

"So it would seem."

Tarzan looked all around at the deserted surroundings, then back at this man who seemed so out of place. His skeptical expression asked all the questions.

"I missed my boat," Joshua explained. "And am waiting for the next."

"Out here, and not in the comfort of a tavern?" Tarzan returned.

"I have had enough of taverns, of all of this," Joshua replied. "It is good to walk in the night alone, I think, though when I heard the cat, I found myself wanting his company." Joshua cocked his head, regarding Tarzan curiously, the set of his back, the ponytail. "I believe you understand," he said with a bright smile.

Tarzan couldn't return that look. Not now; not with the leopard caged right behind him.

"I am returning to my tribe and my family in Africa," Joshua went on. "And you?"

"My family is no longer alive," Tarzan answered. "But I am also returning home."

"I understand," said Joshua. "My father is . . . was, a chief in the Waziri tribe. I was told that he died, and so I must return."

"I hope your trip ends more pleasantly than it is beginning," Tarzan said quietly.

"It will end as it has been determined," Joshua replied, straightening his shoulders. "My destiny is clear to me. I have to serve my tribe."

Tarzan regarded the man for a long, silent moment. He approved of the posture, of the inner strength revealed there. Mugambi's face was soft, delicate almost, dark eyes full of compassion and intelligence. His features were well-proportioned, finely sculpted, though his cheeks seemed almost hinged, so wide was his smile. He held himself with comfortable ease, yet there was little doubt of the strength of his backbone. The Waziri tribe would not suffer for the loss of their last chief, Tarzan judged, though he maintained that Joshua Mugambi certainly looked out of sorts in British finery.

"You have your duty," Tarzan said.

Mugambi, who had been similarly sizing up Tarzan, and who, like his counterpart, approved of what he saw, replied, "I believe you understand."

A movement to the side caught the attention of both men. Tarzan recognized the shuffle and cane movements of Paul D'Arnot, and put a hand out, motioning for Joshua to be at ease. When his companion came into sight, Tarzan nodded to him and began to introduce him, but D'Arnot, who was obviously upset, moved right past Joshua Mugambi, offering only a curt nod, took Tarzan by the arm and pulled him aside. "Rokoff, Paulvitch, and Collette de Coude left for Africa this morning," he explained. "I have arranged our passage for tomorrow morning."

Tarzan was not surprised; he had expected that Rokoff would move quickly. Still, he had hoped to catch the man in France, before he got dangerously close to his destination with that powerful amulet. Uttering a snarl of frustration, Tarzan turned away from D'Arnot, then focused his ire on the cage bars insulting the great panther. He grabbed the padlock and gave it a sharp pull.

"No, please, *mon ami*," D'Arnot had seen this behavior before. "You cannot let a wild animal loose on the streets of Marseilles. He's headed for the zoo—not the best life, perhaps, but life, at least. If you let him loose, he will surely be killed."

"Then I'll let him free in Africa," Tarzan replied angrily.

"Of course," D'Arnot agreed. "Why didn't I think of that? If we weren't already riding steerage, we could get a larger cabin. The three of us could take our meals together at the captain's table. Some after-dinner brandy . . . a cigar, perhaps . . . leg of seaman . . ."

Tarzan's cold expression let D'Arnot know in no uncertain terms that he was finding no humor in his friend's sarcasm, well-intended as it might have been.

"Buy him back," Tarzan said in all seriousness. "He must also return home."

D'Arnot started to reply, but just gave a great, resigned sigh and looked helplessly to Joshua Mugambi.

Joshua answered with a friendly, sincerely amused look, for that simple exchange between Tarzan and D'Arnot had told him much about Jean Tarzan, had shown him something completely unexpected and wonderfully refreshing, coming from any white man. Mugambi's smile became a laugh then, and D'Arnot, defeated, joined in.

Tarzan did not, though. He could not, with the caged leopard so close, with Collette de Coude in so much danger, and with the specter that was the crystal amulet hanging in his thoughts.

"Let us go and find someplace to sleep," D'Arnot said after a few moments, when his laughter became uncomfortable in the face of Tarzan's obvious dismay. "We will be at sea with the rising sun."

Tarzan didn't argue, didn't say another word the rest of the night.

CHAPTER 5

She swirled about the small open area of floor, turning and twisting sensually, feeding off the hunger of the many men seated about the room, moving her veils just right to heighten the allure. Several dancers entertained at the feast, but Rokoff's eyes were fixed on this particular one, a woman of no more than twenty years, but with the wiles and moves of one much older, much more experienced. She had noticed his gaze and locked upon it, moving closer, then swirling away, then moving closer still. She was playing with him, whetting his appetite with the promise of sweets.

Rokoff reached out for her, but she was much too agile for the lunge, and with a graceful spin she was just out of reach, just inches from his fingers. Rokoff nearly overbalanced trying to get his hands on her, nearly went headlong into the huge plates piled with food set about the many plush pillows on the floor.

The dancer smiled and kept teasingly close, rhythmically

swaying those beautiful hips back and forth, back and forth. Rokoff heard a loud laugh from the side, but did not turn his eyes away from the object of his desire.

"You want her?" came a buoyant call, and Rokoff was nudged hard on the shoulder. Now he did turn, first to see the grease the fingers had left on his expensive jacket, then to regard the half-eaten leg of lamb and the bear of a man, Achmet Zek, who was holding it. Zek reached over behind Collette de Coude's shoulders to poke Rokoff again, laughing all the louder.

"Get you some decent clothing, my friend," he was rambling, but Rokoff was hardly listening. Now that his attention had shifted, he was too interested in taking a full measure of the man. Zek reminded Rokoff of Alexis Paulvitch, with that same barrel-shaped torso, same lack of any discernable neck. But Achmet Zek, of course, was Arabian and much darker in complexion than the blotchy-skinned Paulvitch, and Zek, Rokoff continually reminded himself, was much more intelligent.

Much more dangerous.

"You want her?" the huge man asked again, rolling with laughter.

Laughter came easily to Achmet Zek, but with him it was most often a wicked thing indeed, the mirth manufactured at the expense of another.

"She is yours," Zek declared. "I bought her two years ago from the traders. She has great experience in the ways of pleasure, for one so young."

Rokoff nodded and looked back to the girl, his suspicions confirmed.

"You bought her?" Collette de Coude interjected, squirming to get the leaning Achmet Zek away from her. "She's a slave?"

"Be quiet," Rokoff snapped at her. "Remember your place and do no offend our host."

Collette's icy glare went from Zek to Rokoff, then back to Zek, who regarded her with an amused expression.

"I have women who can train this one, if you wish," he said to Rokoff, smiling all the wider at Collette's obvious disgust. To Collette's shock, Zek grabbed her by the cheek and gave her head a sudden jerk. "If they cannot teach her silence, they can easily cut out her tongue."

Collette pulled away and looked back to Rokoff, convinced that even he would not stand for such horrible talk.

"I'll think about it," Rokoff answered, in all seriousness. Then to the stunned Collette, he added, "I hope you heard him well, my dear."

Collette composed herself quickly, purposefully shifting her emotions from incredulity to that defensive wall of anger. She had to be strong, she told herself. Showing her fear—and who would not be frightened by this sudden, overwhelming turn of events—would only fuel Rokoff's wicked nature, and would probably thoroughly amuse the wretch, Achmet Zek. She shifted back against a pillow, removing herself from the line of sight of the two men flanking her. She meant to detach herself thoroughly, to tune her senses completely out of the conversation and out of this decadent place. But then Rokoff unexpectedly placed the amulet, her amulet, on the short-legged table in front of them.

Achmet Zek gasped, barely able to draw his breath. "You have succeeded," he said after a moment.

"That's my father's!" Collette blurted, and despite her resolve, she reached for the item.

Rokoff's hand came down hard, slamming Collette's arm against the closest lip of the table, then holding it there. "Was your father's, my dear," he said. "*Was*. Consider it part of your dowry."

Collette struggled but his grip was too strong. With his free hand Rokoff motioned to one of Zek's many servants. "Take her to her room," he instructed. "And keep her there."

"I will not go!" Collette began, but Rokoff's look, icy cold, somehow less than human, sent her intended tirade right back into her throat.

"Go silently," Rokoff said, with such calm, with such an undertone of malice, that Collette, in light of Achmet Zek's words about cutting out her tongue, didn't dare disobey.

She rose and didn't even try to pull her arm from the servant's grasp—not until she was out of Rokoff's line of sight. She glanced back many times as she was led from the large room, the sights, the sounds, the smells overwhelming her sensibilities, leaving her at a loss to respond. Just a week before, she had been in the safety and comfort of familiar Paris, surrounded by her father and friends. How could she ever have expected this?

Collette had always longed for adventure; it had occurred to her that was why Jean Tarzan had so intrigued her. But this decadence was not what she had in mind, and she did not find this level of fear, cold and clammy, a terror wrought of complete helplessness, in any way exciting.

She just wanted to go home.

Achmet Zek rolled with laughter as Collette was led away, then howled all the louder when he saw that Rokoff apparently wasn't giving her a second thought. He prodded Rokoff with the leg of lamb again, as Rokoff reached once more for the teasing dancer.

"You have recovered the key to the temple," Achmet Zek bellowed. "Ah, what a glorious day!"

"No easy task," Rokoff replied, his eyes never leaving the girl's swiveling hips. "Now you can show us how it is that the amulet will reward us."

"That, too, will be difficult," Achmet Zek stammered.

Rokoff snapped an angry glare over him. "Getting the amulet here was also difficult," he pointed out. "You assured me that it was the key to great wealth, else why would I have gone to the trouble and the cost of retrieving it? Is there a difference in your thinking now?"

Achmet Zek scoffed at him and gnawed a huge hunk out of the leg of lamb. "Would you have brought the amulet here if you did not require my knowledge?" he reminded Rokoff.

"Of course not," Rokoff was quick to reply. "But would you have it at all if it were not for *my* abilities? I have a way of making things happen—good things for my friends, and bad things for my enemies."

Achmet Zek did not respond to the obvious threat, but he did indeed respect this dangerous Russian.

"Like it or not, my friend," Rokoff continued, "we are in a joint venture. If this amulet is as valuable as you claim, there should be more than enough to satisfy our greed—both of us."

Achmet Zek stared at him for a long while, watching Rokoff as he returned his attentions to the dancer. Rokoff almost caught her this time, his hand brushing against her thigh, tearing free one of her many veils as she spun with a giggle. Zek didn't know what to make of the man. Rokoff and his one lackey were surrounded by a hundred of his own men, in his own palatial fortress, hidden amidst the crowded streets of the lowest section of the city. He could have them both killed and dumped into the gutter, and their bodies would not likely ever be identified. Yet here he was, this intriguing Rokoff, sitting calmly, thinking of carnal pleasures, even offering a subtle threat to him, the man who so obviously held all the cards.

"It is from a place called the Temple of the Ancients," Achmet Zek heard himself saying, though he could hardly believe that he was offering the information. "A place of the greatest treasures and greatest dangers, legends say. Many have sought it, but few have returned, and those who have, came back empty-handed and empty-headed."

Rokoff turned to regard him.

"Driven mad," Achmet Zek added gravely. Then he relaxed and his voice took on less dramatic tones. "Of course, these are just rumors. We really don't know how many, if any, have succeeded in even reaching the temple."

"Or if there even is a Temple of the Ancients?" Rokoff put in, his eyes narrowing.

"Oh, but there is," Achmet Zek insisted.

"For the trouble I have already gone through—" Rokoff began.

"If you don't believe it, I will buy the crystal from you now, and be done with it," said Achmet Zek.

Rokoff eyed Zek suspiciously. The man was trying to play both ends against him, trying to frighten him and tantalize him all at once in an attempt to discern his level of commitment and, possibly, his value to the continuing quest. It was all very predictable, and Rokoff was prepared for the tactics. "If I didn't believe it, I would not have gone to the immense trouble of getting the amulet," he said quietly. "I only wish that you had more information than the rambling of frightened amateurs."

"I have the legends," Achmet Zek insisted. "Legends that are older than you or I, older even than the city itself. The Temple of the Ancients is very real, I assure you."

"And the treasure?"

"In the temple there is a pylon of gold that reaches to the sky!" Achmet Zek said emphatically.

Rokoff hid his smile and turned his gaze back to the dancer. He had already coerced Zek into admitting more than the man had ever intended, and had, through a subtle twist in the tone of the dialogue, placed Zek on the defensive, thus elevating himself to a position of authority. No, Achmet Zek would not dispose of him and take the amulet. Not yet.

"I am willing to lead the party to this temple and the pylon of gold," Rokoff said calmly, never looking away from the girl.

"Why would you go?" Achmet Zek asked bluntly.

"Because I have the amulet," Rokoff replied.

Achmet Zek reflexively looked to the item they were discussing, lying there, within his grasp. When he looked back at Rokoff, he found the man studying him closely.

"But you could take the amulet," Rokoff admitted, "to the detriment of us both. I want my share of this, a share I have already earned, but I know the prudence of keeping myself valuable to you."

"My men could go," Achmet Zek reasoned, but his words sounded hollow to both him and to Rokoff. The Russian had intrigued Achmet Zek, had earned the slave lord's respect, first with his cunning in obtaining the amulet and now with his blunt admission, his apparent understanding of their relationship.

"You have the proper man to lead them?" Rokoff asked doubtfully.

"I lead them."

Rokoff nodded, conceding the point. "But you are far removed from the jungle, and need not leave the luxuries of your palace. The heat, the insects, the snakes, the great cats . . ." Rokoff paused, letting the thoughts hang in the air. He had done his homework concerning Achmet Zek, had learned that the man, accustomed to living well, was queasy about such things, particularly the insects.

He waited a bit longer, letting Achmet Zek squirm, then offered graciously, "I will take this uncomfortable journey and return with the treasure."

"My men would accompany you," Achmet Zek said quickly. He smiled widely, too politely. "They would guide your return, of course."

Rokoff matched that smile. "Of course," he agreed. "Then you know the way."

Again the telling pause; Rokoff recognized that he had set Achmet Zek off balance. "Perhaps I have someone who does," the large man admitted.

Rokoff glanced at the side of the room, where Paulvitch was laying back, surrounded by a mountain of pillows and heaps of food. Between bites the large man gulped down spirits, right from the bottle, spilling as much on his shirt as in his mouth.

Rokoff made a mental note to speak with Alexis privately about his behavior. Carelessness would get them killed. A look back to Achmet Zek reassured the Russian, though. His tactics in the discussion had put Zek into a state of paralyzing confusion, and he and Paulvitch were safe enough for the time being. Rokoff let it go at that, and turned his attention, and not just the appearance of his attention, to the swaying belly dancer. He felt a slight twinge of regret concerning Collette de Coude, a prize he did indeed treasure, but that emotion could not hold, not with the young and practiced dancer so close, smelling so sweet. And, even more importantly, with the promise of a pylon of gold dangling before him.

Just as he was falling again under the spell of the dancer, though, he noticed the entrance of another of Achmet Zek's henchmen, a one-eyed Arab named Hadab. The man was scarred and as ugly in appearance as he was in temperament. Rokoff had dealt with this one before, and the man's appearance immediately put him back on his guard. He took one of the pillows and tossed it on top of Paulvitch, getting his attention.

Paulvitch came up groggily on one elbow, pulling away from the woman who had settled on the bed of pillows beside him. He looked back to regard Rokoff, his initial expression showing anger—clearly he was not thrilled at being disturbed at that particular moment. When he followed Rokoff's gaze to Hadab, he calmed considerably and nodded to his master, an assurance that he was prepared for trouble.

Hadab made his way across the room to Achmet Zek, all those in his path willingly scattering before him. With a less-than-hospitable look to Rokoff, the one-eyed man bent low and began whispering in Zek's ear.

Achmet Zek's gaze fell over Rokoff. The slave lord nodded repeatedly, thoughtfully, as Hadab continued his report.

Then Achmet Zek put his hand up and Hadab straightened, his stare, an accusing look, locking on the Russian ex-patriot.

"Is there anyone else awaiting your arrival in this country?" Achmet Zek asked Rokoff.

Rokoff glanced back, for just a split second, to Paulvitch, and the big man pulled himself from the pillows and moved closer.

"No," Rokoff answered Zek. "I left France suddenly, without notice to anyone."

"No friends?" Achmet Zek pressed. "No enemies?"

"Is there a problem?" Rokoff asked bluntly.

Achmet Zek looked to Hadab, then, after a reassuring nod from his primary henchman, turned back to the Russian. "There are two men asking questions about you and your companion and about the location of my palace," he explained.

"No one knows I am here," Rokoff insisted.

Achmet Zek looked to Hadab again, and the Arab bent low in another whispered conversation. Rokoff gave Paulvitch a warning look; even if these two men were not any real threat, their mere appearance might have stolen credibility from Rokoff and Paulvitch, and credibility, Rokoff knew, was the primary thing keeping him alive.

"A man named D'Arnot," Achmet Zek said a moment later. "And another called Tarzan."

Rokoff couldn't hide his surprise, his outrage. His face clouded over. "Tarzan is dead," he replied.

"Then his ghost is hunting for you," Achmet Zek insisted. "He was talking to my man Hadab less than an hour ago. By now he might even know of this location. I am too well known for it to remain a secret."

Rokoff looked to Hadab, judged the man as competent,

then turned his icy glare over Paulvitch. "You seem to have perfected failure," he said evenly.

"He dropped," Paulvitch sputtered. "He was hit—I saw the blood. The monkey . . . if it wasn't for the monkey . . ."

Achmet Zek's laughter turned Rokoff's attention from his fumbling lackey.

"Allow me to extend a courtesy, Nikolas," Achmet Zek said. "This is a very simple matter to handle."

"I'd be most grateful for your services," Rokoff replied. He was thinking otherwise, though, thinking that this situation was not so simple. Achmet Zek would take care of the meddling D'Arnot and the troublesome Tarzan, he did not doubt, but what price would that favor exact?

Achmet Zek smiled widely, and motioned for Rokoff to turn his thoughts back to the dancer, as though all of this was no large matter.

Rokoff knew better, and his last glance at Paulvitch before he did turn back to the girl told Alexis the same.

Paul D'Arnot fumbled with his voluminous white robes, an outfit obviously too large for him.

Tarzan, similarly outfitted in garb they had stolen from two of Achmet Zek's guards, put a hand out to calm him. "Too much noise," he scolded quietly.

D'Arnot finally pulled himself to the edge of the low roof, lying flat on his belly and peering over, as was his larger friend.

"They must be in Achmet Zek's palace," D'Arnot whispered. "But his men are everywhere. We can't get close to the place."

"As long as Rokoff and the amulet are here, we can be patient," Tarzan replied. "Let them make the next move. We don't want to endanger Collette."

D'Arnot looked around doubtfully. They had paid good money for this information, but it had been sold to them, after all, by a street thug, a man who, in D'Arnot's estimation, would sell his own mother—and cheaply. It was quite possible that they had been sent on a wild-goose chase, or even more possible that the thug would then turn around and sell information of them to this Achmet Zek character. "You're sure they're here?" he asked, and when his companion did not make any move to answer, he pressed, "You're sure?"

"The guards patrol for a reason," Tarzan replied.

"It's likely that a man in Achmet Zek's position has made many enemies," D'Arnot reasoned. "That is why he employs guards in the first place, is it not?"

Tarzan gave him a resigned look that conveyed his frustration with D'Arnot's entire argument. Of course Tarzan could not be absolutely certain that Collette, Rokoff, and the amulet were inside Achmet Zek's palace, any more than could D'Arnot, who had been beside Tarzan every step through the city's streets and taverns. But what else did they have to go on? And, by Tarzan's estimation, the sheer number of patrolling guards was certainly a good sign.

"They are here," Tarzan insisted.

"Then you have a plan?"

"We wait," Tarzan said emphatically. "As long as they do not get to the Temple of the Ancients, we have a chance."

D'Arnot once again wanted to inquire further about this mysterious temple to which Tarzan kept referring, but a noise from the back side of the roof stole his attention. He and Tarzan turned to see two men, Achmet Zek's guards, pulling themselves over the edge of the roof.

With a quick glance below, Tarzan grabbed D'Arnot and hauled him over, dropping him as gently as possible. Then Tarzan hooked his hands on a top lip of a trellis and swung down gracefully to land at D'Arnot's side in a ready crouch.

"Left," D'Arnot warned, climbing to his feet.

Tarzan had already noted the two additional guardsmen, coming onto the street down to the left. And they had noted Tarzan and D'Arnot, and began a steady approach.

Tarzan and D'Arnot turned right, to see three more guards coming at them from that direction. There was a side alley directly across from them, but that, too, was blocked by approaching guardsmen.

"Waiting sounded pretty good for about sixty seconds," D'Arnot said dryly. "Right now, I'd suggest running."

Easier said than done, Tarzan realized, as the ring of guards closed tighter. "When I break the circle, you escape," he instructed. "I'll follow."

"I do like simple plans," D'Arnot replied, taking up his cane and assuming a fencer's stance. "When they work!" he added emphatically as the nearest Arabs charged, one of them slapping a club against his palm.

"En garde!" D'Arnot cried, shuffling forward. Tarzan looked at him skeptically, to which the Frenchman only shrugged. His unusual posture did serve to slow the nearest Arab's charge, however, as the man lowered his arms and stared curiously.

D'Arnot's trailing foot came up to his front, then front forward, and again, a quick shuffle that put him in striking distance. A quick poke of the cane caught the Arab in the forehead with a resounding crack, and the man fell away.

Then D'Arnot skittered back, swishing his cane in front of him to fend off the second guard, a true giant of a man.

Tarzan's method was more straightforward. Three guards came at him, arms outstretched to tackle. Tarzan waited until they were right near him, one man ahead of the others, then he leaped up and reached his hands back over his head, catching fast the trellis. Out came his legs in a powerful double kick on the closest man's chest that sent him flying backward into his two companions, the three of them going down in a heap.

Up went Tarzan's legs again, higher, then back down, then up again in rapid succession, gaining momentum with each motion. Out he leaped, springing farther than the charging men could anticipate, leaping right into their midst and bearing them to the ground. Those he had kicked down were rising again, right behind him, but he moved with fluid grace, spinning and punching, spinning back and kicking at his newest foes, and back and forth, keeping all six men off balance, knocking them repeatedly off their feet.

"But I am too quick for you," D'Arnot teased the huge man, slapping his cane repeatedly against the man's futilely reaching hands. "Hah! See how you cannot catch up to my perfect moves?" To accentuate the point, the now-confident D'Arnot slapped his cane to the side, connecting solidly on the Arab's fingers, then stepped ahead and slammed the cane with all his might on the man's bony forehead.

The cane snapped in half; the giant guard seemed not to notice.

The next thing he knew, D'Arnot found himself up in the air above the guard's head and all the world was spinning.

A kick sent one guard sprawling, a quick turn inside a punching arm brought Tarzan against the chest of another. He grabbed the flying forearm and tugged it along, using the man's momentum against him, flipping him right over his shoulder. Even as that one tumbled away, Tarzan leaped into a back kick that connected solidly on the chest of another, knocking him and another unfortunate guard trying to stand up behind him back to the ground.

Then Tarzan saw D'Arnot's unenviable position, the small man about to be hurled into a wall. Tarzan went into a crouch, and then with a powerful spring, like that of a hunting cat, he easily cleared twenty feet to land right beside the giant guard.

The man threw D'Arnot; Tarzan caught him by the arm before he could go very far, and with a subtle twist brought him spinning down, right to his feet. With his other arm, and with the strength of several men, Tarzan caught the giant guard by the throat and held him at bay.

"That way!" Tarzan yelled, holding D'Arnot long enough for the man to find his center of balance, then shoving him along an apparently open route. "Now!"

But before D'Arnot could begin to get going, another half-dozen guardsmen came into view, blocking the route. Hadab led them, his one-eyed visage twisted with apparent glee.

"That is the ugliest man I have ever seen," D'Arnot remarked.

Hadab drew out a huge and curving scimitar and motioned to his men. They came forward slowly, stalking, and all holding long knives, several with blades nearly as long as their leader's.

The stakes had been raised, Tarzan knew, and he dispatched the huge guard with a sudden, vicious chop to the neck that dropped the man, gasping, to the ground.

Then the jungle man was surrounded, guards coming from the roof, others recovering from his earlier strikes to come at him with renewed fury, and with Hadab's men reinforcing their line. But though Achmet Zek's lackeys were stronger now, so was Tarzan. His mind fell into that primal state, that survivalistic instinct that had seen him through most of his life in the jungle. A guard hurtled at him from the left, another from the right, and Tarzan went straight up, leaping high and tucking his legs under him. His attackers slammed into each other, each stumbling back a step. And Tarzan landed in perfect, easy balance between them, lashing out with both hands even as his feet touched the ground. Those two dispatched, he threw an elbow straight out behind him, smashing a nose, then he dove forward, ducking his shoulder and rolling hard into the leg of a charging man, sending him flying over.

Up came Tarzan, finding a low center of balance in a defensive crouch. A knifing strike came in from the left; he caught the hand above the knife blade, pulled it straight down, then let go and reversed his own hand, smashing his cupped palm into the attacker's face. At the same time, Tarzan's right hand weaved in looping circles around the stabbing knife of another man, his movements keeping the attacker too off balance and too distracted to get in close to his intended quarry. Gradually, Tarzan tightened those circles, and then he snapped his hand on the knife-wielder's forearm, catching it tight and twisting it back over so that the man could not maneuver the blade for a strike.

Another man came in hard; Tarzan turned his current captive's arm over even more, bringing the man right across in front of him, twisting him down at the feet of the newest attacker.

Tarzan leaped out to the side, away from the scramble. He was holding his own against a horde of ruffians, but he wasn't gaining any real ground, hadn't scored any definitive hits. And then he looked to D'Arnot, the man held immobile by two guards, and his heart sank.

He caught another movement off to the side in time, though, first falling low in a crouch as if he meant to body-block the man's legs out from under him, then, at the very last moment, leaping high, coming up past the stooping man's surprised expression, then back down with tremendous force, flattening the man.

Tarzan was up as quickly as if he had landed on springy rubber, gaining his feet and balance at once, and rushing out for D'Arnot.

"Behind you!" D'Arnot cried out before Tarzan had gone a full stride.

Tarzan spun to see the ugly, snarling visage of Hadab, to see the deadly scimitar coming straight down over Hadab's head, a mighty chop that would split his skull in half.

But to Tarzan's heightened senses everything seemed to move slowly. Up snapped his hands with perfect timing, slapping on either side of the descending blade, his iron muscles cording immediately, pushing in, in.

Hadab's expression changed to one of sheer incredulity;

several of Hadab's cronies, and D'Arnot, too, gasped out in amazement.

Tarzan had stopped the scimitar in mid-swing!

Hearing nothing, seeing nothing but the deadly blade, Tarzan tightened his muscles even more and began lifting the scimitar. Hadab, his paralyzation stolen by simple fear, growled and pushed down all the harder. It was exactly what Tarzan was counting on.

For the Arab overbalanced, came too far forward on his toes. Tarzan snapped the blade to the right, then back over to the left, the sudden jerking tearing the scimitar free of Hadab's grasp. Tarzan tossed the weapon aside with hardly a thought, then grabbed Hadab by the chest and pulled him in, falling to his back and throwing the man right over.

Tarzan was up in an instant, turning again to D'Arnot and the Arabs, now three, holding him.

The third man, the one mostly in front of D'Arnot, wanted nothing to do with Tarzan, though, and so he lifted his huge knife right to D'Arnot's throat, creasing the skin.

Tarzan stopped in mid-stride, staring, looking for some opening. There was no way he could get to his friend in time, he feared; the frightened guard would slash with the knife at his first obvious move.

"Do not submit to them, Tarzan!" D'Arnot yelled.

Tarzan wasn't listening. He tried to keep a solid measure on the man with the knife, gauging his alertness as he slowly slid one foot a bit closer. The man stiffened, shifted his fingers for a more secure hold on the blade, and Tarzan knew that the game was at its end. He relaxed and straightened, then held his hands out in front of him in a pose of surrender.

Three Arabs were there in an instant, one binding Tarzan's wrists, while the other two put their blades to his throat.

"Tarzan, no," D'Arnot pleaded. "Think of Collette!"

"I am," Tarzan started to say, but his words ended with a grunt as Hadab, having retrieved his scimitar, slammed him on the back of the head with the heavy ball of the pommel, knocking him out cold.

CHAPTER 6

J ean?" he heard, as if from far, far away. "Jean, are you all right?" It was all vaguely familiar to him, coming back from his wounds to hear the sound of that friendly voice.

He could still taste the aftermath of blood in his mouth, that sickly sweet residue. The throbbing on the back of his head took his sensibilities back to the city street, the fight with the Arabs, the one-eyed man. The smells that came to him were different, though, damp and musty now, and the sound, the echo of that familiar voice, told him that he was indoors, probably underground.

With great effort, Tarzan opened his eyes. He was standing, or would have been had his legs been able to support him, chained by the wrists against a rough stone wall. And he was in a cell, a cage lined on three sides by vertical bars sunk into the stone floor. A similar cage was set beside his, and two more across a narrow aisle. There was Paul D'Arnot, across the way. Tarzan knew immediately that it was D'Arnot, though in the minimal light—a couple of smoking torches set high on walls—and with his eyes still half closed from caked blood, he could not make out many details.

D'Arnot was lying on the floor, propped on one elbow and looking his way. D'Arnot started to rise, but then began squirming, moving in jerky motions that Tarzan recognized as fear. Instinctively the jungle man tried to fight through his dizziness and pain to somehow aid his friend, but the chains were heavy and well-secured, and he could hardly stir.

D'Arnot cried out and kicked at something, rolling aside, and Tarzan heard the squeak of a rat. The little creature rushed out through the bars on the front of D'Arnot's cage, scurrying straight across the narrow aisle and into Tarzan's cell. The rat moved right up to Tarzan, stood up on its hind legs and regarded him, its nose and whiskers twitching.

Tarzan could offer no nonverbal communication, could only hang there and hope that the rat would not decide to make a meal of his legs.

"Jean?" D'Arnot called again. "Please answer, *mon ami*."

"Your friend has been unconscious since his arrival," came another voice, a very proper British accent, a voice vaguely familiar to Tarzan, though in his present state of mind he couldn't begin to place it. "However, his breathing is constant," the speaker went on. "There is no reason to believe that he is soon to be deceased." He paused and gave a slight chuckle. "Unless, of course, Achmet Zek—"

"Who is it?" D'Arnot interrupted.

Tarzan saw his friend stand and move to the side of his cage, grasping the bars and peering through them. Tarzan, with a final glance at the rat, who, thankfully, seemed to have lost all interest in him, managed to turn his own head slightly. As his eyes adjusted to the gloom of the dungeon, he saw that he shared his cell with an old man, his bald and pale pate shining in the meager light. The man sat cross-legged, wrists set on his knees, hands upturned. He was deep in a meditative trance, it seemed to Tarzan, and so he had not been the speaker.

"'Oh, yes," D'Arnot said, recognition in his voice. "You were at the docks, by the leopard cage."

"Joshua Mugambi," came the reply, and Tarzan followed the sounds past the sitting old man to another, a black man, standing tall and looking back at D'Arnot with a broad and friendly smile.

"And you were on the boat with us," D'Arnot went on. "You had a cabin, a private room."

"We're all in steerage now, my friend," Mugambi replied. "My vaunted Oxford education proved a meager suit of armor, I am afraid, and did little to deter Achmet Zek from taking me prisoner. And you are Monsieur D'Arnot, I believe."

"Paul D'Arnot," D'Arnot replied. "I would say that it is good to see you, Monsieur Mugambi, but under these conditions . . ."

"Indeed."

Both men looked over at Tarzan. "Are you sure that he is all right?" D'Arnot asked.

"He would have no value to Achmet Zek if he were dead," Mugambi replied.

"Jean?" D'Arnot called again. "Tarzan?"

Tarzan managed a groan in reply, and opened his eyes a bit wider. His sensibilities were beginning to return now, along with his strength, though he feared that would do him little good in his present predicament. The chains were heavy, and even without them, the bars appeared solid. This was a dungeon, a place designed as a prison, and escape, even for one of Tarzan's strength and cunning, would be no easy matter.

"I'm sorry that you are in this situation," D'Arnot said to Mugambi. "I do hope that we are not the reason for your captivity."

"No, no, you are not," Joshua assured him. "I blame my own foolishness. I have been away for a long time, since I was a teenager, and a young teenager at that. I almost forgot about people like Achmet Zek, the rulers of the city bowels. In his demented mind anyone can be bought and sold."

"That is an outrage!" declared D'Arnot, standing tall in an imperious pose and slapping the bars defiantly. "I'll not stand by idly . . ."

Tarzan was too busy studying Mugambi to pay attention to D'Arnot's speech. He noted the man's amused smile, one he had seen often among the Africans when they were dealing with well-intentioned, if a bit condescending, white men such as Paul.

"Slavery is an outrage!" D'Arnot finished powerfully.

"I am no slave," Mugambi assured him. "I am only a prisoner . . . like you."

D'Arnot moved to respond, but only stuttered, the truth of the situation causing his argument to catch in his throat. Tarzan understood Paul's original intentions—to stand tall in defense of the black man against the outrage of slavery—and saw now, by D'Arnot's wide-eyed expression, that his friend had only just realized that this particular situation had nothing to do with the color of Mugambi's skin, or of his own.

The door at the far end of the room creaked open,

drawing the attention of the three prisoners—though Tarzan noted that the old man who sat cross-legged in the cell still didn't stir.

"Rokoff," D'Arnot groaned when the Russian, his lackey Paulvitch, the one-eyed Arab, and a huge Arab, a man even bigger than Paulvitch, entered the dungeon.

"I see you are consistent as an assassin and a thief," D'Arnot spat at Rokoff. "What will be my losses this time?"

"Maybe your life," Rokoff casually replied. "Maybe just your freedom. We shall have to wait and see which will bring me the most value—I already know which would give me the most pleasure."

"You are an insult to your father's family name!" D'Arnot said sternly, but Rokoff only laughed, walking by with apparent unconcern, moving to the bars to stare at the hanging Tarzan.

Tarzan kept his eyes nearly closed and his breathing quiet and steady, wanting to study the group and not provoke them. He was in no condition for confrontation.

"I hope the chain collar did not choke him to death, Achmet," Rokoff remarked.

"Oh, he is not dead, my friend," Achmet Zek replied. He motioned to Hadab and the one-eyed man reached over and picked up a bucket, then threw its contents, filthy, cold water, over Tarzan.

Despite his better judgment, the startled Tarzan erupted into action, struggling and twisting, pulling the chains to their length and cording his muscles, trying to break free. The chains were as solid and unyielding as they were heavy, with links as thick as Tarzan's thumb, and he soon realized the futility of his attempt and calmed.

The four onlookers meanwhile found tremendous enjoyment in the spectacle, laughing riotously.

"This one is strong, and a good size," Achmet Zek remarked. His voice was bubbly, jovial even, and thick with a North African accent. He sounded like one of the many street vendors in the city's vast open market, talking always with a smile. But, considering the goods with which this man bartered, that tone seemed terribly sinister. "He will bring a very good price," Zek finished.

"You are disgusting!" D'Arnot dared to say.

Achmet Zek turned to regard him, smiling widely. "That is a tongue soon to fall to the floor," the large man warned, and his happy grin left little doubt that he would enjoy such an act immensely.

Rokoff never bothered to turn to D'Arnot. He came forward, right to Tarzan's bars, barely five feet from the chained man. "You should have minded your business in Paris, Monsieur Tarzan," he said, putting his face in even closer, right between the bars. "This is the result of your stupidity."

Tarzan lunged forward powerfully, trying to angle so that he could get his foot up into that smirking face. His chains held him back, though, and Rokoff was quick enough and wise enough to take a step away.

"Then let us be glad that he is stupid," Achmet Zek put in. "Our gain!"

"I'll double any bid for all of us," D'Arnot declared suddenly. "I have funds in Paris."

"You are in Africa," Achmet Zek explained to him. "Here we deal in gold." All four were laughing as they started for the next cage in line, the one holding Joshua Mugambi and the old man.

"I can get gold!" D'Arnot cried, moving forward, grasping the bars.

Hadab's scimitar came up fast, the flat of the blade slapping against D'Arnot's fingers, forcing him to step back and to shut up, clutching his stung hands.

Achmet Zek wasn't listening to him anyway, nor was Rokoff. Both of them were bending low to regard the old man.

"This is the man I told you of," Achmet Zek explained. "His memory is the memory of the jungle itself."

Rokoff studied him for a long while, the perfect ease with which he sat, the perfect calm, despite his obviously dire situation. Rokoff reached into a pocket and produced the amulet, holding it up before him, letting the torchlight flicker through it as it rocked, sending splatters of light across the old man's face.

The ancient one's eyes opened slowly; Rokoff moved his hand back and forth hypnotically, then smiled as he noted the man's gaze moving to follow the amulet's course.

"You know what this is, old man?" Achmet Zek asked, coming forward to regard the man from over Rokoff's shoulder.

"I have waited a long time for it to appear," the old man replied in a gasping, scratchy voice. He reached out slowly for the crystal, but Rokoff pulled it away, keeping it just out of the man's reach. "It can now be returned," the old man insisted.

"It will be returned when I say," Rokoff answered. "And not before."

"It must be returned to the pylon," the old man insisted, his voice and movements stronger.

"A pylon of gold?" Rokoff asked.

That unexpectedly brought a smile to the old man's face. He regarded Rokoff and Achmet Zek, then moved his gaze higher, to Hadab and Paulvitch, noting the eagerness of their expressions, the subtle, nervous movements.

"As high as twenty men," he answered dramatically, lifting his arms high above him. "As wide as ten!"

Paulvitch, veritably drooling, came forward suddenly, but Rokoff pushed him back, calming him, calming them all. There were methods for gaining information from unwilling informants, as Rokoff had often instructed Paulvitch, and the first rule of employing those methods was to make sure that one did not seem too hungry. Once the others, particularly his stupid lackey, had been put back in their places, Rokoff turned his stern gaze back on the old man.

"I know the way," the man said solemnly. He gave a little chuckle, then settled back into his previous, meditative pose, his eyes gradually closing.

Rokoff crouched there for a long and quiet while considering the man and the potential gains.

And the potential disaster, he realized suddenly. Rokoff was a merciless man, ultimately selfish, and as such, he almost always viewed others in that same dark light. This old man had just admitted his value, and all seven others in the room had heard it.

"Take him out of this cage," Rokoff instructed Achmet Zek.

Zek balked at the notion. "Should I give him pillows and food?" he asked sarcastically. "Not a morsel, I say, until he proves what he claims!"

Rokoff stared at Zek condescendingly, the man missing his point entirely. "Take him out of this cage," he said again, pausing to emphasize each word, "and put him in that cage." He pointed across the aisle to the one remaining empty cell.

Achmet Zek started to protest, but then caught on to Rokoff's reasoning. If the old man was so valuable to him and Rokoff, what would stop these others from killing him? Achmet Zek motioned to Hadab, and the one-eyed man produced some keys, opened the cell door and roughly grabbed the old man, hauling him to his feet.

Any thoughts Joshua Mugambi had concerning making a break were squashed immediately by the bulk Paulvitch presented, standing warily at the open door. The old man was brought across the aisle and roughly tossed into the empty cell.

Both doors slammed shut with resounding rings. The old man never even tried to rise from where Hadab had thrown him, just shifted over into a sitting position, falling back into his meditative state.

Rokoff and Achmet Zek moved past their hulking henchmen, sweeping the pair up in their wake as they crossed the dungeon toward the exit, with none of the four giving Tarzan or D'Arnot as much as a look as they passed.

"I am prepared to leave immediately," Rokoff said to Zek when they arrived at the door.

"It will be under my authority," Achmet Zek answered.

D'Arnot moved to the closest edge of his cage, attempting to glean some information, trying to find a good measure of the relationship between these two men who had become his enemies.

"Be aware my friend," Achmet Zek went on, "Africa is my land. You will leave it only if I allow it."

D'Arnot glanced across and nodded to Tarzan. Such

rivalry, such open threats, between the two men might prove valuable.

The exterior door slammed shut suddenly, the four men gone, leaving the prisoners alone.

"Jean?" D'Arnot called. "Did you hear?"

Tarzan nodded, then pulled again at his chains, one at a time, but in control this time, testing their strength and not wildly trying to tear them loose.

"Our time runs short," D'Arnot reasoned. "With him"— D'Arnot motioned to the old man—"they have the way to . . ." He paused, considering all that he had seen. "You said the amulet was a key," he said suddenly, realizing only then the implications of it all.

"The Temple of the Ancients," Tarzan replied. "A place of great treasure, it is said."

"And great danger," came the old man's voice. The other three prisoners turned to regard him, but the old man sat quietly again, eyes closed.

"He seems calm enough for one who is about to visit such a place," Joshua Mugambi remarked, bending low and peering through the bars to study the aged face. Not a hint appeared that the old man had even heard Joshua. "He knows something," the black man reasoned.

Tarzan didn't doubt that. The legends of the Temple of the Ancients were many and muddled, whispers in the jungle shadows, secrets that few had learned and fewer had lived to talk about.

"You must not guide them to the temple," Tarzan implored the old man.

"My destiny is to return," the old man replied cryptically. "The amulet must be returned."

Tarzan continued to reason with him, but the old man closed his eyes and did not respond.

Finally, flustered, Tarzan looked across at D'Arnot, who was leaning on his cage, hands grasping the bars, his expression forlorn. Time was running out, they both knew, for Collette de Coude and for them, and, Tarzan understood, perhaps for all the world.

In one of the smoky hallways above the dungeon level, but still belowground, Achmet Zek and Hadab walked and plotted. Rokoff and Paulvitch had gone off, on Achmet Zek's suggestion, to find some pleasures, since their immediate future seemed as if it would offer few of those.

"I do not trust them," Hadab said. "Paulvitch is a bully and a fool, but Rokoff is dangerous."

Achmet Zek only laughed.

"You take lightly this treasure which could secure your place as the most powerful man in all of Africa," Hadab dared to add.

"I take no treasure lightly," Achmet Zek assured him. "It is our Russian friends that I take lightly."

"Do not underestimate Rokoff."

"Not at all!" Achmet Zek roared. "But this is my land," he said, poking his fat thumb into his own chest. "Rokoff will never leave Africa—he cannot secure passage on any ship without my knowledge." The large man patted Hadab on the shoulder as they walked. "In fact," he said, "Rokoff will not leave the jungle. You will take a party of men and accompany them to the temple. Let them assume the danger of the search. Let them lead, let them guide, let Rokoff gain the confidence of command. When the pylon is found and the way secured, you return to me without them. Very simple."

Hadab did not disagree. He had spent the better part of his adult life working as captain of Achmet Zek's guard, and, more importantly, as Achmet Zek's assassin. Many rivals had sprung up in Morocco over the years, and all of them, thanks to the efficient work of Hadab, were now buried deep in the ground.

To vicious Hadab, the trip into the jungle suddenly seemed much more palatable.

Rokoff, a man not unused to luxury, had never seen, had never imagined, anything like the second floor of Achmet Zek's palace. The large building was in the worst section of the city, and seemed unremarkable from the outside—a large and aging warehouse, perhaps. But inside, the place was full of color, of exotic and enticing aromas, of plush cushions and intricate rugs, and of exotic and alluring women. The second floor was even more hedonistic than the first, with every room carpeted wall-to-wall with thick pillows—except those rooms that featured a steaming bathtub—and with beaded curtains hanging across every portal. Women, seductively dressed in tiny outfits and tantalizing veils, seemed to be everywhere, spinning about, laughing, teasing.

A pair of them, including the young dancer he had previously pawed, were with Rokoff now, in a small side room, lounging on the pillows, one lying on either side of him. One nibbled his ear, the other lifted her gentle fingers to stroke his neck, but the obsessed man paid them little heed. Half turned on his side, propped on one elbow, he held the amulet above him, letting it dangle and twist at the end of its gold chain. His eyes sought the flickers of reflected light within its depths; he seemed no less fixated upon it than the old man had been. What treasures would this key bring to him? What power?

One of the women, giggling, reached up for the amulet, but Rokoff was quick to pull it away. "No, my pet, it is not for you," he mockingly scolded her.

Her reply was a pout.

"Ah, but you are the gift to me," Rokoff said, catching up the amulet in his fist, then running an extended knuckle softly down the pouting woman's nose. "Behave, or you'll be whipped," Rokoff whispered, and the other woman tittered. "And I will watch," Rokoff added lewdly, and then both women giggled.

Both went back to their kissing and stroking, but Rokoff, too immersed in dreams of power, brushed them away and stood up. Their protests sounded like a cat's mewling, he noted as he gave them a wry smile. He then exited the room, moving onto the balcony overlooking the main audience chamber on the first floor.

Glancing all about, Rokoff surveyed the area, looking for Achmet Zek's men—or women, for both, he understood, would serve the slave lord as spies. In his quiet pause he heard a not-unexpected sound, for Alexis Paulvitch was never quiet about anything.

Rokoff moved along the balcony and pushed aside the beaded curtain of the next small chamber. There was Paulvitch, wrestling with a woman on the bed, his clothing all disheveled, his mannerisms more those of a rutting elk than of a gentleman.

"Alexis, we must talk," Rokoff announced.

Paulvitch stopped his thrashing as if he had heard the sound of a gun bolt at the back of his head. He looked over his shoulder at Rokoff, his expression one of sheer incredulity. "Now?" he demanded.

"Now," Rokoff answered evenly.

"But—but—" Paulvitch stuttered.

"Now."

Paulvitch rolled off the side of the bed, twisting to his feet. He cast one last look back at the Arab, a girl of no more than seventeen, and with a helpless groan headed for the curtain, straightening and buttoning his pants as he went. The last thing he heard as he exited the room was a soft, complaining whimper from the girl, a sound that stole the strength from his thick legs.

"This must be very important," he said to Rokoff, who was leaning on the balcony, looking over.

"If I say I want to speak to you, it becomes important to you," Rokoff answered without bothering to look at his man. "I am the judge of importance and urgency, and decide when and where you take your pleasures." He gave a curt nod and began walking, wanting to cover their conversation with footsteps, and also to keep any of Achmet Zek's potential spies from hearing any length of the discussion.

"I'm sorry," Paulvitch stuttered a moment later, when they passed Rokoff's room. The two women were still visible, and obviously feeling playful, on the bed of pillows. "This must be important," Paulvitch remarked.

"Do not presume to question me."

"No, no, of course not," the big man immediately responded, spittle flying with every eager word. "It's just that girl," he tried to explain, glancing back toward his room. "That girl. She has some special abilities that are almost hypnotic. I forgot myself."

Rokoff clicked his heel on the hard floor and turned to regard his lackey, his expression stern. "I may just get tired of reminding you," he warned. "Remember that if I do not succeed in my plans, I will not have the power or the wealth to keep the royal executioner from your neck."

Paulvitch paled. Back in the palace at St. Petersburg, he had insulted Rokoff's father, the tsar. A little incident concerning Paulvitch's indiscretion, the large man walking in on Rokoff's father and a young temptress, with Rokoff's mother sitting in the next room. Paulvitch had then made the mistake of thinking that his discovery would bring him some leverage with Rokoff's father. But as it turned out, the tsar's wife already knew of his mistresses, and Paulvitch's intimation of a threat had only prompted the ruler to order him executed. That was where Nikolas had come in, buying a temporary stay, pleading with his father to give him the man as companion for his travels abroad.

How Alexis Paulvitch remembered that moment! His head had been, literally, on the chopping block when Nikolas had interceded. The tsar had agreed with his son, but had not agreed to a permanent pardon and Paulvitch suspected that Nikolas had not wanted him to. Upon their return to St. Petersburg, Paulvitch's fate would rest solely in Nikolas's less-than-merciful hands.

"Forgive me," Paulvitch said, head down. He was no coward, but that moment on the chopping block was one he desperately did not want to repeat! "I would never be disloyal to you," he went on. "You'll return to St. Petersburg and take your rightful place."

"We're going to find this Temple of the Ancients," Rokoff said, once more looking at the tantalizing amulet. "The gold in the pylon will buy me the power I need to assume the throne."

"Your father is still alive," Paulvitch reminded him.

"He's old," Rokoff said coldly. "It is time for him to die."

Paulvitch swallowed hard, not doubting for a moment his companion's murderous intent—and not doubting that Rokoff, so calculating, would be able to pull it off. The future tsar began walking again, and Paulvitch fell into step behind him.

"It's too bad we have to share with this barbarian Zek," Paulvitch dared to say a short time later.

"I have no intention of sharing with anyone," Rokoff quietly replied. He glanced around, making sure they were not being spied upon, then pulled Paulvitch into an empty side room.

"But what about Achmet Zek's men?" Paulvitch asked.

"All I need is the old man," said Rokoff. "Zek's men will be lost in the jungle."

Paulvitch paused, trying to figure out how the two might accomplish such a feat. He knew better than to question Rokoff about the particulars, though, and so turned his thoughts to another delicate matter. "And Collette de Coude?" he asked. "Are we taking her with us?"

Rokoff considered it for just a moment, as though he hadn't been thinking of Collette for some time. "She'd get in our way now," he decided, and then he added with a flourish, "I'll give her as a gift to my good friend, Achmet Zek."

Rokoff moved across the room to look out a small window, the sun low in the sky, casting long shadows across the city streets and turning the grasses of the distant Serengeti a brilliant shade of gold.

Paulvitch was too busy sputtering in disbelief to immediately respond—and he feared that if Rokoff recognized his shock, he might be punished. Still, the large man could hardly believe that his master would be so callous with Collette de Coude! The tsar's son had loved her—even Paulvitch had recognized that—and now . . . to give her to one as wicked as Achmet Zek . . .

The big man shuddered, then dismissed it all as Collette's problem. Joining Rokoff at the window, he stood quietly, sharing the fantasy of power.

CHAPTER 7

I t is time," Joshua Mugambi said solemnly when the door to the dungeon opened and a half dozen of Achmet Zek's henchmen, led by Hadab, entered.

"Time?" D'Arnot asked.

"For auction," Mugambi replied. "Oh, how I love a good sale!"

D'Arnot at first didn't understand what the man was talking about, but then, when he perceived the subtle sarcasm in Mugambi's tone, he figured it out. "This is an outrage!" he said to Hadab. "Selling us as if we were cattle."

His protests were cut short by the ring of a scimitar blade against his cage, and even more so by the look Hadab gave to him, a promise of death.

Joshua Mugambi wasn't quite right with his prediction, though, for the men moved right past the cages holding D'Arnot and Tarzan, and paid him no heed as well, going to the old man. Only the old man.

The ancient, meanwhile, just sat in his meditative pose,

seemingly oblivious to the fact that Hadab and the others had even entered the room. He hardly reacted when he was grabbed by the arms and lifted to his feet, then pulled from his cage and past the others.

Hadab looked back once at the three remaining in the cells, smiling wickedly. Without a word, he and the others, the old man included, left the room, slamming the door behind them.

"Soon enough," Joshua remarked.

"How do you know we will be taken to auction?" D'Arnot asked anxiously. "They might just leave us down here to rot."

Joshua shook his head. "We will bring gold to Achmet Zek," he reasoned. "There will be an auction."

It was a long and quiet morning for the three, Tarzan standing stoically, Joshua leaning against the bars, and D'Arnot pacing, pacing. The dungeon door at last opened again and several guards entered, led once more by the one-eyed Arab, Hadab.

The guards opened Mugambi's cage first, and the black man offered no resistance as they shackled him, wrists and ankles.

Mugambi, walking in slow, short steps, paused as he passed between the cages of the other men. He glanced at D'Arnot, then turned his attention quickly to Tarzan. "You go quiet, my friend," Mugambi offered. "No fighting."

Hadab pushed him along, the one-eyed man smiling Tarzan's way, daring him to battle.

They took D'Arnot next, and though the man moved as if to put up a fight, he was overpowered immediately and shackled before he could get in a single punch.

Then the guards went to Tarzan. Hadab, smiling still,

opened the cage door and entered first, his scimitar in its sheath.

Joshua, D'Arnot, all of them, saw the look on Tarzan's face, like that of a cornered animal seeking an escape, or, barring that, preparing to fight.

"No, my friend," Joshua said to him.

The guard next to Joshua jammed a club hard into his ribs.

"If you fight, they will kill your friend D'Arnot," Joshua said through a grimace, and then he groaned louder and bent lower as the club connected once again. "Not so good a price for him, you see."

Tarzan relaxed visibly, his gaze going past Hadab to D'Arnot. Joshua's reasoning was sound. Tarzan, so strong and able to handle heavy work, might bring a good price at auction, but there was really very little that D'Arnot, a man past middle age, would be able to offer to a prospective slave owner.

"You want to kick me?" Hadab teased Tarzan, moving a little closer, well within range. He snapped his fingers in the air and the man standing next to D'Arnot drove his club into D'Arnot's side, doubling the man over in pain.

Tarzan started forward, snarling, tugging the chains, but he recovered at once and forced himself to relax.

"Yes, yes," Hadab snickered. "You want to kick me. You want to tear out those chains and choke me dead, eh?"

Tarzan's only answer was the continuing stare, his intense steely eyes boring into Hadab. The Arab tried to match that stare, but turned away, covering his discomfort with laughter. "Take him!" he ordered his thugs, who moved at once to Tarzan and shackled his ankles, beating him, twisting his arms painfully.

The jungle man, understanding that D'Arnot would be punished for any disobedience he showed, accepted the abuse stoically.

"You know what to do with them," Hadab said, and then, still laughing, he left the group.

"You insult me!" Collette de Coude snapped when Rokoff came to her that morning. The woman had been forced to dress in the garb of an Arab belly dancer, red top and bottom veiled in pink and white. At first Collette used those veils to keep herself well-covered, but after a moment, after recognizing Rokoff's amusement at her modesty, she let them hang loosely. Collette de Coude was not ashamed of who she was, and she was determined that any unmasking of her physical body would not strip her of her dignity.

"Son of a tsar," she scoffed. "What a foul land your Russia must be to be ruled by such ignobility."

Rokoff raised his arm suddenly, as if to slap her—and she did flinch, though just a bit—but he held it in check. "Perhaps it is that I simply place no value in you, my dear," he mocked her. "Perhaps you are no longer of any use to me."

Collette muttered a curse under her breath. Rokoff's laugh as he walked away showed that he had heard her. He motioned to Paulvitch as he exited the room, and the big man stalked over to Collette, eyeing her lewdly, his gaze never coming above her neck.

Collette resisted the urge to cover herself, stood tall and straight. "Where are we going?" she demanded sharply, drawing Paulvitch's attention.

"To market," the big man answered with a wide and ugly smile. "To see your friends for the last time."

———

Tarzan, D'Arnot, and Mugambi blinked repeatedly when they were led out of the dungeon and out of the house, to a bustling street market. Achmet Zek's men soon handed them over to other Arab guards, men with whips and clubs.

"Keep moving!" one demanded when Tarzan slowed to regard the scene, and he lashed Tarzan across the shoulder, tearing his dirty shirt and drawing a thin line of blood.

Tarzan locked his gaze on the guard and the man backed away a step. But Tarzan did start moving again, wading through a sea of brightly clad buyers. Some pinched him as he passed, as if they were testing fruit; others patted his shoulders, measured his girth. This was perhaps the most degrading part of all, but it was over quickly, with the guards leading the three slaves up some wooden stairs to a stage area.

There were already other slaves up there, chained to huge posts set in the ground. As soon as they reached the platform, D'Arnot was similarly chained to a post, and then Mugambi.

Tarzan realized that time was running short. Two guards came up to him, taking him by the arms and ushering him toward his appointed post.

With a howl, Tarzan dropped suddenly into a squat, then came right back up hard, launching the two men into the air. He spun hard to the side, leading with an elbow to crack the face of a third and lay the man out low.

But then Achmet Zek's guards were there, jamming clubs into Tarzan's ribs, overwhelming him with their sheer numbers. They bore him to the ground, beating him, then dragged him upright and secured his chains to the post.

All the while, the eager crowd howled with pleasure.

They howled even louder when one of the guards tore Tarzan's shirt from his back, leaving him naked from the waist up, his muscled and tanned torso shining with sweat.

"Save your strength," D'Arnot whispered to him, for it was obvious that Tarzan was on the verge of an explosion. "There will be better opportunities to escape."

Tarzan looked at him calmly and nodded. Then he turned to survey the crowd, his eyes widening as he noted a pair making their way through the throng, the scantily dressed Collette de Coude being pushed along by Achmet Zek.

"What is she doing with that pig?" remarked D'Arnot.

Achmet Zek and Collette took their places at the front of the stage, in prepared, comfortable seats. D'Arnot tried to mouth to the young woman that it would be all right, for her eyes were filling with tears, her hope fast fading at the sight of her would-be rescuers, her friends, chained to posts.

Stubbornly, she tried to stand up, but one of Zek's men, standing right behind the seats, grabbed her immediately and forced her back down. She tried to slap at the man, but he pinned her arms quickly.

Achmet Zek's laughter came straight from his huge belly.

"Please, Achmet Zek," Collette pleaded. "I will do whatever you desire, but let my friends go. They have done nothing to you. They are human beings. You cannot treat them like cattle!"

"Shut up and don't annoy me," Achmet Zek warned, his tone deadly serious. "They are what I say they are." He cupped Collette's delicate chin in his plump hand, forcing her to look at him directly. "So are you."

Tarzan watched it all, his rage bubbling, mounting. He

glanced all around, measuring the enemies. He noted that Hadab was nowhere to be seen. Neither were Rokoff and Paulvitch, and while Tarzan considered that to be good news as far as any escape attempt was concerned, he feared what their absence might otherwise signal.

They were already on their way, he realized.

And even without those three dangerous adversaries, he and his friends were badly outnumbered, not even counting the many henchmen Zek no doubt had filtering covertly about the crowd. And they had no weapons. Unless . . .

Tarzan came forward suddenly, powerfully, throwing his shoulder against the post. It shifted, just a bit, but he couldn't take a full measure of its weakness, for a guard was beside him in an instant, jamming the butt of his whip into Tarzan's side, bending him over with pain.

The crowd roared in amusement at the spectacle.

"Whoever buys that man will have his hands full!" Achmet Zek yelled above the tumult, to many approving replies. "Thankfully, it will not be my problem. He is only a sack of gold to me."

A hundred conversations followed, the excitement reaching a fevered pitch.

"I'll buy them," Collette said suddenly, seriously. "I'll buy them all."

"You are a woman," Achmet Zek replied, "and have no power, or even a voice. The next time I hear a sound from you, you will join them on the platform!"

"I'll say what I want, whenever I feel like it!" the ever-defiant Collette snapped right back at him, her anger over-ruling good judgment.

Achmet Zek sat staring as if she had just slapped him. All

those standing near to the pair hushed, stunned by the woman's bravado.

Collette began to suspect that she might have pushed too far.

Achmet Zek's backhand slap stung her across the face, knocking her to the side. She twisted with the momentum, setting her feet under her and recoiling at once, charging at Zek and punching wildly.

She knocked the fat man from his seat. He sprawled out on the ground, and the crowd, despite any well-based fears of the powerful man, couldn't suppress its laughter.

Collette tried to push on, wanting to get atop the wretched man and choke the life out of him, but guards had her then, in full restraint.

"Put her up there!" Achmet Zek roared, pointing to the stage. "Sell her!"

Collette was shoved ahead roughly, into the crowd. She lost her footing, but was caught before she went down, the guards lifting her back to her feet and shoving her again.

Screams of amusement heightened, some turning to fear, when a commotion erupted on the stage.

D'Arnot's first instinct was to scold his friend again, to remind Tarzan that this was neither the time nor the place. But he saw that look, that primal rage, and knew that his friend would not even hear him. The French gentleman pulled back on his chain and fell low to the ground, extending his leg to trip up a guard rushing past behind him. He had bought Tarzan a few seconds, but, he wondered, what good might that do?

Tarzan never saw the encounter, never heard the grunt of the guard as the man tumbled to the stage only a few feet behind him. All his focus, all his rage, went into the heavy post holding him. He repeatedly slammed his shoulder into it, loosening the wooden stage's hold on it, then grasped the post in both hands and twisted, first one way then back the other. Back and forth, growling, roaring. And then, the muscles of his shoulders straining so hard that it seemed as if they would tear right through his skin, the jungle man lifted.

Slowly the post came up from the ground.

"Behind you!" cried someone in the crowd, warning those guards at the front of the platform, who had been watching the movements of Collette and her escort and the growing uneasiness of the mob. They turned about.

There stood Tarzan, holding the heavy post as though it was a baseball bat. With a great sweeping swing, Tarzan took them down, one, two, three, swatting them to the side.

Tarzan turned and thrust the post straight out, blasting the breath from the next man, the guard D'Arnot had tripped, doubling him over and then bringing the post down across his shoulders, flattening him on the platform.

With a primal roar, Tarzan leaped across the stage and slammed the post down atop the post securing D'Arnot, pinching the man's chains, snapping them apart. Then, setting his own post's bottom flat on the ground, roaring again, Tarzan drove his arms out to the side with such force that the eye hook securing his chains to the wood popped free.

Tarzan wouldn't give up the post as a weapon, though, and he took it up once more, spinning about, looking for someone else to hit.

———

The crowd was in full riot now, running and screaming, horrified by the sheer strength and inhuman intensity of the jungle lord, and the guards among the mob could not easily buck the momentum of the riot to get near the stage. Collette, caught in the flow, was torn from the grasp of her jailers. Rather than run for freedom, though, the young woman turned around and ducked low under the bobbing heads, working her way back to the two guards. She got in beside one of the men and reached through the squirming mob to grab the keys from his belt.

He noticed her then and cried out, pushing through the mob to get to her.

Collette stumbled on, toward the stage. She caught sight of Achmet Zek moving to intercept her, two of his men flanking him, and she knew that she would never make it to her friends.

"D'Arnot!" she yelled. "The keys!" And she threw them high and far, over Zek and his men, into D'Arnot's waiting grasp.

Then she ran, trying to melt into the crowd.

Tarzan fought wildly, leaping back and forth to meet any challengers, his mighty swings of the heavy post keeping the guards at bay. One man drew out a scimitar and dared to rush in, but Tarzan smacked the blade from his hand, sending it flying away, then stepped ahead and drove the butt of the post at the man's head. The man lifted his arms to block, but the post blasted past them, slamming his face, launching him backward off the stage.

D'Arnot knew that Tarzan could not hold them all off for

very long, and so he moved along the length of the prisoners, freeing every one. Some ran right to the edge of the platform and leaped off, scattering into the crowd, but others went for the nearest guards, more intent on revenge than on escape.

The guards swarmed Tarzan. One drew out a scimitar and went through a series of dazzling movements, trying to confuse his intended victim before he came leaping ahead with a mighty stroke.

Tarzan, not distracted in the least by the impressive swordplay, met the leap with a club swing that sent the charging man flying off to the side, tumbling into the canvas backdrop of the platform.

Tarzan reversed momentum and brought the post swinging back. He let it go, launching it at the feet of a group of guards, bowling them over, for another had come in from behind, leaping onto his back. His hands now free, Tarzan reached back over his shoulder, grabbed the man and, with a powerful tug, pulled him right over and sent him flying headlong.

Hardly slowing, Tarzan launched a backhand out to his right, smashing the face of another man, then he turned and rushed out that way, shoulder-blocking two more guards from the platform.

"Fight on, *mon ami!*" D'Arnot cried, daring to think that they might indeed win out. His words and hopes were cut short, though, as an Arab leaped in behind him, grabbing him tight, the man's dagger going right for his throat.

Collette's exotic garb and her light skin worked against her. She could not hide among the Arab women, and none in the crowd, so fearful of Achmet Zek, would offer her any help. She scrambled desperately, keeping one step ahead of the guards for some time, but then, suddenly, Achmet Zek had her.

Collette wriggled and managed to get one hand free long enough to punch the man, but Achmet Zek calmed her considerably when he showed her his long knife, its tip barely an inch from her face.

Collette's shoulders slumped; Achmet Zek wrapped her under his free arm and moved away, batting aside any who ventured too near.

Tarzan whipped his arms back and forth. He went up on one foot and pivoted right, kicking out, catching a man on the inside of his knee and sending him sprawling, clutching at the joint.

A man charged from behind, another from the front, another from the left.

Tarzan leaped straight up, tucking his legs, rising above the three attackers. They came together in a heap, Tarzan landing lightly right beside them, grabbing them up in his powerful arms before they could untangle from one another, and running all three of them from the platform.

He turned and saw D'Arnot in the grasp of another, but could not go to help, his attention stolen by still more guards.

He was about to die. He knew it. He could not possibly get the man off his back, could not possibly get the knife away from his throat. And Tarzan, he realized, was too engaged to help him. He grabbed the man's forearm, but had no leverage and could not slow the deadly progression of the blade.

He felt its pinch against his throat.

But then, somehow, it did not push on, did not cut. The man's hold on him lessened, and D'Arnot squirmed free, tumbling down to the ground.

He rolled about and looked back—to see Joshua Mugambi pulling the man back, back, his chains slipping out from under the guard's arm to wrap about his neck. Joshua turned his hands over and over, tightening the hold, bringing the man to his knees. Joshua tugged and tugged and the man went limp.

"Don't kill him!" D'Arnot yelled, and Joshua, who had no intention of choking the life out of the man, just the fight out of him, quickly unwrapped the bonds and let the man slump to the floor.

Joshua rushed over and helped D'Arnot back to his feet. D'Arnot tossed the keys to another freed prisoner, motioning to the few he had not yet freed of their posts, and the man started away. Then the pair went to join Tarzan.

Those few guards remaining, the odds so suddenly shifting, turned and fled into the crowd.

"Well, nothing like a good fight in the morning to get the blood flowing," D'Arnot said.

"My favorite way to wake," Mugambi replied dryly. He turned his smile to Tarzan, only to find that he was gone. He looked back to D'Arnot, who only shrugged, having no idea where his friend was off to this time.

"All very well done," came a voice from a balcony. "All very entertaining."

The two, and most of the others in the crowd, looked up to see Achmet Zek holding Collette de Coude at knifepoint.

"And all very foolish," Achmet Zek went on. "This is my city; there is nowhere for you to run."

D'Arnot glanced all about, then did well to hide his smile as he saw Tarzan moving along in a crouch, walking on the shoulders of the people in the packed crowd!

Tarzan got to the base of the wall, below Collette and Zek, without the big man noticing.

"But where will he go from there?" Mugambi whispered, following D'Arnot's gaze to Tarzan.

"Straight up, I'd say," D'Arnot replied knowingly, and even as he spoke, Tarzan began his scrambling ascent, moving faster up the vertical pitch than most men could run on flat ground.

He came over the railing of the balcony without slowing.

Achmet Zek turned and slashed out at him with the knife, but Tarzan easily caught the man's wrist and bent it backward. And Collette, far from helpless, was fast to curl her hand into a fist and smash the fat man in the face.

Down he went, but more of his men were coming by then, charging up the stairs, weapons drawn.

"Get on my back," Tarzan instructed. He tore the voluminous sleeve from Achmet Zek's shirt, then snapped it up over a guide rope fastened to the wall just to the side of the balcony, catching its ends in both hands. When Collette was securely in place, wrapped tight about him, he jumped out and slid down the angled rope, coming to the ground lightly.

He turned about to find Collette's beautiful face only inches from his own. Her soft lips inviting his kiss . . .

"Well done!" D'Arnot congratulated, he and Mugambi rushing over, stealing the precious moment.

"But I think we should consider leaving," Mugambi added, nodding back to the balcony, where Achmet Zek's men were calling out for their comrades who were still among the crowd. "And save the celebrating"—he eyed Collette and Tarzan knowingly—"for a quieter time."

CHAPTER 8

He is going back to the jungle," Collette de Coude said to D'Arnot late that afternoon. The four escapees, having successfully avoided Achmet Zek's clutches, were taking some rest at a safe house, the residence of a friend of Joshua Mugambi's. The man was a fellow Waziri tribesman who had come to live in the city.

Collette and D'Arnot were on the back balcony, looking past the abrupt end of the city structures and out to the grasses, which were lit up as if on fire by the last slanting rays of day. Though the pair did not know it, they were witnessing a scene hauntingly similar to the one Rokoff and Paulvitch had enjoyed on their first day at Achmet Zek's palace.

"He must go," D'Arnot answered. "Rokoff and his band have half a day's head start." The Frenchman silently cursed the delay they had been forced to encounter in getting away from the slave market and finding a haven—and also in retrieving information about their enemies' movements. The one-eyed Arab and several of his soldiers had left Achmet

"I leave before dusk," Tarzan replied.

"That was my fear," D'Arnot said.

Tarzan reached into one of the saddlebags and pulled out a small bag, handing it to D'Arnot. "My suit," he explained. "Torn and dirty, I am afraid. I wish that I could have returned it to you in better condition."

"Keep it, *mon ami,*" D'Arnot said. "When this is over, you will need it for your return to Paris."

Tarzan said nothing, just continued to hold out the bag, and D'Arnot finally accepted it, realizing the truth of the situation: that Tarzan, even if he took care of this problem with Rokoff and the amulet, had no intention of returning.

While the friends were talking, Joshua moved nearer to the saddlebags, surprised by how little was left in them once the clothing had been removed. "You intend on traveling light," he said.

"And very fast," Tarzan replied.

D'Arnot cleared his throat; Mugambi moved away as soon as Tarzan's attention was diverted.

"I think that I should go with you," D'Arnot said. "We've been through so much together, I should like to see this through to the end."

"You're a terrible rider," Tarzan reminded him.

"I could get a camel," D'Arnot was quick to reply.

Tarzan's look was doubtful.

"A very gentle one," D'Arnot clarified. "Or we could ride double on an even gentler elephant."

"It's important that you get Collette back to her father," Tarzan answered. "Count de Coude is no doubt sick with fear for her."

"I can get word to him," D'Arnot reasoned.

Tarzan's frown showed that he was not impressed by the notion. "The sooner she is back in France, the better," he said.

D'Arnot didn't argue against that logic.

"I'd feel safer if I stayed with you," Collette interjected, moving between the two men, eyeing Tarzan directly. "No offense, Monsieur D'Arnot," she added, glancing back over her shoulder.

D'Arnot only shrugged.

"You would not be safe where I must go," Tarzan said to her when she looked back at him. "The jungle trip alone will be difficult, and then I must deal with Rokoff and his men."

"I am not helpless," Collette protested.

"No," Tarzan agreed, taking her hands in his own. "Not at all. But, like D'Arnot, you cannot move quickly enough in the deep jungle. I must catch Rokoff in time."

"Why the urgency?" D'Arnot interjected. He had pressed the point concerning the amulet several times since they had escaped from Achmet Zek, but Tarzan remained cryptic on the issue. "Collette is safe."

"I have already explained to you as much as I can," Tarzan replied.

"This mysterious temple?" D'Arnot asked.

"I can explain no more," Tarzan said, nodding, "but trust in me when I tell you that Rokoff must not reach the Temple of the Ancients."

Tarzan turned to the horse, grabbing it as if he meant to mount. Collette grabbed his shoulder, however, forcing his attention.

"Will I see you again?" she asked.

"I don't know," Tarzan answered. "But I'll know that you

are safe." Again he turned to the horse, and again Collette stopped him.

"And that will please you?" she asked. "To know that I am safe?"

"Of course," Tarzan answered, and before the words had even left his mouth, Collette's lips were against his, pressing tightly.

"For luck," she explained when she at last broke the kiss.

"It would seem as if he already found a bit of that," D'Arnot put in dryly, then in more serious tones, he said to Tarzan, "You always know where to reach me."

Tarzan swung up onto the saddle. D'Arnot came to his side, extending his hand for a shake, which Tarzan readily accepted.

"Farewell, *mon ami,*" D'Arnot said.

"And you," Tarzan replied. "And you," he added, looking to Collette.

She didn't reply; she didn't have to. Tarzan had touched her heart and her spirit, that much was obvious. And obvious, too, was the fact that she had touched his, as well.

Tarzan let go of D'Arnot's hand and took up the bridle, but when he looked ahead, he saw another horse, ridden by Joshua Mugambi, moving in front of his own.

"I'll be going with you," Joshua explained.

"I'm going alone," Tarzan said.

"You would be doing me a favor," Joshua said. "You are traveling toward my homeland. As am I—and I realize that traveling with you is the fastest and safest way that I can get there."

Tarzan considered the man's words for a moment, then shook his head. "You'll slow me down too much," he decided.

"I am Waziri," Joshua declared, his tone showing more strength and determination than Tarzan had yet heard from the man. "My blood is from the blood of a Waziri chief. I am no stranger to the deep jungle; Waziri warriors have lived in unity with the plants and animals of the land long before the white man put leather on a horse's back and called it a saddle. Let not my acquired accent fool you, Tarzan, son of Kala. I am Waziri."

"If you fall behind, I will leave you," Tarzan warned, and none of the three doubted that claim for a moment.

But Joshua seemed unconcerned. "You will never have to look over your shoulder for me," he promised.

Tarzan turned to D'Arnot and Collette and gave a nod. Then, without belaboring the point, he kicked his horse and galloped away. "I am already ahead of you," he called to Joshua.

The Waziri, true to his word, had his horse at a swift canter in an instant, pacing Tarzan's mount.

D'Arnot and Collette watched them charge off into the grass, and remained for a long while. When the riders were but indistinct dark spots among the shining grass, D'Arnot glanced out of the corner of his eye at Collette. She chewed her bottom lip; he could see that she was trying to be brave but that this parting with Tarzan had stung her deeply. Truly she was intrigued by the mysterious man, D'Arnot knew.

"We'll never see him again," Collette remarked.

"Do not underestimate him," D'Arnot replied, his tone deliberately light.

"But even if he succeeds in stopping Rokoff, we will remain a world away," Collette reasoned.

"But Tarzan has given us his friendship," D'Arnot

explained. "To Jean Tarzan, that is no small matter. He numbers his friends as few, and never, ever forgets them. His whole life is based on that premise."

Collette looked long and hard at D'Arnot, then nodded, satisfied that he spoke the truth. "I would dearly like to speak with him again," she remarked.

"A sentiment that I'm certain Monsieur Tarzan shares," D'Arnot said, and he was glad to see that he had brought a hopeful smile back to the beautiful face of Mademoiselle de Coude.

Tarzan paced about the encampment, the first stars springing to bright life in the clear sky above him.

"With so much energy, you should have kept going," Joshua remarked.

Tarzan looked at him, sitting by the low fire, the horses right behind him. Joshua spoke in jest, but in truth, Tarzan had considered running on through the darkness.

"I could not have kept my horse," he explained in all seriousness. "To ride across the Serengeti at night is foolhardy. There are too many holes, and too many lions."

At that, Joshua turned his bright gaze out to the darkness. Indeed, only a short while before, they had heard the low rumble of a lion's call, though Tarzan, with all confidence, had assured Joshua that the beast was miles away.

"I could have gone out alone," Tarzan went on, "without my horse. But I believe that such a course would have brought me no closer to our goal. Rokoff had a half day lead; if he has moved swiftly, he is already in the deep jungle, and I will need the daylight to track him."

"And if you went out alone, there is still the matter of the lions," Joshua added.

"I do not fear them, not if I am alone," Tarzan replied.

Joshua looked at him doubtfully.

"I have a way with animals" was all the explanation that Tarzan would offer. "Sleep now, for I will depart before the dawn, and if you do not awaken to my one call, you will be left behind."

Joshua nodded and tried to get comfortable on the ground near the fire, not doubting for a moment that Tarzan spoke honestly.

"Snake!" came a cry, followed by a single, resounding gunshot.

Rokoff and Paulvitch ran to the spot, the big man sputtering curses at the Arabs. Hadab was there, too, watching over his men protectively.

All attention focused on one guard, the shooter, the man trembling and pointing to the tangled branches above. "Snake," he said again.

"This is your land," Rokoff said to Hadab. "I should think—"

"This is not our land," Hadab was quick to correct. "This is the jungle. We seldom come here, and never at night."

Rokoff shared the one-eyed man's unspoken exasperation. There had been no rest, not even a short break, since they had left the city. "Tell that to our guide," Rokoff replied, turning to look toward the front of the weary caravan—only to see that their determined guide had moved far ahead of their torchlight.

"The old man never gets tired!" Paulvitch whined. "He just keeps staring at that medallion and keeps walking. There must be some magic in it."

"He sees a different value in the medallion than we do," Rokoff explained. He waved to Hadab and the other Arabs, eight men in all, to move along and catch up with the old man.

"Whatever he sees, it is not natural," Paulvitch remarked.

"As long as he leads the way, he can see whatever he wants," Rokoff said.

"And we will all fall dead trying to keep up."

Rokoff glared at Paulvitch, staring the big man down. "Those who are not strong enough can fall dead, and I care nothing for them," he said coldly. "For me, there is a pylon of gold waiting, twenty men high and ten across!"

Paulvitch knew better than to argue with that point, or with the look in Rokoff's eyes—the same look, it occurred to him, that was in the old man's eyes when he gazed upon the crystal amulet.

On they went, through the night, eating as they walked and trying hard to keep together in the dense brush.

CHAPTER 9

There are your lions," Joshua remarked nervously as he and Tarzan trotted their mounts through the tall grass. Off to the side, dangerously close, reclined a handful of female lions, a pair of playful cubs, and one huge male, its thick black mane shining in stark contrast to its tawny hide.

Tarzan slowed his horse and regarded the pride. He couldn't help but notice the difference in these creatures as compared to the lions he knew in the Paris Zoo. He remembered the ragged fur of the caged male, so different, so lifeless, when compared to the luster of this one's shiny coat.

Everything was different about these lions: their gait, their shining teeth, the sparkle of life in their dark eyes. Even the relationships among the pride were different out here in the wild. In the zoo, the lions moped about, trying to keep out of each other's way. They growled, they snarled, they batted each other in frustration. Out here there were growls and snarls, threats and even fights, but they were the stuff of passion, and the necessity of hierarchy. Tarzan recalled some of the many occasions when he had heard visitors to the zoo proclaim their elation at having seen a living lion.

A false claim, Tarzan knew.

To Joshua's amazement, Tarzan let out a low growl that was promptly answered by the male, the big cat leaping to its feet, fur bristling.

"Telling them we're here?" Joshua asked.

"They knew we were here long before we knew they were here," Tarzan replied.

"So you feel the need to speak to them?" Joshua asked with a snort.

Tarzan nodded, sincerely, and Joshua couldn't stammer out a reply, sarcastic or otherwise.

The lions made no move toward them, though, and the big male soon settled back into the shade of a tree, paying the horsemen no further heed.

Soon after, with the lions far behind, Tarzan and Joshua saw the dense line of the jungle foliage, a barrier of trees springing up from the savannah, appearing as thick as the wall of a man-made fortress. Tarzan went toward it in full gallop, then jumped from his horse, running right to the edge of the jungle and staring reverently into its shadowy depths.

By the time Joshua caught up, he found Tarzan unstrapping the bags from the horse. "A short respite?" he asked hopefully.

Tarzan answered by beginning to unsaddle the horse.

"I was afraid of that," Joshua remarked, sliding down quickly and going to work on his own mount. He had the saddle and bags off as fast as possible, fearing that Tarzan would not wait for him. When he finished, though, sometime after his friend was done, Tarzan was still standing quietly, staring into the jungle.

"Ready to go," Joshua announced.

Tarzan came over at once, moved close to whisper to the horses, then, to Joshua's continued amazement, he slapped them on the rumps, sending them running back the way they had come.

"They are no longer needed" was all the explanation Tarzan offered.

"We could have walked them," Joshua protested.

"They would only slow us."

"But how are we to carry all this gear?" Joshua asked, indicating the saddles and bags.

"Leave it here."

"Supplies?" said Joshua.

"You have been away too long," Tarzan replied. "The jungle will provide all that we require." He was moving before he finished speaking, striding to the base of the nearest large tree. He leaped to the lowest branch, then, with the agility of an ape, he began scrambling higher.

Joshua managed to reach into his pack and pull out some food before rushing to follow. He came under the dense canopy, blinking repeatedly, trying to adjust his eyes to the suddenly different light, and trying hard to locate the ever-elusive Tarzan.

What he found was a pair of khaki pants, floating downward to hook on a branch just above him. Joshua pulled them down and moved along. He spotted Tarzan then, standing on a branch, then leaping away, holding a vine and swinging to a tree deeper into the jungle. Joshua ran to catch up, and found Tarzan's shirt on the ground at the base of the tree. "Is there a bathtub around here that I haven't seen?" he asked quietly.

For Tarzan, running high along the branches, the shedding of his clothing was a freeing experience, both physically and emotionally. It felt good to have his arms and legs unrestricted by too-tight seams or the pull of cloth, and it was good to feel the sun and the wind on his bare skin again.

Even more than that, the shedding of the clothes was, to Tarzan, symbolic of the shedding of all the hypocrisy and foolishness he had experienced during his stay with the "cultured" people of society. So many of them hid behind their clothing! So many of them used their wealth to buy garments beyond the means of ordinary folk, not because the garments were better made or more comfortable, but merely because these expensive clothes separated them, and, in the warped perceptions of civilization, somehow elevated them above the masses.

It was all a game, all a way for some people to feel superior to others.

Tarzan was glad to be rid of it.

For several long minutes Joshua scrambled about, trying to locate Tarzan. Gradually, the son of the Waziri chief began to remember his place here and to grow more comfortable. He had been away for several years, but the jungle was in his blood.

Then he heard the cry, that signature yell of Tarzan, and he followed the sound to see the man standing tall on a branch high above, dressed only in a loincloth, and with his knife strapped about his waist, his bow and quiver over one

shoulder. He held another vine, and Joshua was hardly surprised when the jungle lord leaped away, taking up the vine
in both hands and swinging, to light gracefully on a branch in
another tree.

Now Joshua was smiling widely, thrilled by the amazing
agility. He ran hard to keep up, trying to anticipate Tarzan's
next move. To his delight, when he looked back at Tarzan,
he found his companion smiling down at him, pointing to
guide him.

"Teamwork," Joshua said under his breath, feeling more at
ease with every passing stride. He paused long enough to
retrieve a fallen branch, a sturdy walking staff, and then he
eagerly ran on.

Paulvitch did not feel more at ease. He was tired and the day
was brutally hot, and the last word he would use to describe
the caravan of eleven was "teamwork." The old man continued on his merry way, staring at the amulet and not even
sweating, while Rokoff and Paulvitch and the eight Arabs
struggled hard to keep up.

Rokoff, as obsessed as the old man, did not complain, and
neither, Paulvitch noted, did Hadab. The other seven Arabs,
bearing the brunt of the party's supplies, were grumbling,
though.

"Will you stop him," Paulvitch whispered to Rokoff, indicating the old man, then looking back at the ever-widening
line of weary bearers. "Or slow him at least. The others
grow tired, and their complaints are turning quickly into
threats."

Rokoff smiled at that. "Tired men make mistakes," he

replied. "We press on, with all the speed that our old guide demands."

"Look at him," Paulvitch scoffed, and both men did just that. The ancient guide was only a few yards ahead of them, walking easily around any obstacles, though he seemed to not even look at the ground in front of him, seemed not to look at anything but the amulet, hanging from its chain right before his eyes. "He is more a child, the way he stares at that crystal," Paulvitch sputtered. "It is too valuable for him to have as a plaything."

"I gave it to him to keep him calm," Rokoff explained. "We need him to lead the way. Think of it as a carrot on the end of a stick, held out in front of a mule."

"A boot in his neck would serve the same purpose," Paulvitch muttered.

"Is it his death that you want, or the amulet?" Rokoff asked sharply, stopping and turning on his companion.

"The crystal could be worth a great deal," Paulvitch protested.

Rokoff shook his head in dismay. "You cannot begin to dream, can you?" he asked, his tone condescending. "Very well, then, as soon as the old man delivers us to the temple, you may have the amulet. You may keep it forever, my gift to you."

"The old man will never give it up," Paulvitch noted.

"Then kill him."

Rokoff turned and walked away before Paulvitch could begin to respond, leaving the big man thoroughly flustered. Only for a moment, though, for as soon as Paulvitch considered Rokoff's tone, and knew that his master had not spoken idly, a wide smile of anticipation crossed his round face. He mopped his bald pate with a dirty handkerchief and then rushed to catch up with Rokoff and the old man, all signs of weariness gone from his step.

The day wore on, one hour following another in the steamy jungle. Even though Rokoff allowed them to drop most of their supplies, the bearers could hardly keep up to the old man.

It got worse with each passing moment. By early afternoon Paulvitch was circling the line of bearers, yelling at them to keep up. "Go on, move!" he commanded.

The Arabs mumbled amongst themselves in their own language, and though he couldn't understand their exact words, Paulvitch recognized the fear in their tones.

"Can't you even keep up with an old man?" he yelled at them, and they all glanced about nervously at the volume of his voice.

Paulvitch turned about to see that the old man, too, had stopped with Hadab in front of him, kneeling and peering into the dense jungle. Rokoff was off to the side, resting against a tree.

"What is it?" Paulvitch asked, joining Hadab.

"We are in Kikuyu territory," their guide replied with an amused smile.

"Kikuyu or not, move on!" Paulvitch roared. "I'm not afraid of any tribe of naked natives." He held his rifle up before the old man. "I have enough firepower here to destroy anything that gets in our way."

"That is yet to be determined," said the old man.

Paulvitch's face was beet red with rage. "All you have to concern yourself with is finding the temple," he growled. "Or you will find yourself back in Achmet Zek's dungeon."

"A bit quieter would be wise," Hadab warned.

Paulvitch was about to explode again, but then Rokoff was there, calming him and moving in front of the old man, locking him with an icy stare.

"You do not have to fear the dungeon, old man," he said calmly. "You only have to fear for your life."

"Death is a daily possibility," the old man replied, unconcerned.

"It will be a very painful departure," Rokoff promised.

The old man chuckled. "I'm sure that your friend would enjoy that. But I do not have the stamina of youth, with which to bear pain for more than a few moments. I am afraid that I will be gone quickly."

Rokoff didn't blink. "We will see if I am better at pain than you are at dying."

The old man's expression, a combination of amusement and deep serenity, placed Rokoff off balance. He got the feeling then, and so did Hadab and Paulvitch, that something very strange, even supernatural, was going on here.

"The Kikuyu will not find us," the old man assured him. "The amulet has guided us safely past their warriors."

"How can you know—" Paulvitch began to ask as he came forward, but Rokoff stretched his arm across the big man's chest and held him at bay.

"Without the amulet to guide us, our heads would be shrunken, I fear," the old man quipped, and he ended with that typical, aggravating chuckle.

Joshua Mugambi leaned heavily on a tree, then pushed himself away, rushing forward, trying to keep up with his graceful friend. He would have had no chance of staying close—even though Tarzan was as often running along the branches of trees as on the ground—except that Tarzan had to stop often to check for signs of Rokoff's passage.

Tarzan was similarly pausing now, crouching at a bush, checking its leaves and sniffing the air.

"We should—" Mugambi started to say, but Tarzan was up like a springing cat, running on.

"Do you ever get tired?" a frustrated Joshua asked.

Tarzan skidded to a stop and glanced back. "When I do, I sleep," he replied with simple logic.

"How about 'rest'?" Joshua asked. " 'Reprieve, repose, loaf!' "

"You know a great many words," Tarzan congratulated. "I only know what I must do."

The flatness of his tone warned Joshua, as did his body language as he abruptly turned to run off once more. "Then take my words as mere entertainment," Joshua said, "and do not allow them to offend you."

"They don't," Tarzan replied and started away. "Nor do they slow me."

"Slow you?" echoed the Waziri incredulously. "At this pace I'll be home in record time!" With a groan of protest, Joshua pushed himself off once more, running as hard as he could, to try and keep the elusive jungle man in sight.

He did spot Tarzan again, almost immediately. The ape-man was standing very still, muscles tensed, just a short distance ahead. Joshua wisely held his tongue and eased nearer.

A spear whistled out of the brush, embedding itself in the ground right at Tarzan's feet. Or at least, right in front of where Tarzan's feet had been, for he reacted with a great leap that put him onto a branch six feet off the ground.

Joshua, too, scrambled to the base of the tree, trying to

climb, but not taking enough time and slipping all over the place, never keeping both feet off the ground for more than a second or two.

Tarzan dropped back down in front of him defensively and eyed the spear, noting its markings. "Kikuyu," he said.

"I've been away a long time," Joshua replied. "Are they at peace with the Waziri?"

Tarzan stood very straight, eyes darting all about. "Maybe you'll get a chance to ask," he replied, and then snapped his hand up to catch a second spear, this one flying only inches from his chest.

"That's incredible!" Joshua gasped, hardly able to get the words out. His companion glanced all about. "But what if he reloads? Or what if there are others?"

As if on cue, all the foliage around the two men erupted with the movements of Kikuyu warriors. Camouflaged with paint and plumage, they immediately formed a circle about the intruders, a ring of spear tips holding Tarzan and Mugambi at bay.

Joshua tried to take his cues from Tarzan, who was standing perfectly still, holding the spear. Joshua considered his own weapon, the thick walking stick, and realized that it wouldn't be of much use against the many razor-tipped spears pointing at him.

Then another Kikuyu, large and square-shouldered, more heavily painted than the others and wearing a great headdress of exotic plumes, emerged from the brush. The other warriors backed off a bit, deferring to him, and he and Tarzan locked stares.

To Joshua's horror, Tarzan flipped the spear in his hand and hurled it at the Kikuyu leader. The missile soared in, embedding into a tree just inches from the tall man's head—and he never even flinched.

"Oh, why did you do that?" Joshua mumbled, thinking they were about to be impaled.

"You missed," said the Kikuyu leader, in perfect English.

"You almost didn't," Tarzan replied.

The Kikuyu, smiling broadly, walked up before Tarzan. "It has been a long time, my friend," he said.

"It no longer seems that way," Tarzan replied, clasping the Kikuyu's hand, sharing his warm smile.

The other Kikuyus began laughing and lowered their spears, many clapping Tarzan on the back as they moved aside.

"Does this mean that I'm not going to be dinner?" Joshua asked meekly, the poor man's sensibilities overwhelmed.

"Maybe yes, maybe no," Tarzan answered. "Either way it will be fast. We have little time to waste." His tone as he finished was serious, his eyes locking on those of the Kikuyu leader.

"This is Joshua Mugambi," Tarzan explained.

"Waziri?" asked the Kikuyu.

"Son of their chief, who has recently died," Tarzan explained.

The Kikuyu warrior gave a meaningful nod.

"Jakar is chief of the Kikuyu," Tarzan said to Joshua. "He would like us for dinner." As he spoke that double-edged phrase, Tarzan turned with Jakar, the two of them hiding their smiles.

"Oh, well yes," Joshua replied, and then his brow furrowed as he considered the words. "And about the relations between the two tribes . . ."

"At least it is a rest," Alexis Paulvitch remarked, trying to calm the boiling anger of the impatient Rokoff. Night had fallen, but the moon was full and the sudden stop, the first real respite since they had left the city, had come as quite a surprise—especially since the distant beat of tribal drums could be clearly heard.

"A rest at a dead end," Rokoff snarled back at him. They had come to a small clearing that ended at a pool and a thundering waterfall.

"We will find a path around—" Paulvitch started to say.

"He does not want to go around!" Rokoff interrupted, waving his hand at the back of the old man, who stood on the edge of the pool, staring into the waterfall.

Behind them and to the side, the Arabs, glad to have set their packs down for a while, stretched and relaxed, several falling to the ground from sheer exhaustion. Hadab, though, seemed as impatient as Rokoff. He stood staring at the old man, his expression nothing short of murderous.

"Maybe he knows that we needed a rest," Paulvitch offered, but Rokoff was no longer listening. He stormed up to the old man, Paulvitch rushing to keep up.

"We are here," the old man said before Rokoff could begin his tirade. "Our journey has ended."

Rokoff glanced all about, at the waterfall, at the surrounding jungle, a solid wall of flora, it seemed. "What do you mean it has ended?" he demanded. "There is nothing here but jungle and the waterfall. Where is this Temple of the Ancients?"

"It is before your eyes, yet you do not see," the old man answered cryptically. "Is it greed that blocks your vision?"

"I have no more time to waste on you," Rokoff said sharply. "Take me to the gold pylon now, or you will not see it, either!"

The old man grinned at him, that detached amused smile that so bothered Rokoff and so unnerved Paulvitch. "I do not fear," he said simply. "We are at the place you seek." As he finished he held up the amulet, the *glowing* amulet!

Rokoff and Paulvitch stared at it dumbfoundedly. Even Hadab and a couple of the other Arabs noticed its light from several steps away. It was glowing, and of its own accord, the stunned onlookers recognized. This was no reflection of the moonlight, no trick of the water glistening before them. The amulet shone of an inner light.

Paulvitch stepped right in front of the old man. "Then we no longer need you," he said. "And the amulet is mine." He reached for the crystal and grasped it tightly, then cried out in pain and fell away, clutching his hand.

Hadab was there in an instant, he and Rokoff trying to determine what had happened to Paulvitch. To their amazement, the big man upturned his palm, revealing a burned imprint, a perfect representation of the six-sided amulet.

All three looked at the old man, to see that too-calm grin once again.

"You're dead, old man!" Paulvitch roared, drawing out his revolver.

Rokoff immediately slapped his arm upward and the gun discharged harmlessly into the air, echoing and echoing, a foreign sound in the jungle night. All the world seemed to go eerily still for a moment, even the distant drumming pausing.

"You kill him when I say so, and not before!" Rokoff yelled

in Paulvitch's fat face. He turned almost immediately to the old man. "But you will still be dead," he warned.

The old man's grin disappeared, replaced by a look so serious and intense that it gave unshakable Rokoff pause. "Only in this world," the old man answered calmly. "Only in this world."

"We are tired of your riddles!" Paulvitch yelled, shoving past Rokoff and grabbing the old man, jamming the barrel of his revolver into the man's gut. "Where is the temple?"

The old man's gaze never left Rokoff. He held the stare for a long moment, then relinquished it with a great sigh. "It is beyond the falls," he admitted. He turned away from Paulvitch and started around the pool. Rokoff motioned for Paulvitch to follow, and Hadab signaled to his men, who were already hauling up their gear and falling in line.

"I want to kill him," Paulvitch muttered to Rokoff.

Rokoff didn't bother to reply. Paulvitch was a fine lackey, strong and stupid, but one who had to be constantly monitored.

The fire, the dancing, and the pounding of the drums brought Tarzan, and Joshua Mugambi, as well, back into the mindset of their previous lives, reminded them of who they were. In the Kikuyu encampment they were shown again the intensity of jungle life, the primal alertness, the vivid colors, a life heightened because it was ever on the very edge of disaster.

Tarzan silently compared this place with the world he had left behind. He compared the dance of the Kikuyus, wild and passionate, the flow of muscles moving in instinctual response to the varying rhythms of the drums, to the practiced, rigid dances of the cultured. It was akin to having the roaring bonfire of the Kikuyu encampment measured against the contained hearth fires in Paul's house, akin to the obvious difference between the lackluster mane of the zoo lion and the shining black mane of his wild counterpart.

Indeed it was good to be home.

Tarzan blew the thoughts away with a sigh and turned his attention back to the blazing bonfire, the ring of Kikuyus spinning and leaping about it.

Yes, it was good to be home, good to be back in a place where man better understood, and fully accepted, his relationship with nature, and better admitted the passions locked within him. Even the food, by Tarzan's estimate, was superior. Real food, honestly earned and wholesome. But still, Tarzan, too excited about Rokoff and the temple, ate sparingly.

Nerves seemed to have the opposite effect on Joshua Mugambi, Tarzan noted, watching the man cram large quantities into his mouth.

"You could have told me they weren't cannibals," Joshua remarked through a mouthful of food when he noticed that Tarzan was looking his way.

"Maybe I wasn't sure of that," Tarzan answered. "As a guest, I never ask what is put on the plate in front of me."

The leading manner of the response, the suggestive nature that perhaps Joshua was jumping to false conclusions, gave the man pause. He stopped chewing and stared down at his food, poking at it gingerly.

"Eat, my friend," Jakar interjected, taking a cue from Tarzan. "It is 'takanda,' a large and healthy specimen."

Joshua smiled and nodded at Jakar, an obvious facade. As soon as the chieftain turned away, Joshua moved closer to Tarzan. "What is takanda?" he asked nervously.

"Something that lived yesterday," Tarzan replied.

"Something," Joshua asked, "or *someone*?"

Tarzan merely shrugged.

"On two legs?" Joshua pressed, growing more animated. "With a heartbeat?"

"On roots," Tarzan finally answered. "Takanda is a palm tree. We are eating the core of it."

"And it is very good," Joshua replied at once, stuffing his mouth and visibly relaxing.

Jakar roared with laughter, and Tarzan would have, too, except for a sound that came from the distant jungle, a foreign sound, one with which Tarzan had become far too familiar.

He stood straight, peering out into the darkness. Then he darted away, out of the encampment, Joshua scrambling to follow.

"Thank you," the confused Joshua managed to stammer, and then he, too, was gone.

The Kikuyus hardly noticed and simply continued with their evening revelry.

In another place, in a world that seemed so far, far away, Collette de Coude and Paul D'Arnot stood at the rail of a great ship, staring at the pale break of the prow wave and at the millions of stars that dotted the sky above them.

"He is looking at the same sky," Collette remarked, and D'Arnot did not have to ask her who she was talking about. His thoughts, too, had been dominated by Jean Tarzan ever since the man had ridden away.

"The world is not so big a place," he said to Collette.

The woman snickered at the notion. "Would that there was truth in your claim, Monsieur D'Arnot," she said.

"But there is," D'Arnot insisted. "The trains run fast, the ships sail hard. We will be back in Marseilles before you know it, and back to Paris soon after that."

"And Monsieur Tarzan will still be in the jungle."

D'Arnot could offer no answer to that. He had seen this all before, with Jane. He had thought that Tarzan and Jane would be married, and what a wonderful union that might have been! But Collette was right, he knew, the world was a large place, inhabited by peoples of widely varying aspirations and societies. It hadn't worked out between Tarzan and Jane because, though many believed they belonged together, their worlds most certainly did not.

Collette, so obviously enchanted with the jungle man, faced the same problem.

"I should like to touch him," she said after a long moment of quiet.

"Collette?" D'Arnot responded, his tone showing surprise and more than a bit of shock.

"Touch his heart," the woman promptly clarified, and she couldn't suppress a giggle. "I should like to give to Monsieur Tarzan what he gave to me."

"And what is that?"

"Hope," she replied.

D'Arnot nodded and smiled, and then he had an idea. "Perhaps there is a way," he said slyly.

Collette, staring up at the stars, taking some comfort that Jean Tarzan was likely eyeing the very same sky, begged him to explain.

CHAPTER 10

True to his word, the old man brought them through the misty spray of a narrow channel around the side of the rushing water, and into a wide and shallow cave in the stone behind the waterfall. It took them some time to get their torches lit in the damp confines, but when they had the fires going, they noticed a darker entrance that opened into the stone. Walking single file, the old man in the lead and Rokoff right behind him, they moved into a long and dark tunnel. Their torches seemed meager indeed against the darkness of that place. Uneven walls cast wild shadows and they came upon many side passages, but the old man, holding the glowing amulet up before him, led them on unerringly.

At last they came upon the tunnel exit, the old man moving out onto a narrow clearing, surrounded on all sides by towering walls. Moonlight filtered down through the tangle of vines and branches partially blocking the top of the ravine far, far above them.

And in front of them loomed the Temple of the Ancients, a pyramid structure thirty feet high, with great carved steps climbing to its flat top on all four sides.

"We never would have seen this from up there," Rokoff commented, glancing up the towering walls of stone. He understood then how the location of this temple had remained secret through all the years.

"Unless we fell through the tangle," Paulvitch commented, nearing the end of the tunnel behind Rokoff. "Then we would have seen the place, but only for the seconds it took us to hit the ground!" He ended with a laugh and lowered his gaze, and then his words were caught in his throat as he glimpsed the ancient temple.

The eight Arabs came out behind the Russians, then filtered out in a wide arc, all of them mesmerized by the spectacular sight.

"Lead us in," Rokoff said to the old man. He knew the danger of delaying, for he understood that Achmet Zek was every bit as greedy as he; Hadab undoubtedly had orders to get rid of him and Paulvitch. Rokoff could delay the inevitable encounter—though he was not afraid of that fight—by keeping them moving. He might yet need the Arabs, both to carry the gold and to serve as fodder for any traps that might be in place within the ancient structure.

"Stay alert," Rokoff said to all of them. "Such treasures are not unusually unprotected."

As if on cue, there came a great hissing noise, out of the passage behind them. They turned as one—except for the old man, who had already started for the temple—to see the head of a snake coming out of the tunnel—the head of a gigantic snake that nearly filled the six-foot diameter opening!

Paulvitch dove to the side, tucked his shoulders and rolled, just getting clear of the snapping jaws. He was halfway around on the ground when he had his revolver out and began firing, every shot striking the supernatural serpent.

Hadab and his men were in full retreat, racing for the temple, the bearers dropping their packs and taking out their rifles, pumping round after round into the snake.

The snake hardly seemed to notice, just slithered on, coming out, out, out of the tunnel endlessly.

Paulvitch was up and running, Rokoff pulling him along. "What is it? What is it?" the terrified big man cried over and over.

Some of Hadab's men, their weapons so obviously ineffective, began scaling the side of the temple, screaming in terror.

The snake was stretching twenty feet out of the tunnel by then, and judging from its girth, Rokoff figured that to be less than one-fifth its length. Their guns were useless against such a beast, he finally acknowledged, and so he reached into a pouch and pulled forth a grenade.

On came the snake; Rokoff pulled the pin and tossed the explosive device right in its path. Then he, too, ran for the temple.

The blast lifted the serpent's head right from the ground. It came down with a bounce and seemed unhurt. But, to the relief of all, it began to recede back into the tunnel.

"Stop your firing!" Rokoff said to the Arabs. "Save your ammunition!"

"You didn't even draw your sword," Paulvitch remarked to Hadab.

The one-eyed man looked at him incredulously; what good would a scimitar do against such a beast as that? Hadab's confusion didn't last, though, for he quickly realized that Paulvitch was merely mocking him.

"We must find a way in," Rokoff said loudly to all the group. "And where is the old man?"

"He went back there," one of the Arabs answered.

Rokoff, Paulvitch, and Hadab ran around the temple and found an opening, barely more than a slit in the wall.

"Send one of your men in," Rokoff said to Hadab.

The Arab eyed him suspiciously for a moment, but did motion for one of the bearers to take up his torch and lead the way in. The man did not disobey, though he moved tentatively, waving the torch before him every step.

"Your man next," Hadab said.

Rokoff smiled at him, then nodded for Paulvitch to move along.

"It opens up," came a call from within. "The pylon!" The Arab ended with a grunt, as though all of the air had suddenly left his lungs, and when Paulvitch and the others caught up to him, they understood.

He stood pinned to the wall, alive and writhing in agony, a spike driven right through his belly, extending from the opposite wall of the narrow tunnel.

"Pressure trap in the floor," Paulvitch remarked callously, batting aside the dying man's reaching arms.

"Open it," Hadab demanded. "Free my man!"

"How might we do that?" Rokoff replied.

Hadab considered the situation for a moment, then nodded his agreement. "End his suffering, then," the Arab instructed.

Rokoff nodded to Paulvitch, who immediately drew out his revolver and put a bullet through the squirming Arab's head.

It was no easy task for the bulky Paulvitch to squeeze

by the impaled man, but he managed it, coming onto a balcony overlooking a roughly circular chamber. A staircase descended in front of him, twin braziers burning at the corners of the bottom step. Paulvitch moved to the stone railing of the balcony. Down below him stood the old man, but Paulvitch hardly noticed him.

"It is beautiful," Paulvitch gasped, forgetting the danger and leaning forward, for in front of the old man loomed the legendary pylon, its gold gleaming brilliantly even in the dim light of the twin braziers.

"That was rather rude, wouldn't you say?" Joshua Mugambi remarked when he finally caught up to Tarzan, nearly a mile from the Kikuyu camp.

Tarzan made no move to reply, just stood perfectly still, sniffing the air, glancing all about.

"What is it, my friend," Joshua said more seriously, sensing that something must be very wrong.

"A sound," Tarzan replied. "A sound that does not belong. Not here."

Joshua considered the words for a moment, and the hostility brewing within his friend. He didn't know Tarzan that well, of course, having only met him recently, but he believed that he understood the basic tenets that guided Tarzan, and he could guess easily enough what sound would most offend this man in his treasured jungle. "A gunshot?" he asked.

Tarzan started away swiftly, with Joshua running to keep up. "At least let me stop and light a torch," he begged, but Tarzan wasn't listening.

Another gunshot crackled through the night, and then several more right behind it.

"Rokoff," Joshua reasoned. "It must be Rokoff."

Then came the thunderous explosion of a hand grenade, and Tarzan ran on, but Joshua skidded to a stop. "A very big gun," he remarked quietly to himself. "Perhaps it would be better to wait until morning." He knew that he would get no reply, and so he turned about, thinking that he would return to the Kikuyus. In the moonlight every jungle trail looked the same, and the fires of the encampment were too far away, and with too much brush in between, to be seen, and the sounds of the drums were too distant to follow.

"Sometimes you are very stupid, Joshua Mugambi," Joshua scolded, and he swung around again and ran off after Tarzan. He called his friend's name repeatedly, then thought the better of making too much noise. All he could do was put his head down and run at full speed, and he knew that even then he would be losing ground to his amazingly agile companion.

He crashed out of the brush suddenly, nearly toppling with the abrupt change of terrain. Across a small meadow, he came to the edge of a pool, a waterfall thundering across the way, and he glimpsed, for just an instant, the movement of a large man, Tarzan, going behind the curtain of falling water.

"This gets better and better," Joshua grumbled, and on he ran, around the edge of the pool and under the waterfall.

He skidded to a stop; Tarzan was in the hollow behind the falls, lighting a makeshift torch.

"You had the time to stop and gather fronds?" Joshua asked incredulously.

"I collected them as I went," Tarzan answered. His torch blazed to life and he stood up, nodding to the tunnel entrance just ahead.

"I am not so fond of tunnels," Joshua remarked. "I wonder if there is a way around it."

"Only if we can swim to the top of the waterfall," Tarzan replied dryly.

Joshua looked at him long and hard, wondering if Tarzan might be able to do just that. "Do you know this place?" he asked.

"I know of it," Tarzan replied. "Take care now, for we have found the entrance to the Temple of the Ancients, and it is likely guarded."

"Take care *now*?" Joshua echoed and he nearly burst out in laughter. "I have been taking care all along. It is you—"

Tarzan quieted him by putting a finger to pursed lips. He pointed to the tunnel, then led the way in, Joshua moving close behind.

"What are you doing?" Paulvitch demanded of the old man, but Rokoff moved up beside him and hushed him. Down below them in the room, the old man moved nearer the pylon of gold, reaching up to it, the crystal amulet glowing even more brightly in his hand.

"Achmet Zek said it was a key," Rokoff reminded his companion. "A key to what, I wonder?"

Even as he spoke, the old man placed the amulet in a notch on the pylon. The fit was perfect. The old man left the amulet there and stepped back, his eyes full of wonder.

As were the eyes of Rokoff and Paulvitch, and of Hadab and the other Arabs who filtered onto the balcony behind them. The amulet's glow seemed to become less distinct, as though it was melding into the pylon, and suddenly the glow went away, then abruptly returned, yellowish now and much brighter, glowing from all of the surface of the huge pylon, lighting the astonished faces of all the would-be thieves and the serene visage of the old man.

All thoughts of the slithering monster they had just left behind were gone now; all thoughts of the inevitable conflict between Hadab and Rokoff seemed inconsequential. As one, the men moved closer, staring, unblinking, bathed in the magical light.

"We are whole again," the old man proclaimed, turning to Rokoff and drawing the Russian from his almost trancelike state. A shaft of light beamed from the narrow pinnacle of the pylon, striking the old man's head, and all his form became limned in the golden hue.

For some of the Arabs this was too much. They shrank back, one even started for the exit, but then, remembering the serpent outside, he held his ground, crouching at the end of the tunnel.

Rokoff only moved closer to the pylon, though. He even started down the stairs, and his courage prompted Paulvitch and Hadab to keep pace with him.

"How long I . . . we have waited," the old man said, and his voice seemed distant somehow, though resonant still. He closed his eyes and, before the disbelieving stares of the stunned men, began to fade.

Paulvitch sputtered a dozen curses, then a like number of prayers.

The old man was transparent! They were looking right through him to the pylon of gold!

"A trick of the light," Hadab declared, and he had to believe that.

But then the old man vanished, was simply gone, and the shaft of light retracted, leaving Rokoff, Paulvitch, and the seven Arabs without a clue. Still the pylon glowed, the richest hue of gold.

"What happened to him?" Paulvitch sputtered.

Rokoff spun on his heel and slapped the lackey across the face, yelling, "He's gone, you idiot!"

The outburst surprised Hadab, and even Rokoff, who quickly realized that his anger was wrought of fear and of a level of excitement he had never before known.

"But where?" Paulvitch whined.

"I don't care!" Rokoff screamed in his face. "We have what we need. It is standing before you. Why does the fate of a foolish old man interest you?"

Paulvitch smiled unconvincingly, but then took a deep breath and considered his master's words. There it was, the pylon of pure gold, a treasure greater than anything he had ever imagined. There was the power that would bring Nikolas to the throne, and would keep his own fat head from the chopping block. In the face of this, Paulvitch's fears concerning the old man could not take root. He moved past Rokoff, down the rest of the stairs and right to the base of the magnificent pylon. "Gold," he said breathlessly. "Look how it shines! We will have to break it up to carry it back, but oh, it is so magnificent!"

Rokoff looked to Hadab, who was staring at Paulvitch, as mesmerized as the big man.

"There is more than gold here, Alexis," Rokoff announced, and he was speaking as much to Hadab as to his lackey. "There is power here, a greater power than anything I have ever felt before."

"Wealth is power," Hadab remarked.

"Beyond wealth," Rokoff replied without hesitation, and

indeed he could feel it, a subtle undercurrent of energy. He knew that the disappearance of the old man was no trick of the light. It was magic—no, not magic, but some power beyond the norm, beyond anything known in all the world.

Rokoff's eyes shone with more than reflected light as he admired the pylon, for soon, he believed, that power would be his.

Tarzan tried to move quickly, but the tunnel was narrow and twisting, and the last thing he wanted to do was turn a corner and stumble into a handful of Rokoff's armed men. He stopped and sniffed the air. Nothing, no smell, no sound of men, save the labored breathing of Joshua Mugambi a few steps behind him. Tarzan reached back and handed Joshua the torch, then went on, crouching low.

He led the way past a side passage, and he did smell something, some scent vaguely familiar, but very wrong in intensity. He had no time to stop and analyze it, though, for ahead of him, around another slight bend in the tunnel, he saw the pale glow of dim moonlight.

Tarzan motioned to Joshua to stay back with the torch, then he went on, around the corner and out of the tunnel. Now he smelled gunpowder and he saw the scar on the ground, a shallow depression of torn, blasted earth.

"What is this?" he heard behind him, and he turned to see Joshua standing in the tunnel exit, touching some gooey substance that was clinging to one of the walls. "Like spittle," Joshua remarked. "But thicker."

The picture was just starting to become clear for Tarzan, the smell, the slime, the gunfire, when an enormous serpentine head came into view, right behind Joshua and closing on the man fast.

With the reflexes of a mongoose, Tarzan leaped forward, grabbing the surprised, and still oblivious, Joshua, and throwing him to the ground to the side.

But the movement cost him time, too much time, and the great snake rushed forward, maw opened wide, and though he eluded the venom-covered fangs, each as long as one of his arms, Tarzan could not get out of harm's way and the mouth closed over him, the snake trying to swallow him whole.

"Tarzan," Joshua tried to stammer, but only gurgling sounds came forth, the Waziri man too overwhelmed by the spectacle. He scrambled backward on his elbows, trying to get out of reach. He stared at the snake's giant head, at the great maw, closed now and showing no sign at all of Tarzan, not even a bulge in the snake's body behind the head.

The great snake, its appetite hardly sated, followed Mugambi, though it had to take a more roundabout course to keep its tremendous body flowing out of the tunnel.

Joshua wondered where he might run; he knew that he was doomed.

CHAPTER 11

Standing right in front of the pylon, Rokoff and Paulvitch saw that it was much more than piled gold. There was a magnificent design here, the whole of the tower appearing much like the flared and decorated tip of a ceremonial spear. It was indeed as wide as many men at the base, but the sides came up at an angle, narrowing the pillar. Then they flared out once more, briefly, before rolling around on themselves, turning straight in, forming shelves on either side of the pillar's second tier. Up on his tiptoes, Rokoff could reach those shelves, could have pulled himself up, to sit atop the pillar's first tier like a king on his golden throne.

Or like a tsar, he mused. Greater than a tsar.

In the middle, between these shelves and from the second tier, the tower rose, beginning as wide as a man's outstretched arms, running up to a point like the blade of a dagger, ending some twenty-five feet off the ground.

Truly the pylon was a magnificent artwork, and even more

so when viewed up close. For it was not simple gold, as beautiful as that would have been, but was embellished with many designs, with accentuating ridges and pleasing geometric twists. In the exact center of the wide base was a circle, nearly six feet in diameter, and just above that, where the old man had set the glowing amulet, were four more huge gemstones, one red, one yellow, one blue, and one green, brilliant and lustrous, flawless as far as Rokoff could discern, and seeming almost alive with their flowing colors swirling about the gold.

Rokoff could hardly imagine taking apart this work of art, but he saw no other possible way for them to get the pylon out of the temple, let alone out of the jungle, without breaking it down. Still, there was something about the whole of it, something that transcended the value of its gold and gems, something that transcended mere wealth.

Paulvitch moved nearer to the pylon, transfixed by the luminous glow of the jewels, particularly of the lowest stone, the red one. A beautiful ruby, it seemed, shining crimson and perfectly cut, itself worth a king's treasure or more. As his more practical nature came back to him, as he considered how he might extract the ruby, Paulvitch realized that it was not set upon the gold, but rather, that it seemed to be *within* the gold.

He didn't understand that, had never heard of anything like it, but he was too fascinated, to pause and study, and instead simply reached up for the coveted prize.

His hand slipped through the gold as if it was liquid, closing on the gem. Hardly registering the impossibility of it, Paulvitch pulled back with his prize. He smiled from ear to ear and turned to show off the loot, but before he got his hand up before him, a great wind began, spinning and churning like a cyclone.

Behind the Russian the circular center of the pylon transformed, changed in color and in texture, like a thick liquid, swirling and spinning.

"What?" was all Paulvitch managed to stammer before the wind yanked him into the liquid center.

Rokoff, who had watched the transformation, dove down and wrapped his arms about a nearby column. Hadab came sliding past, reaching out to him, but Rokoff wouldn't risk his grip to offer the Arab his hand, and away Hadab went, following Paulvitch into the pylon's liquid depths.

Another Arab came flying by, and two more behind him, all pulled right from the balcony. The remaining three screamed and tried to find a hold, but they, too, slid inevitably toward the liquid hole.

Then only Rokoff was in the room, the cyclone beating him, pulling, pulling. His arms tired, his grip weakened.

Then he, too, was sliding, flying, screaming, into the unknown.

Joshua heard the raging tumult inside the temple and felt a stiff breeze, but his more immediate problem, the gigantic snake, kept him backing, backing, until he felt one of the stone walls behind him and had nowhere else to run. He looked to the temple, thinking that he should have gone for the stairs, but now it was too late, for the snake had cut him off.

On came the serpent; its head was fully forty feet from the tunnel where it had emerged, and still its body continued to flow out.

But then it stopped, head swaying hypnotically, back and forth and in small circles.

The great maw began to open, and Joshua's mouth dropped open, too, for the snake was not trying to bite. In fact, it was trying to keep its mouth closed, but it could not, for inside the mouth Tarzan stood nearly upright and pushed on it with all his strength.

"The stick!" he cried. But Joshua was too stunned by merely seeing him alive to hear his words.

"The stick!" Tarzan yelled more insistently.

"Stick what?" Joshua cried back, looking all around.

"The walking stick!" Tarzan clarified. "Prop open its jaws!"

Joshua took up his stout stick, but then hesitated, looking at the pole, a meager thing indeed when measured against the serpent's maw. He gave Tarzan a disbelieving look.

"Prop it," Tarzan commanded. "Its mouth will be open too wide for it to gain any momentum for its bite."

Joshua wasn't sure that he agreed, wasn't sure that the monstrous snake would need any leverage at all to snap the pitiful walking stick in half. But he went forward boldly, setting the wooden staff firmly in place at the side of the serpent's jaw. Then he ran back, and Tarzan, covered in slime, dove out of the mouth and rolled to join him. The snake backed away a bit and whipped its head back and forth, but as Tarzan had predicted, the staff held firm and it could not close its jaws.

"I thought you had a way with animals," Joshua remarked, helping Tarzan to his feet.

"So did I," Tarzan replied. He shook his head and began wiping the slime from his arms, then from his bow and quiver.

"I think we can get past the monster now that he can't close his jaws," Joshua remarked. "Unless, of course, it decides to roll on us!" He shuddered as he visualized that possibility. "I believe that our friend Rokoff is already within the temple," he added, changing the unpleasant subject. "If we are quick, we will get by." He started off, but Tarzan grabbed him by the shoulder.

Joshua looked at the slimy hand and his now slimy shirt with a disgusted frown.

"We could," Tarzan agreed. "But we have to take the stick out or the snake will not survive."

"Are you crazy?" Joshua shot back. "He'll get the both of us this time!"

Tarzan wasn't sure that he disagreed with Joshua, but in looking at the snake, at this creature that had obviously lived for so many years, centuries, perhaps, he found that he could not leave it thus, that he could not willingly bring about its death. "Don't worry," he said in a deadpan voice while offering a little smile, "I have a way with animals."

Tarzan drew out his knife and cautiously approached.

"You aren't really going to take that stick out, are you?" Joshua whined behind him.

"It has a right to live," Tarzan replied.

"So do we!" Joshua reasoned. "Let it live with its mouth open; I know many people who do."

"It can't." Tarzan paused and motioned for Joshua to run ahead, to the safety of the temple's stairs, and the Waziri readily agreed, sprinting away.

The snake wriggled its head furiously, but the stick was wedged in place and would not budge.

Tarzan figured that he had one swipe, and given the size

and strength of the stick, he knew it would have to be powerful and perfectly aimed. He moved in a bit closer, eyeing the serpent directly.

The snake came forward suddenly, and so did Tarzan, leaping into position and slicing his knife across in a powerful backhand. The blade dug into the stick and altered its angle as it cracked wood, and that, combined with the continuing press of the snake's jaws, snapped the staff in half, both pieces flying free.

Tarzan stood straight, unafraid, staring at the freed serpent, its waving head barely three feet from him. With a slight rush, the snake could obviously swallow him whole again.

"Now what?" Joshua asked as Tarzan slowly and unthreateningly moved away.

Tarzan didn't answer, just locked stares with the snake.

"Now what?" Joshua asked more urgently, but then he calmed as the serpent began to recede, its great body slithering back into the tunnel opening.

"It is no longer a threat to us," Tarzan announced.

"Does the snake know that?"

In response, Tarzan walked right toward the snake. It flicked its forked tongue out at him several times, then continued its retreat into the tunnel.

"Now we can go to the temple," Tarzan said. "And return with confidence that the guardian will not hinder us."

"I can't believe it," Joshua replied. "The thing's afraid of you!"

"Not afraid," Tarzan corrected. "We understand each other."

"Then he must understand me," Joshua stated. He

assumed a heroic pose and puffed out his chest. "I'm the one who put the stick in his mouth."

Tarzan gave a low bow and motioned for Joshua to lead on. "Then after you, my hero," he said.

"I'll let you have the credit," Joshua replied without missing a beat, skidding to a stop as he regarded the mysterious temple.

Hiding his smile, Tarzan stepped past and started around the pyramid's base, seeking an entrance.

Joshua waited a few moments, standing behind, looking to the snake, to the sheer stone walls, then finally back to Tarzan. "I thought I was in Africa," he said quietly. "My home. Instead, I'm somewhere in the middle of a mysterious mountain with a snake that is the size of a river and possesses teeth as long as my arm." He let out a great sigh. "I miss Oxford," he lamented. "Even during exam week!"

He was in a tunnel of stars, it seemed, swirling and spinning through a winding vortex. Down, down—or perhaps it was up, for there seemed to be no real direction, no gravity tugging at him, no visible point of reference.

Rokoff fought hard to get his bearings, but there was nothing to guide his senses. All around him seemed like the clearest of night skies, but wrapped tightly, somehow pressing in on his sensibilities. And the sound was like the wind, but with a low, resonating undertone, like the mantra of a thousand, thousand chanting monks.

Then it was over; a tree branch hooked his arm as he tumbled, rolling about and slamming another branch and then landing unceremoniously on the ground. He sprang up, ready to run, momentarily terrified. He saw Paulvitch and the Arabs, some standing, some still cowering where they had fallen. He saw . . .

He saw a scene that made no sense, a horizon that bent upward, reaching for the sun. "The sun?" Rokoff asked skeptically, for the glowing ball of red that lit this place bore little resemblance to the sun of his world. Only the wind, blowing, swirling in the trees above him, seemed the same. Terror fast shifted to intrigue for the always-curious man. He stepped forward, ahead of the others, eyes wide, mouth ajar.

"Where are we?" a frantic Paulvitch asked, moving to stand beside him. "What is this place?"

"Control yourself," Rokoff scolded. "Your questions are the ramblings of a fool."

"But look," Paulvitch went on. "There is no horizon! The earth blends into the sky! It was night when we went into the temple, but now it is day." He jumped around, growing more animated, more frantic. "Everything is strange," he cried. "Have we fallen to the opposite side of the earth?"

Rokoff's demeaning stare settled him somewhat, as if reminding him that, in their travels together, they had been everywhere from Mongolia to England. What "other side of the earth" might Paulvitch be talking about?

"It is different," Rokoff agreed, no trace of panic in his voice. "But there is always an explanation."

"We are here," Paulvitch argued flatly, waving his hand at the upturning horizon. "There is no rationale!"

"It was that red stone," Rokoff said. "There is some power in that stone that can transport us to a place like this." He looked up into the pair of trees through which he and the others had fallen, to the swirling branches there, the apparent center of the vortex.

Paulvitch held up the ruby, which was shining a deeper shade of red in the strange hue of this place. "Then we must use the stone to get us out of here," he said.

"Not yet!" Rokoff was quick to reply, to Paulvitch and to the Arabs, who were listening intently to his every word. "The old man has led us to more than a pile of gold. He has given us the key to some mystical power. Between the pylon and that red stone, we have stumbled into something amazing."

"It's dangerous," Paulvitch remarked.

"Power always is," Rokoff replied without hesitation. He looked straight at Hadab, looking for some signal of acquiescence as he finished the thought. "And power is always worth it."

Hadab nodded slightly; Rokoff understood then that whatever conflict had been arranged by Achmet Zek between them would wait until this strange situation was sorted out.

"What is that?" Paulvitch asked.

Rokoff followed his gaze upward, to the hanging, red-glowing ball in the unnatural sky. Rokoff couldn't be sure if the man was referring specifically to the glowing "sun," or to the sky itself, which seemed, somehow, smaller, somehow contained.

"It is getting bigger!" Paulvitch exclaimed.

Rokoff peered closer, focusing on the red ball, and saw, in its center, a black dot, growing, growing.

No, Rokoff realized suddenly, not bigger, but closer! Something large was speeding their way! It was still a long way off, Rokoff realized, and continuing to close, continuing to grow. It nearly blocked out the sun, and took form, birdlike.

But no bird, Rokoff realized. Its wings were more batlike, but huge, twenty feet across and shining dark red! And its torso seemed human, except that its legs were long, storklike, and ended with tremendous claws.

On it came; a few of the Arabs dove for cover, but Rokoff held his ground, studying the creature as more of its gruesome features came clear. The body was indeed roughly human in form, but ridged with rippling muscle and armored by a tough orange and black hide. A ridge of small horns ran front to back over the top of its head, which was so black as to appear purple and shaped like that of a snoutless lizard. Red eyes glowed at him, rows of formidable teeth gleamed evilly. Even worse were the creature's two horns set at the sides of its mouth, great and curving, hooking back over the gleaming teeth.

Paulvitch tackled Rokoff suddenly, driving him to the side, to cover.

The flying creature shrieked, a bloodcurdling, bone-shivering howl that split the air more powerfully than the roar of the largest lion or the trumpet of the largest elephant.

"No light," Tarzan said to Joshua, who was trying to get the torch burning again.

"It's very dark," Joshua replied, staring into the opening in the wall, which seemed to be barely a crack.

"No light, and no sound," Tarzan said, and before Joshua could argue, he started in, creeping along, trusting senses other than his sight.

A few twists and turns later, and both he and Joshua could see again, for the tunnel was bathed in golden light. Around a last bend they saw the dead Arab impaled against the wall, a bullet hole in his temple.

"Poor man," Joshua said sincerely.

Tarzan nodded and crept past, bending low to slip under the wall-to-wall spike. His hair started blowing about as soon as he came to the other side, to the opening for the balcony overlooking the pylon of gold, though the wind was not nearly as powerful as it had first been.

"Where does this wind come from?" Joshua asked, having to shout as he stepped out on the balcony beside Tarzan and surveyed the room, which seemed intact and fully enclosed, except for the one entrance they had used. "And where are Rokoff and his men?"

"A secret door, perhaps," Tarzan replied. He stepped in a bit farther, dared to go around the railing of the balcony to the stairs that led down to the pylon. The wind buffeted him, but then seemed to diminish even more, and Tarzan walked on, right up to the pillar of gold and then around it, checking all potential hiding spots.

"It is beautiful," Joshua remarked from the balcony. "But I don't think Rokoff would willingly leave it. Is it solid gold?"

"It would appear so," Tarzan answered. "But these things are not always as they seem."

"Tarzan!' Joshua called suddenly, and Tarzan turned to see him moving to the side. He bent low below the balcony's solid stone rail and came back up holding a burnoose, a piece of cloth that had not lain there for long. "See? They were in here."

"Their scent spoor is strong," Tarzan agreed.

A flash of light interrupted their conversation and spun them both about to regard the pylon, or rather, a shaft of light beaming out from its tip to spotlight a point on the floor in front of it. Within that circle of light appeared a form familiar to them, the old man, except that he was cleaner now, and dressed in a splendid white robe. He seemed perfectly at ease, perfectly serene.

"Tarzan of the apes," he said solemnly, "you have found your way back to our place."

"How do you know me?" Tarzan asked.

"We have always known you," the old man replied. "We also shared a dungeon when I was in human form."

Joshua Mugambi held the railing for support, feeling as if he would faint away.

Tarzan nodded at the old man, showing that he recognized him. "I'm glad that you are still alive, old man," he replied. "But where are the ones who kidnapped you? Where are Rokoff and the amulet?"

"The amulet has been returned to us," said the old man. He turned and pointed to the pylon, above the circle, where the amulet was set, along with three of the four gemstones. "But the one you call Rokoff and his companions have opened a portal to the core of the earth. They are in Pellucidar. You must follow them and retrieve the stolen stone to close the portal."

"Wherever this Pellucidar is, let them stay there," Joshua Mugambi replied.

"No!" the old man snapped angrily. "Tarzan, you must go. You must retrieve the red stone."

"Let them have the stone," Joshua said.

"The portal cannot be closed without it," the old man

explained. "If it remains open, it remains open both ways—or many ways, perhaps. I have not the time to explain. Such a portal cannot remain. Creatures will come through, Tarzan, and they will destroy your world."

"What is this talk of a portal?" Joshua wanted to know. "What creatures?"

"I have heard the legends of Pellucidar," Tarzan replied. "They do speak of monsters and animals larger than the largest elephants." He turned to the old man. "Are these legends true?" he asked. "These creatures exist?"

"They are and they do," the old man answered grimly. "And I warn you that more than the creatures of Pellucidar, formidable as they might be, will find their way through the open portal. The missing gemstone must be returned to its place before the wind ceases or it will turn to vapor, leaving the portal open forever. Your world will not survive."

CHAPTER 12

A couple of the Arabs turned their rifles skyward and opened fire on the diving monster; others cowered in the bushes, scrambling to get away.

Paulvitch didn't give an inch. He stood his ground firmly, revolver in hand, picking his shots.

Despite the barrage, the creature continued downward, diving, diving, straight for Alexis Paulvitch.

"Die!" the big man yelled, emptying the last shot. He was certain that this bullet, at least, had hit the mark, and yet, the beast continued its swoop.

Paulvitch pulled the trigger again, then, hearing the click of the empty chamber, he turned and ran, diving and rolling. The creature was on him, right above him, and so he threw his arms up defensively to block, slapping at the grasping talons.

A claw raked his hand, sending the ruby gemstone flying. It skidded to the side, near a bush, and an Arab hiding there could not resist. He scrambled out and snatched the stone, then turned to run back under cover.

Too late, for as soon as the stone went flying, the creature left Paulvitch in pursuit of it. Now the Arab had it, but in an instant the creature had the Arab in its clutches, easily lifting him from the ground. Off it flew, followed by yet another volley of futile gunshots.

"The ruby!" Paulvitch wailed. "Oh, my treasure." He scrambled in the direction the creature had flown, holding his empty hands up in frustration. Then he turned on the Arabs, cursing them for being too frightened to pause and pick good shots. "And my treasure!" he wailed again.

"More than that," Rokoff sneered, coming from behind a tree. Even as he spoke, the wind seemed to diminish a bit more. Rokoff looked back to the pair of trees, but the vortex there had lessened considerably as the magical stone was carted far from the spot.

Unbeknownst to Rokoff and the others, three people, garbed in animal skins and armed with hooked clubs, witnessed the battle from a hilltop not so far away. In fact, one of the many errant gunshots ricocheted near to them, skipping off the stone near one man's face.

"Those sticks that shoot fire," he gasped, rubbing his finger against the deep chip in the stone, "they break rock!"

"But still they did not stop the mahar," answered a tall and strong woman, the only female in the group. "It flew away without any harm."

"We do not know that, Jana," the first man responded, an edge of anger in his voice. "These strangers still have stronger weapons than we do." To emphasize the point, he held up his club and gave it a frustrated shake. "And there are many of them. They are a new danger."

"A new danger that may help us," Jana replied, a cunning smile coming to her fair face. "If they separate, we can take them a few at a time. Then their weapons will be ours."

"I say it is better if we just stay hidden from them," the man argued. "The boom sticks can destroy us."

"And if they did not have the boom sticks?"

The man eyed her suspiciously, guessing that he was being baited. "I would consider an attack," he answered. "On a few of them."

"Truly you are a brave warrior, Turro," Jana remarked. "You would hide from all the world, if you could find a deep enough hole."

"And you, Jana, are insolent and disrespectful," Turro came back. He stepped toward her forcefully, fighting the urge to strike her.

"Yes I am," the woman replied, smiling as if he had just complimented her. She turned away briskly, dismissing Turro with a wave. Her thick, shoulder-length blond hair bouncing, her blue eyes sparkling eagerly, she scanned for the men with the coveted boom sticks. They were already on the move, she noted, running fast in the same general direction the mahar had flown.

Jana was a bit unnerved at the fact that the boom sticks had not brought down the mahar, even though they could apparently break stone. She had to hope that the mahar had indeed been injured, or that the men had just aimed badly. More than anything in all the world, Jana wanted a weapon with which she could fight back against the evil mahars, the bane of her tribe's existence.

If she had to kill a few intruders to get such a weapon, then so be it.

"They're in there?" Joshua groaned, pointing to the circular design in the pylon's base, the place the old man had indicated as the portal to Pellucidar. "Rokoff and his bunch are in there?" He moved next to Tarzan, his expression showing that he was not happy with this situation. Not at all.

"Not in there," the old man explained. "Through there."

"In some other world?" Joshua balked. "I'm not going to some other world!"

"The world of Pellucidar is part of your world until the portal is closed," the old man reasoned. "This man you call Rokoff and his party can come and go as they please, as can the creatures of the earth's core."

"As can we," Tarzan reasoned.

"It is time for you to enter the portal and stop them before they bring about destruction," the old man said. "If the red stone is not returned in time . . ." His voice faded as his image faded, leaving the unsettling thought hanging in the air.

"I'd rather be in London," Joshua remarked.

Tarzan wasn't even listening. He walked boldly toward the portal, and with no more than a finger-touch test to ensure that it was not solid, he stepped right through, disappearing from sight.

"I've also heard some good things about the United States," Joshua went on. With a frustrated groan and a slap of his hands, he, too, went to the portal, though he inspected it much more cautiously than had Tarzan, first poking his finger into it, then his whole hand, then his whole arm. For all his inspection, though, Joshua knew no more about the strange liquidlike gate than had Tarzan, and so, with a final, resigned grunt, he dove through.

That grunt turned into a scream for help as Joshua spun through the swirling star tunnel, and became a yelp of surprise as he found himself suddenly crashing through the low branches of a pair of trees. He reached out and caught one as he fell, but he could not fully break his momentum and his effort did no more than to spin him over so that he was facing the weird sky. And in that pose, he dropped the last few feet to land sprawling on his back, his breath coming out in a great "whoosh!" of air.

Joshua's mind was whirling too fast for his mouth to keep up, and over the next few seconds nothing but gibberish came forth from his sputtering lips.

Then he noticed Tarzan, and the sight of the powerful man, standing alert and ready, already scanning the area, calmed him somewhat. Joshua pulled himself up from the ground and dusted himself off, then went to join his friend.

"What is this place?" he asked.

"You heard the old one," Tarzan replied. "It is Pellucidar, the earth's core." As he explained, he pointed to the up-curving horizon and the glowing red ball that served as Pellucidar's sun.

"It's true," Joshua muttered, shaking his head. "And if it's true about this world, then it follows that—" He stopped, for Tarzan was already answering his next question, the jungle man pointing to a depression in the ground, a footstep several inches deep and nearly seven feet in diameter.

Joshua's mouth and eyes popped open wide. He wanted to

scream, but couldn't find the breath for it. He looked to Tarzan, who held his finger over pursed lips and with his other hand was pointing off into some distant brush and trees.

As he concentrated, tilting his head in that direction, Joshua caught the sounds of an animal munching, rather like a cow, he thought.

"A cow?" he whispered under his breath, but then he looked back to the footstep, and noted another depression moving in the direction of the chewing sound. Joshua grabbed Tarzan's arm. "When do we run?" he asked.

"We don't," Tarzan replied. "Stand perfectly still."

"We've done this before," Joshua said. "I hate this part."

"Still your lips as well," Tarzan said.

"They're attached to my fear," Joshua explained.

"We do not want to appear as a threat to anything watching us," Tarzan insisted.

"Do I look threatening?" Joshua asked incredulously. "What could I do to a 'footprint' that size?" As he finished, the beast in the brush shifted, coming into clearer view. Joshua blinked with sudden confusion, and then his heart nearly stopped. He had thought the creature to be behind a hill that rested among the trees; imagine his surprise when he learned that the creature *was* the hill in the trees!

Tarzan grabbed him as he backed. "Stand perfectly still," the jungle man ordered quietly. "And stay calm. There is no danger here."

"How do you know?" Joshua asked.

"The animal is grazing," Tarzan replied. "It eats grasses and plants, not meat. It will not attack unless we frighten it."

"I have enough fear for him and me," Joshua was quick to

point out, but Tarzan, in studying him, knew that Joshua wasn't speaking entirely truthfully, that he was indeed finding his nerve. Joshua had seen renderings of such a creature at Oxford, and he was amazed at how accurate the paleontologists had been. This creature was called a brontosaurus, he remembered, or at least, this creature looked an awful lot like what the paleontologists said a brontosaurus would look like.

"If any were alive," Joshua mumbled aloud. "Of course, none can be alive, since they're long extinct. Right?" he asked, turning to Tarzan, who had not been in on the private conversation.

"So of course there really is no such creature as that," Joshua rambled, and Tarzan wondered if he was going to have to slap the man across the face to calm him down.

Finally, with a sigh, Joshua quieted. "Nothing to worry about," he announced.

Tarzan nodded and motioned for Joshua to quietly follow.

As he fell in behind the cautiously moving Tarzan, Joshua's thoughts again went back to his studies at Oxford. He remembered the text accompanying the drawings of the brontosaurus, which pointed out what Tarzan had already told him: that the creature was a huge and docile eating machine, and also that it was incredibly stupid, with a minuscule brain cavity.

Still, despite the reassurances, Joshua jumped—and Tarzan did a bit, too—when the brontosaurus grabbed the end of a branch and tore it down, nearly pulling the tree from the ground.

"The old man is right," Tarzan said. "Nothing could stop these beasts. They would destroy everything we know, just to survive."

There came a noise then, a sudden rushing of air, rumbling like a small train. The burst of wind hit Tarzan and Joshua, backing Joshua several steps. And then it was gone.

"What was that?" Joshua asked.

"It must be the ruby," Tarzan reasoned. "Perhaps Rokoff is experimenting with it. Who knows what trouble he might cause? We're running out of time, I fear; we have to find him and the missing stone, now."

Tarzan held perfectly still, sniffing the air.

"How can you smell anything with that beast so near?" Joshua asked.

Without a word, Tarzan started away, and his deliberate pace told Joshua that he was on to something.

Somehow, Joshua wasn't surprised.

"We must slow down!" Paulvitch insisted. "We do not even know where we are, or what we are running into!"

Rokoff, in the lead, spun about, suddenly stopping Paulvitch, who was right behind him, and cutting off the man's blabbering with an icy stare. Behind them the Arabs paused as well, grumbling and complaining. These were men, Rokoff feared, teetering on the very edge of hysteria. A few more dangerous surprises from this unknown land might put them over the edge, might send them running wildly. Except for Hadab. Rokoff's suspicions of that one seemed on the mark. The one-eyed man appeared as composed as ever, moving along, not protesting, and if he was scared at all, he did not show it.

In truth, Rokoff had to admit that Hadab was handling himself better than Paulvitch. For the big man was sweating and swearing profusely, waving his hand around to show anyone who cared to look at the now-useless item he carried.

"Enough," Rokoff finally said to him, growing embarrassed by his companion's rambling.

"But look," Paulvitch protested, holding up a compass. "It has no reading. It simply spins around and around like a broken clock."

Rokoff glanced at the wildly spinning compass needle and gave a shrug. His lack of concern only frustrated Paulvitch all the more, and with the big Russian, frustration always led to sheer anger.

Rokoff jumped back in surprise as Paulvitch snapped the compass shut and tossed it into some bushes.

"Throwing it away will certainly be helpful," Rokoff said dryly.

"You don't seem to need it," Paulvitch dared to say. "You're moving us along like you have some idea of where you're going. But you don't, of course."

Rokoff's look went from cold to purely threatening, stealing some of Paulvitch's bluster. "If you had not lost the stone," he snarled, "we would have something of great value and the key to an escape route. Now, because of your incompetence, we must find both."

"And how are we going to do that?" Paulvitch asked.

"By following the direction taken by that flying monster," Rokoff answered. "It must end its flight somewhere."

Paulvitch glanced around at the strange surroundings, at the upturning horizon. "Are you sure of that?" he asked. "Are you sure of anything at all?"

"Only that you are an idiot," Rokoff replied. "Concerning this world, I am sure of nothing. But we must find that creature if we are to retrieve the stone, and I am convinced that we must regain the stone if we are to find a way out of here. Do you have a better idea?"

"No," Paulvitch replied. "No, no, no! I have no ideas, except to get out of this place, to get away from all of this!"

"Then shut up and do as you are told," Rokoff finished, turning away and, with a look to Hadab, moving on. "Now follow!" he commanded.

He hadn't gone more than a few steps, moving between two thick trees, when the brush at his feet snapped wildly and a snare tightened about his ankle, yanking him to the ground, then dragging him upside down, finally lifting him to hang several feet from the ground.

Hadab leaped forward, next to Paulvitch, drawing his scimitar even as the large Russian pulled his rifle from his shoulder. Neither completed the move, though, as a weighted net fell over them, followed by two humanoid forms, slamming against them, knocking them to the ground.

The other Arabs scrambled, some coming forward, most retreating, but not one of them got more than a couple of strides before he was similarly overwhelmed, as all the foliage erupted suddenly with squat and powerful humanoid forms. They resembled humans, but seemed more primitive somehow, with ridged, furrowed brows and heavy jowls, and a low, arm-swinging, apelike gait.

Paulvitch and Hadab struggled under the net, managing to toss the first couple of attackers aside, but then they were both forcibly calmed as spear tips, crude but undeniably effective, came in to point at them, barely inches from their faces.

Beyond the two trees, Rokoff doubled up and was trying to work on the snare line with his pocketknife. A club strike to the back of his head ended that.

He hung limp, upside down, thoroughly helpless.

CHAPTER 13

The cave was brutally hot, and a noxious, sulfuric odor permeated the place, burning Rokoff's throat whenever he inhaled. His party was down to six now; the cavemanlike humanoids had dragged him, Paulvitch, Hadab, and three of the Arab guards to this place. The remaining three had been dragged off in a different direction in this underground complex of twisting tunnels. The sounds that had subsequently come from that direction, screams like none any of the men had ever heard, led them to believe that their three companions were no longer alive.

The nets were gone and no ropes bound any of the men, but there was no thought of escape. Their squat and powerful captors watched them carefully, and even if they could overpower this bunch, they had no idea of how to escape the labyrinth of passages.

"What will they do with us?" Paulvitch kept asking Rokoff, who dismissed the question each time with a wave of his hand.

Paulvitch's anger mounted with each brush-off. The big man was not usually afraid, and never before had he been this terrified. Paulvitch had been a fighter all of his life, a brawler that the other kids on the streets of Moscow did well to avoid. By the time he had reached his mid-teens, so great was his reputation that local businesses paid him for protection. The other young men, even those banded in gangs, avoided him at all costs, as did the local police. The tough Paulvitch had ruled his small section of Moscow, and so great did his reputation become that the tsar himself had taken notice, bringing the fighter under his wing and elevating him quickly all the way to the palace guard.

Even among that select group of warriors, the bear-shaped Paulvitch had a reputation for toughness. But now Alexis Paulvitch found himself in the most uncontrollable and nerve-wracking situation of his entire life, more frightened even than on the day he was led out of a jail cell to have his head placed on an execution block. At least on that occasion, he was able to comprehend what was happening, could understand the logical process that would, he believed, lead to his death.

This, however, was too bizarre.

"I could kill that one," Paulvitch growled at Rokoff, pointing at one of the thick-browed humanoids. "And that one. And that one. On your word, I could snap their necks, or bash their heads into the stone."

"Silence," Rokoff commanded. "I have no time or patience for your stupidity now."

"But—"

"But where would we run?" Rokoff interrupted sarcastically. He waved his hand alternately at each of the many exits to the chamber—and each of those passages appeared as if they had many more passages running off of them, an absolute maze. "And how many more of these creatures would we have to fight?"

"You heard the three Arabs," Paulvitch reminded.

"And if they had wanted to kill us all, then they would already have done so," Rokoff reasoned. He meant to go on, but stopped when he heard shuffling footsteps approaching.

He saw her then, up to the side of the chamber's main floor, on a higher tier of stone, and Rokoff knew at once, without the slightest doubt, that she ruled in this place. She was tall, above six feet, and exotically beautiful, with straight, raven-black hair and penetrating dark eyes. The skin on one side of her face and neck was decorated with a pattern of dark dotted tattoos. She wore little, a simple one-piece outfit of some smooth, dark orange-hued material that Rokoff could not identify, cut high on her legs, up above her hips on both sides and low in front. Her physique was not typically feminine, not soft and round in the least, her shoulders broad and all her body covered with sinewy, corded muscles. Yet there was a sensuality to her, a promise of powerful passion beyond anything the Russian had ever known. Her movements were the most unique thing of all, swift and darting, almost lizardlike, almost as if her body was possessed of too much energy and strength to be contained within its fleshy limits.

Behind the woman stood three others, tall and exotic, beautiful all, with the same dark features, the same powerful bodies, the same uncontrollable inner strength, though not to the degree of the first.

Yes, she was the leader, Rokoff knew, a belief that was

strengthened when he noted the item she wore about her neck.

"She has the red stone!" Paulvitch spouted in his ear as the big man, too, noticed the gem. It had been set as a pendant, dangling on a gold chain. "She's wearing it!"

"Shut up, Alexis," Rokoff replied quietly. "I'm not blind."

The woman smiled wickedly, having heard every word, and circled around, moving down the natural steps from the tier. Two of the larger apelike humanoids moved to flank her immediately, and Rokoff noted that as they followed her, they carefully remained a respectful step behind.

"This one is royalty," the Russian said quietly.

The other three women came to the very front of the higher tier, leering down at the captives, staring too eagerly. Like starving carnivores viewing an easy kill, Rokoff thought, and he remembered again the screams of the three men who had not made it to this room.

The leader came down among the prisoners, walking with confidence, completely unafraid. She moved to Hadab, and for the first time Rokoff believed the one-eyed man to be shaken. This man, this warrior, who had calmly walked into every battle, who had battled Tarzan and had kept his cool even when the magical portal had deposited him in this alien land, could not look the woman in the eye!

She paused for a moment, scrutinizing Hadab, staring him down. Then she moved to study the other Arabs, one at a time, staring each of them down, then moving on. Paulvitch straightened his back and tried to meet that penetrating gaze, but the woman snickered and with one hand and hardly an effort, casually pushed him aside, coming at last to stand before Rokoff.

"It is obvious that you are the leader of this group," she said, and her command of English caught Rokoff off his guard. "Do you admit that?"

"Why would I deny that which is obvious?" Rokoff replied, composing himself quickly.

The woman glared down at him and chuckled in superior tones. "I am Mora," she announced proudly. "Queen of the Mahars."

Rokoff straightened and tried to match her arrogance. "I am Captain Nikolas Rokoff," he said, "son of Nikolas the Second, Tsar of Russia."

If Mora was impressed in the least, she hid it well. "I have never heard of this 'Russia' anywhere in Pellucidar," she answered.

"And I have never heard of Pellucidar," Rokoff replied.

Mora nodded, conceding the point. "Yet you are here," she reasoned, "in *my* land."

Rokoff considered the less-than-subtle threat in her tone. In truth, though, that threat only offered him more hope. Mora was trying to intimidate him, which, if she meant to kill him soon, made little sense. No, Rokoff realized, the Queen of the Mahars was intrigued, at the very least, by these strangers who had come into her land, and that curiosity would keep him alive, at least for the time being.

"If we are not welcome, we will leave," he offered calmly.

Mora's expression showed her surprise. "You have come into my land bearing strange weapons," she snapped back at him. "And you wounded Tikka; for that alone I should destroy you."

"We did not," Alexis Paulvitch sputtered. "We have hurt no one, only that—"

Rokoff wisely cut him short, putting an icy glare over the man. He suspected that if Paulvitch finished the thought, Mora would finish all of them in an instant. "And Tikka is?" he prompted, again in a calm and controlled tone.

Mora eyed him contemptuously, making no move to answer.

He knew the answer anyway. Rokoff was not surprised to discover that Mora was somehow connected to the monster that had assailed them when first they had come into Pellucidar. She was wearing the ruby, after all, and even more than that, something about the way she moved revealed to him that she was different from him, from any human he had ever known.

"Your pet?" he went on, for he wanted to learn more about this Tikka creature, and discover what relationship Mora might have with it.

"My friend," Mora replied, and she smiled wickedly at Rokoff's curious expression. He had figured out much, she realized, but not the whole truth.

"But enough of that matter," the Queen of the Mahars declared. "Your weapons were pitiful against the like of Tikka, pitiful against the powers of the mahars."

Rokoff glanced to Paulvitch, who stood with his mouth hanging open, confused and stunned by the implications of Mora's words. When he was confident that his blustery friend would say nothing, Rokoff then went on to replay the battle in his mind. He remembered clearly the confusion, the screaming, the wild shooting. The weapons were not pitiful, he decided, the shooters were. In all the confusion, the Arabs seemed as likely to hit each other as the flying creature, and Paulvitch, the only seasoned fighter among them—except for

Hadab, who had carried only his scimitar—had been engaged too quickly to put his rifle to use. And considering the accuracy of the pistol, he really hadn't gotten off more than one effective shot—likely the one that had wounded Tikka.

Also, Rokoff considered Mora's tone when she spoke of the weapons. There was indeed a subtle undercurrent of anger there—likely based on fear. These inhabitants of Pellucidar had never seen the power of guns before, he believed.

"I rule here," Mora sneered.

"I offered to leave," replied Rokoff.

"You are not permitted to come and go at your whim," Mora said. She came forward as she spoke, and seemed to grow taller somehow, towering over Rokoff.

The proud Russian did not back down an inch, and matched Mora's glare with a cunning smile. "Then maybe I would prefer to stay," he replied, trying to keep her off balance, "if you could tell me the nature of this strange place, and what it might offer me."

Mora's expression, for just an instant, was one of sheer incredulity, as if to ask what this intruder, this mere prisoner, might be talking about. That expression quickly transformed, though, into one of anger, and Rokoff knew that she had recognized her obvious surprise as a show of weakness. "Your statements are stupid," she snapped, walking around him, studying him, glaring at him. "You are in Pellucidar. Tell me why you are here."

Rokoff, reading her explosive nature, knew that he could not press this game too far. Keeping Mora off her guard was a fine tactic, but pushing it to the point where he frightened her would surely get him killed. The time had come for him to be more candid, for him to tease Mora with a bit of the truth. "My party was drawn into a tunnel that took us on a trip like no other," he answered. "We were deposited here, in your Pellucidar."

"A strange tunnel?" Mora questioned, showing more than a little interest. "Tell me more about it."

"I will tell you nothing more until I have a clear understanding of my situation here," Rokoff dared to reply, trying to draw on that apparent intrigue. "I demand to know."

"You demand?" Mora stuttered, and then she laughed wickedly. "You are an interesting human, Nikolas Rokoff."

"Human?" Paulvitch echoed under his breath. What an odd way for the woman to describe him, he thought. Unless . . .

Paulvitch sucked in his breath. Unless she was not human.

Rokoff, who had already come to that conclusion, was not surprised by the phrase. Tikka, the winged creature, was her friend, she had said, and so her reference to Tikka as a "human" was likely not simply an unusual manner of speaking.

"You are either very brave, or very stupid," Mora finished.

"I also demand that you return my property," Rokoff pressed. He had taken Mora to the limits, he knew, but there was no turning back without showing weakness. And Rokoff suspected that showing weakness to Mora was to invite death. "You have the red stone around your neck that was taken from me. It is mine."

Mora relaxed and smiled disarmingly, then, in a movement too quick for Rokoff to even follow, she slapped him hard across the face. His knees went weak from the strength of the blow, but he stubbornly held his ground.

"The Crimson Eye belongs to my people," Mora snarled at

him. "It was taken from Queen Roma many lifetimes ago. Its power gives back what was lost." She motioned sharply to the guards, then turned to glare once more at Rokoff. "Your trial is over."

Rokoff and the others were immediately overpowered by the deceptively strong humanoids, dozens of the squat and powerful creatures coming in through every entrance. Even Paulvitch and Hadab could offer little resistance, and within seconds the whole group was knocked down and dragged away.

He sprinted ahead, then stopped and sniffed the air and scanned the ground and brush. Then he ran on again, repeating the process. Those short respites were the only reason that Joshua Mugambi could keep up with Tarzan. Still, the Waziri was running hard, and running short of breath.

"I have the utmost confidence in your ability to know where we are going," he panted. "So that's not the reason I'm questioning you."

That last comment got Tarzan's attention. He stood straight and looked back, waiting for Joshua to catch up.

"Could you tell me why we are traveling in this specific direction?" Joshua asked. "I have seen few tracks or other signs of passage."

"I am following a spoor," Tarzan explained.

"A fungus seed?" Joshua asked incredulously.

"No, a scent spoor," Tarzan replied. "It remains strong even in the wind."

"The old adage 'follow your nose' applies, then," Joshua said, trying to lighten things up.

Tarzan, though, remained stern. He said nothing to Joshua, just went back to his hunting. But then he froze suddenly, straightening and sniffing the air repeatedly, his expression curious.

"What is it?" Joshua asked.

"A new scent," Tarzan replied. "One I do not know."

"I'm not surprised," Joshua said dryly. "In this country, it could be a twelve-legged purple horse with horns and a soprano voice!"

Tarzan started off again, but more slowly, more cautiously, with Joshua right on his heels. Only a dozen strides later Tarzan stopped again, abruptly, and stood perfectly still, his expression once again showing that he was truly perplexed. "The scent," he explained, before Joshua could even ask. "It has changed again."

"Perhaps it is the purple horse," Joshua remarked.

"This is a confusing world," Tarzan admitted.

"And you, my friend, are a master of understatement!" Joshua said, chuckling. He didn't realize how true his words were until he turned and looked around, as had Tarzan, only to find a sandy-haired man standing right behind him. Joshua jumped, but not quickly enough, and the man slugged him hard in the chest, knocking him to the ground.

Tarzan spun about, instinctively throwing his forearm up high to deflect the attack of a second man who had appeared on the scene. His other hand knifed in under the upraised arm, catching the man by the chin, then his blocking arm spun out and about the man's arm, catching a hold on the back of the man's head. Turning his right hand out to the right, his left out to the left and down, Tarzan had little trouble in spinning the man down to the ground.

When he turned back, though, thinking to go after Joshua's attacker, he found the sandy-haired man atop his friend, a knife tucked neatly under Joshua's chin.

Tarzan studied the young man intently, sensed his fear, and guessed that the man would hesitate if he attacked boldly. He could get to Joshua in time, he decided.

But before he could make the move, a third attacker leaped out at him from the rear, kicking him hard on the hip. He turned into a roll to absorb the hit, then came back to his feet, only to find the second attacker coming at him again, shoulder down.

The man slammed into Tarzan, who set his feet wide apart and behind him and held his ground. He reached under, around the man's chest, slid his arm down a bit to the man's belly, then heaved with his great strength, breaking the hold and inverting the man.

But then a knife was at his throat, and a woman's voice whispered in his ear, "Do not move or you will die."

Tarzan gauged her tone, the steadiness of her hand. Unlike the man standing over Joshua, unlike the man he now held upside down, there was nothing tentative about her voice, no trace of paralyzing fear.

Tarzan eased his captive back to the ground, the man immediately scrambling to the side of his companion, helping him to hold Joshua steady.

"Your nose was right, Tarzan," Joshua remarked. "Something still smells rotten."

"Silence!" commanded the woman. "I will tell you when to speak!"

"And you are—" Tarzan started to ask, but he wisely went silent as the woman's knife bit deeper into his throat.

"Who are you?" she asked through gritted teeth.

"I am Tarzan," he replied calmly, "as my friend just said. We are not here as enemies."

"Liar!" The knife came in tighter and Tarzan was thinking that he might have to do something about it—though any move against the woman might cost Joshua dearly.

"We mean you no harm," he said.

"Then why are you here?" she demanded.

Tarzan hesitated, trying to see things from the perspective of these people. They did not seem to be thieves or murderers; from the nervous and jittery way they were acting, particularly the two men, they seemed, at best, reluctant defenders. "I am following a man named Nikolas Rokoff," Tarzan admitted, going with his instincts.

The man holding the knife to Joshua's throat stood up suddenly. "Following?" he said loudly. "Or are you a part of his band?"

Tarzan understood then that these people had indeed seen Rokoff, and hadn't liked the view. They probably hadn't actually encountered the Russian, however, for if they had, there would likely have been a fight. Given that scenario, they would have treated any strangers as enemies; Joshua would be dead by now, and Tarzan knew he would be battling for his life. "Following," he insisted. "Rokoff does not name me among his friends."

"How are we to know that?" the nervous man asked.

"Rokoff could cause great damage in my world," Tarzan tried to explain. "A different place than this. So, you see, I am not here to help you. But I warn you that Rokoff could cause damage to your land, as well. Believe me, we both seek the same ends."

"You admit that you are not of Pellucidar," the woman reasoned, tightening the squeeze of the knife.

"It's not for you to question anyone, Jana!" the man snapped at her suddenly, surprising Tarzan most of all. Among the three, he would have guessed the female to be the leader.

"You are a woman," the man went on, speaking with his pride and not his heart. "Be silent!"

Tarzan could see the woman's strong profile out of the corner of his eye. He recognized the frustration there, the explosive rage. But he saw, too, the steady nerve, and understood that he could not use his wit to twist the man's words to cause any potentially divisive rift among the group.

"Let him answer first," was all that she replied.

"It's true," Tarzan put in before the man could scold her some more. "I am not from Pellucidar."

"Then you are like the others with the boom sticks," Jana said. "You have declared your own sentence!"

It wasn't hard for Tarzan to figure out what that sentence might be, and he had already discerned enough of these desperate people to realize that they would not be formal in carrying out the execution. So when Jana recoiled her arm, just a bit, for the killing strike, Tarzan was ready. Quicker than she could react, he brought his hands up under her arm, one catching the inside of her wrist, the other the outside of her elbow. A simple twist and thrust motion sent her flying, to crash hard into the sandy-haired man, and he, in turn, to tumble over both his companion and Joshua.

Joshua, far from surprised at Tarzan's little trick,

scrambled out of the pile, spinning to his feet. He saw the woman's knife lying in the sand and snatched it up. By the time the Waziri chief had regained his feet, Tarzan had already pulled the woman from the ground and was standing calmly, holding her much as she had held him, with his knife to her throat.

"Do you now feel what it is like to be next to death?" he asked her, his words spoken in a dangerous, casual manner.

"It's not new to me," Jana proclaimed, her steady tone showing that she spoke the truth. "The mahars raid and take us constantly. I have been next to death for all of my life."

"You know I can kill you if I wish?"

"So what?"

The simple manner in which she replied, with absolute resignation and acceptance, tore at Tarzan's heart. What must this woman's life be like for her to accept death so readily? He held the pose for a few moments, waiting to see if her emotions could withstand the tension. And then, as the seconds passed without any movement from Jana to show fear or protest, he simply released her and slipped his knife back into its sheath on his hip, and motioned for Joshua to similarly relax.

"I am not an enemy and mean you no harm," Tarzan reiterated. "I only seek a man named Rokoff, a man who does not belong in Pellucidar, and whose very appearance here creates danger for your world and for mine. Once I have found Rokoff, I will leave, in peace, and I mean to take him, and all those of his party, with me."

The woman did not move for a some time, except to turn and stare hard at the ape-man.

Tarzan did likewise, taking a full measure of her. In many

ways, she looked very young. Her skin was smooth, her blond mane bouncy with life, and her blue eyes sparkled. Yes, she was beautiful, Tarzan decided, but there was something else in her eyes, an intelligence that showed experience beyond her years, a deep sense of pride and determination. He couldn't understand at first what so drew him to this woman, but then he figured it out. He had met someone so much like her before, in another world, for though Jana's hair was golden and not silky brown, the comparison to Collette de Coude was unmistakable.

Jana was possessed of that same inner beauty, that same resolve and strength. Tarzan had only known her for a matter of minutes, and certainly not in the best of situations, but he knew without doubt that if she had been raised in French society, she would behave as Collette behaved, and that if Collette had come of age in the fierce land of Pellucidar, she would have put the knife to his throat with the same casual assurance as had Jana.

Looking at this woman now, with her wearing little more than Collette had been when she had been shackled to Achmet Zek, Tarzan couldn't help but be attracted to her.

"Get away from him!" the sandy-haired man yelled, startling Tarzan out of his contemplations. The man scrambled forward a step and Tarzan wondered if he meant to charge. This man loved Jana, that much was obvious, but even though he feared for her now, he showed not the courage to throw himself in harm's way.

Jana didn't move, didn't blink once as she continued to measure this stranger to her world. "Maybe you could have killed me," she said evenly. "You did not."

"Jana!" the sandy-haired man protested.

"Be quiet, Turro," she scolded, still looking at Tarzan.

"Run!" Turro commanded.

Jana didn't move. "I'm tired of running," she said. Then to Tarzan, she went on, "I am Jana of the Zorham. Do you need help in your search?"

"Jana!" Now Turro did come forward, far enough to grab at Jana's elbow. She shrugged him away, though, and continued to look at Tarzan.

"I know little of your world," Tarzan admitted.

Turro started to protest yet again, but Jana turned on him fiercely, her look silencing him. "I'm willing to take a chance," she said flatly, and when he couldn't stammer out an immediate response, she turned her attention back to Tarzan.

"He's not one of us," Turro managed to say, inching closer to Tarzan.

Tarzan readied himself. Turro wouldn't charge at him to save Jana, perhaps, but now the jealous man's pride was at stake and that was a different matter altogether.

"So what?" Jana answered sharply. "I believe his tale." Seeing the same danger as Tarzan, she stepped in front of Turro, blocking his path, staring him down before turning to regard Tarzan once more. "I will help you," she offered.

She couldn't have been more than a foot away, and the electricity passing between her and Tarzan was obvious to both of them. It was obvious to grumbling Turro, too, hovering uneasily right behind Jana.

At that point, Joshua, standing to the side, cleared his throat loudly. "Well," he said, "it seems as if this whole matter could have been handled in a much calmer and more dignified manner."

CHAPTER 14

The insults suffered by the would-be Tsar of Russia stung him worse than the pain of the tight, rough vines that bound his hands behind his back and dug into his waist. Rokoff and the other members of his rapidly dwindling party had been hung like slabs of beef, twisting and turning over the jagged rock floor. To make matters worse, the ugly humanoid guards—sagoths, Mora had called them—kept poking at the men, or kicking them, not to injure them, but to simply enjoy the spectacle of their helplessness.

A sagoth moved over and prodded Paulvitch with his club. The big Russian responded by spitting on the sagoth, which only got Paulvitch a vicious smack across the knees. He yelped and twisted, and spun all the more, to the delight of his jailers.

"Well, your excellency," Paulvitch growled at Rokoff, a tone that Rokoff had never heard the big man direct his way before. "Son of the Tsar of Russia!" Paulvitch spat derisively.

"Do you think we should have the national symphony or the army band play at your coronation?"

Rokoff shifted his weight, turning slightly so that he could glare at Paulvitch out of the corner of his eye. "If I cut off your head, you will hear neither," he remarked. "Spend your energy trying to free us, and not on futile attempts at witticisms."

"I have tried!" Paulvitch protested. "It is impossible. These vine ropes will not break and they have been expertly tied." He gave a great, resigned sigh, ending in a low growl that sounded almost like a moan. "I wonder how they are going to kill us."

Now Rokoff shifted more violently, spinning his hanging frame about to face Paulvitch directly. "My destiny is to rule, not to die in a damp cave with a flock of morons," he said. "Are you a coward, then? Have you so readily surrendered?"

"I did not surrender," Paulvitch reminded him, the big man missing Rokoff's point entirely. "I was captured, as were you!"

"I am not speaking of a physical surrender," Rokoff clarified. "Where is your heart?"

Paulvitch thought about it for a moment, then shook his head and growled once more, this time with a bit more determination. Then he went back to wriggling his hands, trying to pull them loose from the bindings. He stopped almost as soon as he had begun, though, fearing that he would be caught, for Mora and two other beautiful, black-haired women had entered the chamber.

"Tikka," Rokoff whispered, noting that one of them held her left arm limp at her side, and carried a small round scab on her shoulder, a gunshot wound, by all appearances.

"Huh?" Paulvitch asked, not catching on.

Rokoff ignored him.

Mora came to stand directly in front of Rokoff, though he was elevated several feet up in the air. The Queen of the Mahars held the coveted magical ruby up teasingly, fondling it in her long fingers. Then she motioned to one of the sagoths, and Rokoff was lowered to her eye level—though this still left his feet several inches from the floor.

"Now do you know who rules, Rokoff?" Mora asked.

"I admit that in Pellucidar it is you," he answered. "I never doubted that, never questioned that. This is your domain, where you reign supreme, but there is much more to the world, Queen Mora, that you know nothing about."

Mora laughed at him. "Do I need more?" she asked incredulously, holding up her arms and turning to regard her two companions. The women took her cue immediately, smiles broadening. "I am supreme in Pellucidar," Mora went on. "There is no threat to me in this domain."

"Then if you are so all-powerful, why do you worry about a mere human like me?" Rokoff asked. "You must feel that I am strong enough to be a threat." As he finished, he focused his stare on Tikka and her gunshot wound, hoping to lead Mora's stare there in a subtle reminder.

"Do you feel like you could be any danger to me swinging from a rope?" Mora teased, giving him a little push. "You certainly don't look frightening." She turned to her companions. "Does he frighten you?"

Again they both laughed on cue.

"Then perhaps you are intelligent enough to know that I could be of some aid," Rokoff went on. Mora had lowered him for a reason, he suspected. She was more than a bit intrigued, and despite her bravado, she was more than a bit afraid.

"What could you offer to a·queen?" she asked.

"What you do not already have," Rokoff was quick to answer. "Another mind. Another brain. A plan, perhaps."

"A plan?"

"To make your domain even greater," Rokoff said with as much enthusiasm as he could muster—he wished that he could lift his arms high and wide for dramatic effect, but of course the binding vines denied that option.

"I already have all that I need," Mora replied calmly, though with just a hint of intrigue edging her tone. She held up the ruby again, spinning it in the flickering light. "Including the Crimson Eye."

"And I can show you how to use it," Rokoff cried. "How to control other places: Africa, Russia, France, all of Europe."

"To do what with them?"

"To rule," Rokoff said, his voice like the hungry growl of a wolf that has trapped its prey. "To have the one thing that is the most exhilarating feeling known." He gave a dramatic pause. "To have power over everything."

Paulvitch listened carefully to his friend, to the tone of Rokoff's voice. He knew that the man was not acting. In all his life, Alexis Paulvitch had never met anyone as driven as Rokoff. Rokoff would give up anything, Collette de Coude included, to satisfy his need for power. And no matter how much he garnered, it would never be enough to keep Nikolas Rokoff satisfied.

"These places, Africa, Russia, they are human places?" Mora asked.

"Millions of humans," Rokoff replied. "Millions of slaves for Queen Mora."

"And if I would want this," she said before he could build any momentum, "why would I share it with you? You are nothing but a weak and feeble human." As she spoke she began to walk around him, forcing him to struggle if he wanted to keep watching her. Halfway around, she gave him another little push to start him swaying, for no other reason than to make things a bit more difficult for him, and a bit more humiliating.

"We could learn each other's ways," Rokoff reasoned.

"Not likely," Mora said with a laugh.

Rokoff continued to try and turn about, but then, suddenly, Mora reversed direction and was right in front of him, her intense—too intense!—gaze boring into him, her face only inches from his. Rokoff, a man of no small willpower, matched that stare. "I still believe you need me," he said. "I also believe that you know it."

Then he went silent, for no more words were needed. Mora was in his mind, communicating telepathically. She caught him off guard with the sudden intrusion, and tried to take advantage of that initial shock and disorientation, pressing her thoughts over his, trying to dominate him. Rokoff understood many things in that instant: first, why his weak-willed companions had shot so badly against Tikka.

Even more importantly, he understood perfectly that this moment was his trial. If he now failed to show Mora enough willpower to impress her, she would surely kill him.

No, it went beyond simple killing, Rokoff came to understand, when Mora let him see into her thoughts. As he had suspected, she was not human, despite the fleshy trappings. Mora, like Tikka, like all of the beautiful and mysterious women of this clan, was a mahar, winged and taloned, and with those gruesome, curving horns.

Mora conjured a recent memory concerning herself and three other mahars, and the three Arabs who had been taken from the party when first they were captured. In his mind Rokoff heard those screams again, and now he understood them fully. Mahars ate humans!

With great discipline, Rokoff sublimated his horror. To recoil, even mentally, was to show weakness, and to show weakness was to die as horrible a death as Nikolas Rokoff had ever imagined.

"You are part of a tribe?" Tarzan asked Jana as she and the two Zorham males led him and Joshua along forested trails.

Jana started to respond, but Turro, ever the nervous one, promptly intercepted. "Do not answer!" he commanded, his tone desperate.

All four of the others, even the other Zorham man, who seemed just as uneasy as Turro, looked at Turro in surprise.

"He could be gathering information," Turro reasoned. "He could be a spy, sent to find out all about us so that his people can come and destroy us. Perhaps that was why he did not kill you, because you were not the only prize he sought."

"Is he always like that?" Joshua asked.

Jana was not amused, by Turro's interruption or by Joshua's flippant attitude.

"I was merely asking a simple question," Tarzan explained, speaking directly to Jana.

"To what end?" Turro demanded.

"Always?" the irrepressible Joshua said with a snort.

"I am no spy," Tarzan started to say, but Jana's upraised palm told him that there was no need for that. He had already earned her trust.

"The Zorham are not numerous," she admitted. "We have never been. Not with the mahars' constant raids."

"How long has this been going on?" Tarzan asked.

"Forever," Turro put in.

Jana only shrugged helplessly.

Tarzan knew a little about tribal warfare, for he had witnessed it in the jungle. There was something strange about the attitude of Jana and Turro, something out of place, for if the mahars were so dominant over the Zorham, then this warfare should have ended long ago. And given the way in which the three discussed the dreaded mahars, Tarzan assumed that it had been a long time since the Zorham had held the upper hand in the contest.

"They take your people as slaves?" Joshua asked. He was carrying another stick, this one sharpened as a spear, and he leaned on it heavily, glad for the break. It had been quite an adventure for the Waziri heir, who had spent several years in the calm lifestyle of Oxford, mostly sitting comfortably in leather chairs. He could hardly believe how many miles he had ridden, and had run, over the last couple of days. Joshua had spent years acquiring a bit of a potbelly, but already he could feel it withering away.

"They take us as food," Jana replied grimly.

That answer caught Tarzan completely off guard, and Joshua nearly fell to the ground—and would have, if he had not been leaning on the sturdy staff.

"Sounds like your Kikuyu friends," he whispered to Tarzan. "Perhaps we can teach the mahars to eat takanda."

"You can teach the mahars nothing," Jana insisted in all seriousness. The sarcasm in Joshua's voice was lost on her, for the Zorham never considered anything about the mahars the least bit funny. "You cannot teach them. You cannot reason with them. You cannot fight them."

Tarzan looked at her long and hard. Who were these mahars, he had to wonder, to evoke such terror in so brave a warrior? Up to that point, Tarzan had thought the mahars to be another tribe of people, but now he was beginning to wonder. Pellucidar was full of strange and powerful creatures, that much he already knew. Might it be that one race kept the humans here like cattle?

"You can always fight," he said grimly.

"Not against mahars," Turro was quick to put in. "We have no weapons that might harm a mahar, and we are fools to be going near to their caverns."

Tarzan stopped abruptly. "Is that where you're taking us?" he asked Jana.

"You said that you had to get to the man named Rokoff," she replied. "Rokoff was taken by the sagoths, and the sagoths serve Mora, Queen of the Mahars." She stopped and pointed to a cave entrance, barely a dark slit in a hillside, partially covered by scrub. "That tunnel will lead us to the mahars. The men you seek are in there."

"How can you be sure?" Joshua asked. "Did I miss something?"

"Some signals from other Zorham on distant hilltops," Tarzan said.

"Very observant," Jana congratulated. "In there, in the caverns of the mahars, you had better be."

"You speak as if you have been in there," Tarzan remarked.

"She has," Turro interjected, an angry edge now coming to his voice. "Jana prowls the caverns alone and somehow comes back in one piece." He glared over Jana as he finished the thought. "She obeys no one."

"Especially not you," Jana replied without the slightest hesitation.

Tarzan liked her spirit, though he thought she might be taunting Turro a bit too far. On that note, he figured that standing in one place talking could only lead to no good, and so he started for the tunnel entrance.

Jana stopped him. "It is dangerous in there," she said. "No one returns."

"Except Jana," spat Turro.

"Only the mahars come and go as they please," Jana went on, ignoring the comment. "They come out to hunt us, then return to the safety of their caverns, surrounded by a river of fire."

"Then you should not permit it," Tarzan said matter-of-factly. "You must stop them."

"We are defenseless against them," said Jana. "They kill us as they please."

"No one is defenseless," Tarzan said. "I saw your fighting abilities out there, when we first met."

"You are not mahars."

"It doesn't matter," said Tarzan. "All you need is the will, then you can learn how to fight them."

"That is easy for someone to say who has not met them," Turro put in.

"I intend to face them now," Tarzan reminded him.

"Why?" Turro asked suspiciously.

Tarzan studied him for a long while.

"Why would you go into the caverns of the mahars?" Turro asked.

"I told you that I must stop Rokoff," Tarzan replied.

"Stop him from what?" Turro asked. "If he really is in there with the mahars, he is probably already dead and eaten."

"I have to find out," said Tarzan. "And even if that much is true, I . . ." He paused, considering the wisdom of continuing with his story.

"What?" Turro prompted, but it was Jana's questioning stare that most affected Tarzan. She had been honest and open with him, after all.

"Rokoff possesses something that is dangerous to both our worlds," Tarzan admitted.

"The boom sticks?" Jana asked.

"They, the boom sticks, are called guns," Tarzan explained. "But that is not what I seek; in my world there are millions of guns." He paused and looked to Joshua, who offered a supportive nod.

"Rokoff took a gemstone," Tarzan tried to explain. "And that stone, removed from its rightful place, created an opening between our worlds."

Jana looked to Turro, and Tarzan did not miss the fact that the sandy-haired man seemed more than a bit intrigued.

"This portal will bring ruin to my world and to Pellucidar," Tarzan assured them, "for it is an opening to other worlds as well, worlds full of creatures even more dangerous than the mahars."

Joshua's eyes widened with surprise, for Tarzan could not know if he spoke truthfully or not, and it certainly was not like Tarzan to lie. When he looked at Turro once more, he understood. Turro, like most of the Zorham, was a desperate man—and who could blame him? It was possible that he would want to keep the portal open, at least long enough for him to get through.

"I have to find the stone that will close the portal," Tarzan said determinedly. "Rokoff has it, and if he is with the mahars . . ."

"Then the mahars have it," Turro said.

"Then I will fight the mahars" was Tarzan's logical response. He started again for the tunnel, but was stopped again, this time by Joshua.

"We will fight them," Joshua declared. "I couldn't turn back now even if I knew where to turn back to!"

"You won't find your way through there alone," said Jana. She looked to Turro and the other Zorham. "We will lead you."

Tarzan exchanged a glance with Joshua, then both eyed Turro and the other man, neither of whom seemed thrilled by the prospect of entering the caverns of the mahars.

"There is no need for you to endanger yourself," Tarzan said.

"You let me live when you could have killed me," Jana said, her tone and posture leaving little doubt that she meant to lead them in. She gave a laugh. "I am already one life ahead." With a nod, she moved in front of Tarzan, starting deliberately for the entrance.

"Jana, wait!" cried Turro. "To die because of them is stupid."

"If you're afraid, you don't have to go," Jana replied.

"You are my woman," said Turro. "I forbid you to go!"

"I am no one's woman," Jana shot back. "No one can forbid me or permit me. I do as I choose, not as Turro chooses for me."

"I can go alone," Tarzan interjected, trying to defuse the situation. "Or with Joshua; we can find the way."

"I just told you," Jana said angrily, her dangerous gaze jumping from Tarzan to Turro, then back again, "I will do as I please. Right now it pleases me to lead you." Again she stepped by Tarzan, glancing back to look him directly in the eye. "If *you* are afraid, do not follow me." And before Turro or Tarzan could argue, she slipped into the dark crack.

"I wish she would have made me that offer," Joshua remarked quietly, but, true to his loyal nature, he followed Tarzan into the dark opening.

Just inside the crack the cavern widened out, and Tarzan and Joshua paused to see if the other two Zorham would follow. Jana wasn't waiting; they saw her moving cautiously down another dark passage, away from the meager daylight, though she had no torch in hand. Tarzan started to follow, while Joshua moved back for one last glance outside.

"Turro and the other man are leaving," the Waziri announced. "Going back into the jungle."

Tarzan was not surprised. "Come," he bade Joshua, guessing correctly that Jana would not wait for them.

They moved along a lightless corridor. Joshua struggled in the dark, but Tarzan, who was more attuned with his senses other than sight, had no difficulty in keeping up with the Zorham woman. The darkness didn't last long anyway, for around a few bends the tunnels brightened with an orange light, as if some giant torch was glowing right through the very stone walls. The air grew noticeably warmer and a sulfuric smell permeated their nostrils.

Jana continued to lead, with Tarzan in the middle and Joshua bringing up the rear. They went along quietly, making good time, but then Tarzan stopped suddenly, standing straight, eyes and ears straining. He jerked his head about to regard a crevice along the side of the tunnel, a small side passage opening. He noted the darting movement of a shadow, and reached back and took Joshua's spear. Then he went into a low, defensive crouch, staring hard down the side passage.

Jana noticed his pose and turned about, moving close and studying him, as was Joshua. Both were fascinated by the silent game between this man and the unseen creature.

Tarzan held the pose, perfectly still, not even drawing breath, for a long while. Then, noting another movement, he came forward with lightning speed, jabbing the spear into the crevice. A shrill scream cut the air, followed by the shuffling sounds of the retreating creature.

"What was that?" Joshua asked as Tarzan relaxed and straightened, handing him back his spear.

"A noise," Tarzan replied.

"It was more than just a noise," Joshua protested. "It was a 'something.' And it left proof," he commented, noting a stain of blood on the spear tip.

"There are many strange things in the caverns of the mahars," Jana interjected.

"I know all about strange things," Joshua said with a great exaggerated sigh. "My life has become a series of strange things."

"Then they will soon not seem to be strange anymore," Jana said.

"That's less than satisfying," Joshua replied dryly. "And how long will it take me to get used to these things?"

"Not very long if we don't get out of here," said Tarzan.

"Why's that?" both Joshua and Jana asked together.

"Because there are more of those 'somethings' hiding in the crevices," Tarzan replied calmly. "Many more."

"That's less than satisfying," Joshua said again. Then, when he considered the look and smile that passed between Tarzan and Jana, he realized that they were playing with him.

Despite the revelation, Joshua moved closer to Tarzan, clutching his spear tightly, and he was more than a little glad when Jana started off again, getting them farther away from the hidden creature or creatures.

CHAPTER 15

You are not totally unpleasant to look at," Queen Mora purred, moving about Rokoff, studying every inch of his six-foot frame. She ran her finger along his shoulder blade and down his spine. "Desssed properly and at my side, you could present yourself accordingly."

Whatever that might mean, Rokoff thought, wisely keeping the notion to himself. Or had he kept the thought private? he had to wonder, and to worry, for Mora had quite easily gotten into his mind once before. Of all the wonders Rokoff had seen since finding the gold pylon in the Temple of the Ancients, of all the promises of potential power, nothing intrigued him more than the telepathic prowess of the mahar race. In their brief mental joining, Rokoff realized that Mora could not only enter his mind and read his thoughts, she could influence them.

Only his willpower—and Rokoff believed his willpower to be superior to the vast majority of humans—had prevented

Mora from dominating him, a precipice to which even he had been pushed dangerously close. Mora had almost broken him, and he could only imagine the depths of slavery such dominance would have produced.

And now he could only imagine the power such ability to dominate might offer to him. If he could learn that mental prowess, or use Mora's proficiency with it, the potential seemed unlimited. People might disguise their words, but not their thoughts. If Rokoff could find a way into minds, he could discover the plans of international traders and beat them at their own fickle game. He could influence his father into early retirement and avoid the messy murder and the inevitable enemies that such an act would breed. He could create an army of loyal, unthinking lackeys, men even more committed to him than Paulvitch.

Most interesting of all, as the new tsar, Rokoff thought, he could dominate other national leaders, forcing them into adopting policies favorable to his regime, winning unnoticed wars, willpower wars, without ever firing a shot.

All these thoughts whetted Rokoff's appetite, but he was wise enough not to let his daydreaming get ahead of the realities, not to fool himself into thinking any of these possibilities represented a done deal. He still had the formidable Mora to contend with, and held no doubts that she might kill him on a whim—or on a hunger pang.

She had other things on her mind now, he realized as he watched her continue to circle him, one hand fingering the gemstone, the other caressing the curves of his body. She seemed an animal on the prowl, primal and vicious. But also incredibly seductive, for she was prowling not for food, but for passion.

Rokoff hardly considered the setting romantic. They were on a secluded tier of an immense cavern, surrounded by bare stone. The air was hot, reeking of sulfur, and the only light was that eerie orange glow, lavalike, that seemed to illuminate most of the mahar homeland. There was no soft bed about, no soft anything, but somehow, with Mora, that seemed fitting indeed.

And despite the hard surroundings, Rokoff couldn't deny the allure of the mahar queen. She might kiss him; she might bite him. She might embrace him; she might squeeze the life out of him. She was the promise of passion and of death. There was nothing tender about her.

Rokoff could hardly believe how much he desired that. For him, power was the greatest aphrodisiac, and never had he seen a more concentrated frame of power than Mora of the mahars.

"Yes," Mora said, "perhaps you will be suitable."

"Then you have decided correctly," Rokoff replied, trying hard to relax. "With me at your side, you can reach new levels of glory and wealth."

"Perhaps," Mora said, striking a seductive and dangerous pose, one hip out to the side, the chain of the Crimson Eye hooked under one thumb and pulled out to its limit. "My subjects wish to kill you and your followers." she announced. "To keep you alive will not please them."

"If you order it, would they dare disobey their queen?" Rokoff asked.

"Why should I deny them their pleasure?"

"I can think of reasons," said Rokoff, locking her gaze with his own. She was teasing him, he knew—or at least, he hoped. Again, that fear brought with it an undeniable surge of passion. "And so can you." As he finished he narrowed his eyes and tilted his head toward her, thinking to draw her into a kiss.

Mora slipped away and laughed at his feeble attempt to seduce her.

"The rewards outweigh the losses," Rokoff went on, quickly composing himself. "You could have millions of humans at your disposal. Why throw away such long-term potential for the short-term satisfaction you might find by devouring one man?"

"There is truth in that," Mora admitted.

"I need only my servant, Paulvitch," Rokoff pressed, thinking he might have found a chink in Mora's resilience.

"The fat one?"

"The fat one," Rokoff confirmed.

Mora pouted at that. "A pity," she said. "Tikka had a special plan devised for that one."

Rokoff tried hard to let that pass, but he couldn't help but visualize Paulvitch served up like a holiday pig, an apple shoved into his mouth. That led to images of Mora and her companions feasting on the three Arabs, images that Mora had shared during their telepathic link, and he fought hard not to gag.

He was back under control quickly—he had to be. "And the one-eyed man, Hadab," he said as an afterthought. "He is dangerous, but might prove quite useful to both of us. Do as you wish with the others; they mean nothing to me."

"You are truly ruthless," Mora noted.

"A trait I also respect in you," Rokoff replied.

"Yes, we are very much alike."

"Yet different enough to please each other," Rokoff said,

and again he put that intense, promising stare over Mora, reaching out to her.

This time she didn't laugh, didn't even smile. And instead of slipping away, she came closer, draping one arm over each of Rokoff's shoulders, staring deeply into his eyes. Still she came closer; her tongue, too long for any human woman, flicked out to lick him on the tip of his nose.

"You will please me," she purred, "or you will die trying, won't you?" Mora laughed then, and Rokoff wisely joined in, though he didn't doubt for a moment that the merciless mahar queen was deadly serious.

Mora ended that by pulling Rokoff close suddenly, hungrily, then turning him about and pushing him down to the hard stone. There was no doubt about who would lead this dance.

"She is always stubborn!" Turro growled, slapping his club against the side of a tree.

"She is brave," the other Zorham male replied.

Turro turned on him, his blue eyes flashing dangerously.

"Does it bother Turro that Jana has disobeyed," the other man asked, "or is it because she disobeyed to help the man called Tarzan?"

"Speak plainly, Althor," Turro demanded.

"You are jealous," Althor replied. "You fear—"

"We are right to fear the mahars," Turro interrupted. "And Jana is a fool to invite their wrath!"

"You fear that you have no control over Jana," Althor finished.

That straightened Turro as surely as if Althor had slapped

him across the face with a cold and wet cloth. "We were promised," Turro stuttered. "Our paths were arranged when we were but young children."

"Jana will not follow that path," Althor said bluntly. "Jana follows only Jana's will." The Zorham backed a cautious step, for it seemed as if Turro meant to strike him.

Turro calmed quickly, though, for in truth he could not dispute Althor's words. He and Jana had been promised to each other by his father and her mother, their only living parents, when they were mere babes. But both of those parents were dead now, both taken by the mahars, and the intended joining should have happened nearly a year before.

Jana had delayed it. Always it was Jana, and of late the woman seemed to be even more headstrong and independent. Turro had once accused her of going into the mahar caverns because she preferred death to life with him, and she had not answered.

She had not answered!

"She does not respect you, Turro," Althor said, "because you are wise."

Turro looked at him curiously.

"You are a man of thought, but Jana is a woman of action," Althor explained. "She would have us all go into the caverns of the mahars and wage war against them, though every Zorham of Pellucidar would be easily destroyed. Forget her, I say. Let Jana tempt the mahars once too often, and then let Turro find himself a woman who knows her place."

Turro came forward suddenly, lifting his forearm in a powerful strike that dropped Althor to the ground. The man lay there, staring up incredulously.

And Turro had no answer for that questioning stare. He

didn't know why he had struck Althor. The man had spoken against Jana and that had brought an anger bubbling within him, a rage that forced him to act before he could think.

He wanted to apologize now, to offer Althor his hand, to do something to make amends. But he didn't. He just turned on his heel and walked off into the jungle, backtracking the course that the two strangers, and Rokoff's party before them, had taken.

Sometime later, Mora and Rokoff walked together through the twisting and confusing caverns. Mora led the way, striding determinedly and not even responding to Rokoff's questions. The Russian, curious and anxious as he was, quieted quickly, realizing that any conversation would not be welcomed now. Mora was thinking, was holding a private debate in light of the new revelations she had uncovered about Rokoff.

He prayed that his performance had been acceptable.

They went through a series of small chambers all in a row. Sagoths milled about them, giving Mora a respectably wide berth, many falling to their knees and bowing their heads. Even the few women they saw, Mora's mahar subjects, moved quietly and respectfully aside.

They were acting out of respect—and fear—for Mora, and not for him, Rokoff knew, but he basked in the feeling anyway. Someday soon he, too, would command such respect, and let all the people of Moscow fall to their knees when he passed! And let all the people of Paris and London fear him! And let—

Rokoff's daydreams were stolen as he and Mora passed

through yet another small chamber, his attention grabbed when he noted the weapon a sagoth carried: a club fashioned of a rifle barrel. Another sagoth was whittling a knife from the wooden stock of a different rifle.

Mora's people had destroyed the guns. That thought struck Rokoff as profound indeed. The mahars might have studied the weapons, might have put them to use. They were, as far as Rokoff could tell, more powerful physical weapons than could be found anywhere in Pellucidar. Why, then, had Mora chosen to destroy them?

He almost asked her about it, but held his tongue as the truth of it all came clear to him, confirming his earlier suspicions that Mora had indeed feared him, and had feared these weapons his party had brought into her domain. In Pellucidar she was supreme, her power all but uncontested, but if guns came to this world, and those guns fell into the hands of her enemies, then she would be threatened.

So she had ordered them torn apart, had reduced them to typical weapons of Pellucidar, weapons that posed no threat to the mahars.

She was a pragmatic leader, Rokoff realized. But in leaders, pragmatism often equated to plodding. While pragmatism might ensure longevity, his and hers, it did little to bring about the vision of greater glories.

He would supply that vision to her, Rokoff decided. He would carefully tease her with images of absolute rulership, of wealth beyond her belief. He would guide her and coax her, to his gain.

But only if she tolerated him, he realized. Only if his performance had satisfied her. Only if he, reduced, temporarily, to a role as her consort, could hold her interest.

Otherwise, Rokoff realized, he would end up much like his guns.

The path was treacherous, no more than three feet across at its widest points. The wall on their left was uneven, jagged in many spots, sometimes leaning out to cover most of the narrow trail, and on their right loomed a sheer drop, fifty feet at least, to sharp stones. All three fought hard to hold their concentration—to make an error now would certainly mean death. But it was hot, brutally so, and the sulfuric smell burned their throats and made their minds spin. The only good point was that the eerie orange glow had intensified, so they could see clearly enough.

"I have something to tell you," Joshua announced. He grabbed Tarzan with a sweaty hand, falling back for support against the wall, then running his other arm over his sweat-soaked forehead.

"Now?" Tarzan asked.

"I just remembered it," Joshua explained, laboring for breath. "Did I ever tell you that I have scotophobia?"

"No," Tarzan said with finality. He turned about and moved along the trail in pursuit of Jana, concentrating on keeping his footsteps sure.

"Don't you want to know what scotophobia is?" Joshua asked, scurrying to keep up.

Tarzan, having no time for Joshua's incessant wit, didn't bother to answer. He knew that he didn't have to; Joshua was going to tell him whether he wanted to know or not.

"Scotophobia is the fear of dark, small places, such as caves," Joshua predictably announced.

"And how long have you had this fear?" Tarzan asked, playing along in his role as straight man.

"About fifteen minutes, give or take a few," Joshua replied in a deadpan voice.

Tarzan paused and turned to him, and gave a nod. He got the joke, but he knew that if he pretended that he did not, it would bother Joshua all the more. Satisfied by Joshua's frustrated grunt, Tarzan moved along. Jana wasn't far ahead, having stopped at one particularly troublesome outcropping, and she welcomed Tarzan's assistance in getting her over it to the path on the other side. Then she, in turn, helped Tarzan to cross over, and, as Jana started off once more, Tarzan waited to assist Joshua.

"The temperature has increased at least twenty degrees in the last ten minutes," Joshua said in all seriousness as Tarzan steadied him on the far side of the rocky blockage.

Tarzan nodded, for Joshua wasn't exaggerating; Tarzan put the increase at more than that, at around thirty degrees.

Jana came back to them, having heard their conversation. "We are approaching the River of Fire," she explained.

"Sounds promising," Joshua remarked, but no one was listening.

"It will become even hotter," Jana finished.

"You have been this route before," Tarzan stated. "This far?"

"Once," Jana replied. "When I was a young girl and ventured out alone for the first time." She looked back down the trail, deeper into the caverns, her expression pained. "But I got frightened."

"With good reason," muttered Joshua.

"And turned back," Jana finished.

"Did the mahars attack you?" Tarzan asked.

"No," Jana admitted, and it seemed to Tarzan and Joshua that the woman was embarrassed by what she perceived as cowardice.

"I wouldn't have come down here at all," Joshua offered.

"They did not attack me," Jana went on, and if she had even heard Joshua, she made no indication. "But I thought they would. In my mind, the mahars were all about me, ready to kill me, and so I became frightened."

"When you run, you cannot see what you must fight," Tarzan said. "You must face your enemies to see their weaknesses."

"The mahars have no weaknesses," Jana insisted.

"You will never know until you fight them," Tarzan answered.

"My people tried to, in ages past, so my mother once told me," Jana said, and in a lower voice she added, "before she was taken by the mahars. We fought them, and we were slaughtered."

"As you are now," reasoned Tarzan. "Because your people failed many years ago does not mean that you will fail now." He studied Jana's look and was pleased to see that there was some hope there. Sooner or later, she and her people would have to realize that they had nothing to lose by fighting back against the mahars. To sit and wait for the slaughter, like the zebras of the Serengeti, made no sense for humans—for humans who could build weapons and set traps. A zebra could not fight against the lions or the hyenas, had not the weapons nor the cunning, but Tarzan could not believe that there was any foe so powerful that humans could not stand against it.

Jana chewed her lower lip. She didn't miss the logic of his words, but, as Turro had said, he had never seen the horror of the mahars. This was a conversation for another day, she believed, and so she turned away and continued down the tunnel.

Tarzan looked to Joshua.

"You ask much of them," Joshua said.

"This world demands much of them," Tarzan corrected. "I ask for nothing, but hope that the Zorham will see the folly of their ways and the error of their fears."

"Fear is not a conscious choice," Joshua answered.

"But overcoming that fear is," Tarzan was fast to reply.

Joshua considered that for a moment, then nodded his agreement, and he and Tarzan started off after Jana.

They went through a low archway, down a narrow and low tunnel, and back out onto another open ledge, again with a sheer cliff on one side and a sheer drop on the other. The temperature jumped again, the heat fed by waves of thick steam wafting up over the narrow ledge. The heat source was right below them, they realized, but they could not see it through that opaque veil of steam.

"Scotophobia," Joshua mumbled.

"What?" asked Tarzan, turning to face him.

"I'm looking for the logical construction of the word," Joshua explained. "Trying to break it apart to its roots that I might figure out another appropriate word."

Tarzan eyed him curiously, not understanding.

"I don't think there is a word for 'fear of burning to death,'" Joshua explained.

"You can make one up," Tarzan offered. "We will never know."

Joshua smiled widely, and so did Tarzan, the tension momentarily dispelled.

"You may not know it, my friend, but you just told a joke," Joshua said. "I'm sure that fact is a surprise to all of us."

"To those of you, at least, who rank quantity of wit above quality of words," said Tarzan, and both he and Joshua smiled all the wider.

Their grins were short-lived, though, stolen by Jana's scream.

Tarzan spun about, to see the ledge give way beneath the woman. The muscles in his legs instinctively twitched, launching him headlong as he dove flat out to the stone. Stretched to his very limit and hanging over the break, he caught her by the forearm and held her fast, though she was hanging in the empty air. As Tarzan tried to brace himself, as he looked over the lip, the steam veil below Jana broke apart for just a moment. Tarzan gasped, seeing for the first time the heat source, the River of Fire Jana had spoken of, a river of molten stone flowing fifty feet below the ledge.

"Hold her!" Joshua cried. He tried to come forward to Tarzan's aid, but the ledge was too narrow to accommodate both men. Joshua did get close enough to see the lava flow below Jana, and he was frantic indeed when he cried out, "For God's sake, man, don't let her go!"

Tarzan tightened his grip, the corded muscles on his forearm bulging. Normally, hoisting one as lithe as Jana would not have been a problem for the strong man, but now, in the steamy heat, both his hand and her arm were slick with sweat. She gave another cry as she began to slide down, down, coming to where their hands met and holding there.

"I can't hold on!" Jana cried, her face a mask of panic. "Not like this!" she said. "I do not want to die like this!"

Tarzan dug his fingers into her wrist with all the strength he could muster, the muscles on his arm bulging even more. Lines of sweat streamed along his face and neck and arms. Jana was talking again, so was Joshua, but Tarzan blocked out their words, blocked out all distractions, and found a meditative trance, a deep concentration that tightened his grip even more, that locked his fingers like a metal vise about the woman's hand.

Slowly, impossibly, he began to lift her.

"Please, please," she said, quietly.

Tarzan opened his eyes. He saw that Jana was high enough now, and knew that his hand might slip from hers at any moment. So he let go of the ledge with his other hand, gave a great heave, and caught Jana by both arms. He scrambled to turn his legs under him and rolled back to a sitting position, hauling Jana halfway over the ledge. Then he planted his feet and stood up, taking her all the way over, putting her right up against him, tight in his arms.

They stood there together for a long time, feeling the closeness of each other's body, the sudden tension in their muscles, their pounding hearts joining in a rhythmic pulse. Jana looked at Tarzan long and hard, her expression showing gratitude . . . and something else, something inviting. Their mouths were barely an inch apart; Tarzan could feel Jana's breath on his lips, a gentle puff, inviting him to move closer.

Joshua cleared his throat, saving them both. "Oh, er, Jana," he stuttered. "I think a simple thank you would suffice."

Jana smiled and backed away, but her hands lingered as

they came back across Tarzan's neck. "Thank you," she said sincerely. "That's twice."

"Now you're two lives ahead," Tarzan said with a sheepish grin. He coughed and moved past her, taking the lead, first bending low to inspect the integrity of the ledge farther on, then springing easily across the small gap and motioning for Jana and Joshua to follow.

Jana went over without hesitation, but Joshua stopped at the break, staring down. Plumes of hot white steam came up at him, but every so often they cleared enough for him to get a good look at the flowing lava beneath.

"And they were thinking of kissing," Joshua remarked dryly under his breath. "Indeed, what a romantic place this is!"

"We're waiting," Tarzan remarked.

Joshua backed up three steps, took a deep breath, and skittered ahead, but changed his mind at the last instant and skidded to a stop at the very edge of the precipice. "Perhaps you should go on without me," he offered sheepishly.

"It is not even two meters," Tarzan replied. "You can jump it, I assure you."

Joshua looked down at the lava and shook his head.

"You must," Tarzan prompted.

"I can't," Joshua replied. "I think it's time for me to invent that new word we spoke about."

"Silence!" Jana commanded suddenly, harshly. Both men looked at her. She stood poised as if for battle, head cocked slightly, looking back up the path, past Joshua.

"What is it?" Joshua demanded after a few uncomfortable seconds slipped by.

"Those creatures," Jana replied earnestly. "Those scurrying creatures in the crevices."

Joshua's eyes widened.

"There!" Jana yelled, pointing her finger at Joshua.

He was standing beside her in an instant, stuttering, scrambling. He got past her and dared glance back—to see an empty path.

Joshua stared at Jana, then at Tarzan, and both were grinning. "She's good," the fooled man admitted.

A short distance ahead, the three rounded a sharp bend in the path that took them away from the lava river. They went through a tunnel that was so low they had to go down to their knees in several places and crawl through. The tunnel wasn't long, and they soon came out, back onto another open ledge, only to find that the lava river was once again below them.

They were not as high up now, and could hear the hissing, grating flow of the molten stone, and the heat and odor were even more intense.

The three companions had no time to dwell on that, however, for looking across the lava river and down to the opposing bank, they saw a chamber, or more particularly, they saw a handful of men hanging from vines in a chamber, with ugly humanoids prodding them and pushing them.

One man in particular roared out in protest, cursing in a language that Tarzan had heard before.

"Paulvitch," he noted, falling flat to the ledge and peering over.

"Rokoff's man," agreed Joshua, recognizing the man from Achmet Zek's dungeons.

"But where is Rokoff?" Tarzan pondered aloud.

"And what are those?" Joshua added, pointing at the sagoths.

"Sagoths," Jana explained. "Enemies of the Zorham. They serve Queen Mora."

"Ugly," Joshua remarked.

"In temperament as well as appearance," Jana agreed.

Tarzan began visually scanning for a way to get down to the chamber. He had a path picked out—though it would not be an easy descent, and he would have to leap a narrow bend of the lava river at one point. Even more dangerous, he realized that it would be nearly impossible to keep hidden from the view of the sagoths, for the path was wide open to the lower chamber in many places.

He would go anyway, he decided. He had not come this far just to turn around and leave. "You wait here," he instructed Joshua and Jana.

Tarzan put his feet under him, but before he could get going, he noticed some movement off to the side of the lower chamber and he fell back flat to the stone.

"Rokoff," Joshua Mugambi said grimly.

CHAPTER 16

Turro and Althor stood in the clearing, staring at the strangely swirling tree branches.

"This is where they appeared?" Althor asked. "I see no tunnel."

Turro shrugged. There was something strange about this place, he sensed. The wind ended here, up between those trees, but how could that be?

The two Zorham moved to the base of the trees and looked up at the dancing limbs. They could feel the pull of the swirling air, though it was no longer overly strong, not with the Crimson Eye so far away, tucked deep in the tunnels of the mahars.

"Nothing," Althor grumbled.

Turro wasn't so sure. Tentatively, he began to climb. "The wind grows stronger up here," he announced, though he was just a few feet off the ground. "Come and see."

Althor started up the tree; Turro went a bit higher. "It gets even stronger," he said, having to yell through the sudden tumult of air. He went to the next higher branch, and then, suddenly, he was holding on desperately as the wind grabbed at him, trying to pull him up.

"Althor!" he cried.

The other Zorham scrambled higher, trying to get to Turro. The wind buffeted him, too, as he neared his companion, reaching, reaching.

Turro let go to take his hand, but as soon as he loosened his grip on the tree he was gone, taken upward and then vanishing.

Althor cried out and leaped to catch him—and he never came back down, grabbed by the wind and pulled into the swirling vortex right behind his friend, into the starry tunnel.

"How can you walk around free?" Paulvitch whined when Rokoff calmly strode into the prisoner chamber.

The sagoths apparently wanted to know that as well, for they came forward, brandishing their clubs in a threatening manner. They backed away immediately, though, when they saw Queen Mora enter right behind the human.

"The fat one?" she asked again.

Rokoff nodded. "Alexis Paulvitch," he said.

Mora shook her head and sighed, not pleased to be losing one of such girth. She motioned to the sagoths and pointed to Paulvitch, and the primitive creatures scurried for the vines. Paulvitch was down to the ground in a matter of seconds, on his knees, Rokoff moving behind him to untie his hands.

Once they were free, Paulvitch went to work on his other bindings, then began rubbing the circulation back into his limbs and shifting as if he meant to stand.

Rokoff grabbed his shoulder hard and held him down. "Stay on your knees and pay homage to your leader, Queen Mora!" he instructed.

"Are you crazy?" Paulvitch asked.

"Do it!" Rokoff demanded and, as stubborn Paulvitch came up again, he slapped the man hard on the back of his head.

Paulvitch looked at him, stunned, then turned to regard Mora, and three other women and a handful of sagoths who had also entered, all of them closely watching his every move. Finally Paulvitch understood: pay homage or be killed then and there. He dropped back to one knee and bowed his head. "Queen Mora," he said.

Mora looked at Rokoff and gave a nod of acceptance.

"And the one-eyed man?" Rokoff asked.

Mora motioned to the sagoths to let Hadab down, then turned to her fellow mahars. "I will be following the great wind on a journey," she announced. "To a place unknown to us, a place this man, Rokoff, calls Russia. If it is as he says, we will be able to dominate and expand our numbers."

"How can you trust him, my queen?" Tikka asked.

"I know his mind," Mora replied, glancing back over her shoulder at Rokoff. "He is as hungry for power as we are."

"Is he as hungry for flesh?" Tikka asked with a smile.

All the mahars grinned, except for Mora, who remained deadly serious.

"I am told that the world at the end of the wind will afford us vast new lands that will provide us unlimited sources of food," she explained. "Millions of humans live there, so Rokoff says."

"We should all go," one of the others offered eagerly.

"No," Mora said. "I will go and see, then return to lead you all there. Until then," she continued pointing to the Arabs still hanging by the vines, "I have left you a sufficient supply of nourishment."

"What is she talking about?" asked Joshua.

"Humans," Jana whispered back. "As I told you. That is Mora, Queen of the Mahars. Mahars feed on human flesh." She pointed to the unfortunate Arabs. "What hangs above them is their next meal."

"You still in the mood for kissing?" a sick-looking Joshua asked Tarzan.

Tarzan motioned for Joshua to be quiet and still, for he was shifting about on the narrow ledge, trying to get into a better position in case he had to run down to try to rescue the prisoners.

"If these humans are any indication," Mora went on, "there will be an unlimited supply of plump humans for us to feed on."

Paulvitch snapped a disbelieving look at her. "Feed on?" he echoed. "You eat humans?" He looked at Rokoff in horror. "They eat humans?"

"Be quiet," Rokoff instructed.

Mora, obviously enjoying the fat man's discomfort, walked up between the two Russians. She stroked Rokoff's chin with a long finger and snapped her teeth teasingly in the empty air. "I have not eaten you," she said casually. "Or your plump friend." She turned to face Paulvitch and licked her lips hungrily, and the big man nearly swooned. "Not yet," Mora finished.

Up on the ledge, Tarzan eased closer. So did Joshua, trying to remain silent though he was gasping for breath, overwhelmed by the mahar's words. The stunned Joshua wasn't paying enough attention to his own movements, though, and he inadvertently dislodged a few pebbles, sending them tumbling down the steep slope.

The eyes of Mora and the other mahars, and of Rokoff, Paulvitch, and the just-freed Hadab, scanned up to the ledge, to a now-scrambling Joshua, Jana, and Tarzan.

"Him again!" Rokoff cried at the sight of the jungle man, this man who was fast becoming his chief nemesis. He turned angrily to Paulvitch, yelling for him to kill Tarzan.

But the words were trapped in Rokoff's throat, stolen by the sight of Paulvitch, trembling and stuttering, sweating profusely and wobbling shakily on his feet. Rokoff followed Paulvitch's gaze to Mora, and then he understood.

Her eyes glowed—not just sparkled, but truly *glowed*, with inner fires that were far from human. She held her arms out wide, and they contorted weirdly and grew darker; no thicker, but more sinewy, reptilelike. And with a sickening crackle her arms split and rolled over on themselves, sprouting leathery wings. Her sculptured human face, angular and beautiful, bulged and popped, her mouth becoming a sharp-toothed maw, curving tusks tearing through her skin.

Rokoff had suspected something like this, of course, since he had met Tikka, Mora's friend with the gunshot wound. And when he and the mahar queen had joined minds, he had glimpsed Mora's true nature. But actually seeing the transformation of the mahar, from human female to this hideous monster, stole the strength from his legs. He leaned heavily on Paulvitch, who was in even worse shape, both of them groaning and gasping. Finally, Paulvitch fell to his knees, and Rokoff staggered several steps to the side. Behind them the hanging Arabs began screaming horribly and the sagoths jumped about, excited and pleased to see the terrible glory of their god-figure revealed in all its terrible splendor.

Turro stepped out of the pylon, into the chamber in the Temple of the Ancients. The twin braziers burned at the base of the stairwell, but the main light in the room was the pylon itself, glowing with power. The wind remained on this side of the portal, but it was not strong.

Too mesmerized to consider his actions, Turro dared to move away from the spot, circling the pylon, studying its intricate designs, its sheer beauty.

Althor came out next and fell to his knees, panting, gasping. "Turro! Turro!" he cried over and over.

"Here," the other Zorham replied, finishing a complete circuit of the pylon. He offered Althor his hand, helping the man to stand.

"Where are we?" Althor asked.

"Tarzan's world, I would guess," Turro replied.

"We must go back!" Althor cried, turning for the pylon.

Turro grabbed him and held him fast. "No!" he yelled, and when Althor finally calmed and looked at him, he added quietly, "Not yet."

"We do not know the dangers of this place," Althor warned.

"We do not know that there are any dangers in this place," Turro corrected, a hint of a smile turning up the corners of his mouth. "Do you not understand? This could be the refuge that the Zorham have forever sought. This world, this place, away from the mahars."

Althor stopped his struggling, and was suddenly not so anxious to go back through the magical portal.

"We must learn what we can of this world," Turro went on. "And decide if it is fitting. Then we can go back to Pellucidar and lead the Zorham out of there."

Althor looked long and hard at his friend, finally catching on. "Jana will be pleased," he said.

Turro's expression soured. "Jana is probably already dead," he said coarsely, "a fate she deserves for tempting the mahars." Turro turned on his heel and started up the stairs.

Althor didn't believe a word of what his friend had said. He knew that Turro's main source of strength now was Jana, that impressing the woman with his courage was at least as important to him as any notion of leading the Zorham from Pellucidar.

At the one exit from the pylon chamber, the two began to understand that this place might not be the refuge they had hoped for. There stood the dead Arab, brutally impaled.

Turro pushed past anyway, moving down the tunnel and out of the temple, onto the grass of the high-walled clearing. Up above, dawn was breaking, tilting rays slipping through the tangled canopy.

"This way," Althor called, spotting the tunnel entrance. The Zorham stopped when he got there, though, inspecting the slimy substance covering the walls. "What—" he started to ask, but then his voice was stolen and his eyes went wide.

"Run!" Althor screamed, spinning on his heel and nearly bowling over poor Turro.

Turro understood fully as the man ran past him, as the gigantic serpent came straight for him.

In mere seconds the two Zorham men were back into the temple, scurrying past the dead Arab, leaping down the stairs and running headlong into the liquid center of the pylon.

Both came out of the gate in a tumble, crashing down through the trees, Althor landing hard on the ground, Turro landing hard on top of Althor.

Turro scrambled to his feet and pulled Althor up behind him. Both ran for the cover of the jungle, both thinking that Turro's vision of a haven for their beleaguered people was a perfectly stupid idea.

Up on the ledge, the other three were no less in shock than Paulvitch and Rokoff. Tarzan controlled his fear well, pulling his bow from his shoulder and quickly stringing it. Jana, while she was not surprised in the least, was still in awe of the mahars, and called continually for the other two to run away with her.

And poor Joshua Mugambi! The man shook so badly that the spear in his hands seemed as if it was made of some rubberlike substance.

"Now is the time to find your heart," Tarzan said to Jana.

"You cannot fight them!" Jana insisted.

"We'll never know that until we try!"

As Tarzan finished speaking, a pair of Mora's companions followed the queen's lead and transformed, then lifted into the air, gliding on the hot currents straight for the ledge.

"Do not look into their eyes!" Jana warned. "They can steal your thoughts and your heart."

Tarzan, who had dealt many times with the hypnotic stare of snakes, understood well. He focused on the chest of the nearest creature, bow bent way back, and held his shot until the very last moment.

The mahar, ignorant of the foreign weapon, came straight in, swooping up over the ledge, wings wide, presenting a perfect target, and Tarzan let fly, point-blank, his arrow diving deep into the armored chest of the monster.

Still the mahar came on, its trumpeting shriek now wrought as much of pain as of hunting excitement. Tarzan threw his arms up to block, expecting to get pinned in the rush, but Joshua was beside him, stabbing with the spear, and Jana was on his other side, screaming as loudly as the mahar, pounding hard with her hooked club.

The mahar's momentum was stolen, and Tarzan's arrow, deep into the monster's vital organs, was doing its grim work. The mahar tried to gain the ledge with its taloned feet, but it couldn't find a hold and fell away, spiraling down, trying to control its descent but swerving, inevitably, for the lava river.

The three on the ledge, facing a second monster coming in, couldn't watch the fall, but they could guess easily enough what had happened when the falling creature's shrieks abruptly ceased.

Mora loomed over Rokoff, staring down at him with those fiery eyes, her wings spread wide to enhance the effect of her impressive body. "You will come with me!" she commanded.

Rokoff shook his head. "Alexis!" he cried, but Paulvitch

was facedown on the floor, whimpering. Rokoff yelled and tried to fall away, but Mora lifted into a short hop, her great clawed feet catching the man by the front of his vest and hauling him away. She circled upward, riding the hot currents of air, and swooped out of the chamber, along passageways that she knew all too well.

"Get up!" Hadab demanded, kicking Paulvitch in the side. "Now is our chance! Our only chance!"

Paulvitch peeked up at the Arab. "Behind you!" he cried, and just in time.

Hadab reacted with deadly efficiency. He turned to the right and fell back a step, inside the wide-swinging blow of the sagoth's club. He caught the sagoth by wrist and elbow, using his momentum to snap the humanoid's arm out awkwardly. Had he finished the move, he surely would have broken the sagoth's arm, but he let his leading hand slip under the wrist of the primitive creature, catching the club even as the humanoid let it fall.

Hadab lifted the sagoth's arm up high as he turned about, smashing the humanoid's exposed ribs with its own weapon. Then, in the same fluid movement, he brought the club back in to his chest, took it up in both hands, and jabbed it straight out like a spear, slamming the surprised sagoth under the chin and knocking it away.

Bolstered by his companion's fighting prowess, Paulvitch scrambled up from the floor and hit the next charging sagoth with a flying tackle, burying it under his great weight.

"Back out!" Tarzan instructed. "They have no room to turn in these tight quarters. We can escape."

His reasoning seemed sound enough. The second mahar had veered when the first fell, and now was having a hard time manipulating her wide body to come back around. The third creature, Tikka, was having an even more difficult time, her injured shoulder barely supporting her in flight. She flapped awkwardly but could not gain the height of the ledge.

Jana ran back along the ledge, toward the bend that would get them out of this room. Joshua was right on her heels, and Tarzan, defensively, remained a few steps behind. Had the tunnel opening been wide enough for them to pass through unhindered, they would have gotten free, but Jana lost precious time, sliding down to her knees and trying to scramble through, hooking the belt of her skin skirt on a jagged rock.

Joshua turned back to see the second mahar swooping in at Tarzan's back.

"Look out!" he cried.

Too late. Tarzan spun about, trying to get his bow up, but the creature was too close, crashing against him and bearing him to the ground under its great weight.

Half dazed, Tarzan looked up to see the boarlike tusks of the horrid mahar looming over his exposed face.

"That is my scimitar," Hadab yelled at the next sagoth in line. The humanoid came straight in, holding the curving blade more like a spear than a sword.

Hadab sent the club back over his right shoulder, snapped his right hand down to catch it on the other end and shifted its momentum, sending it wrapping about his back, where he caught it in his left hand and launched it, spinning over his left shoulder. He caught it in his right hand again as it came around and snapped it out diagonally in front of him, blasting the scimitar out to the side.

Hadab reversed the flow of the club, smacking the humanoid across the face, then again with a vicious back-hand. The stubborn brute still stood, staring dumbly from under its ridged brow, so Hadab grasped the club, out far to the right in both hands, and brought it smashing back, then back again on the backhand.

The sagoth staggered a few steps, did a short, weird hop, and finally fell to the ground.

A shriek turned Hadab about. He saw the fluttering Tikka, who had given up on gaining the ledge, coming back for him and Paulvitch. He threw the club at her, and as she instinctively swerved, he went for his scimitar.

It took wounded Tikka a long time to recover from that dodge, and by the time she had straightened, she saw Hadab pulling Paulvitch from the ground and running on for a low tunnel exit from the chamber. The Arab dispatched yet another sagoth with a series of short, chopping cuts, then deftly slashed the three lines holding the remaining prisoners, dropping the bound men to the floor.

Tikka couldn't get to Hadab and Paulvitch in time, she realized. But what did it matter? she mused. This was Pellucidar, the domain of the mahars. Where could they run?

She went instead for the three thrashing men, flopping down on the closest, her claws and terrible tusks making short work of him.

Paulvitch had no intention of turning back to try and help the Arabs, and neither did Hadab. The Russian understood then that Hadab had only cut the men down as a diversion, had fed them up to the creature to facilitate his own escape.

If Paulvitch could have paused long enough to catch his breath, he would have congratulated Hadab for a job well done.

Up snapped Tarzan's hands, one grabbing each tusk. It was pure survival now for him, purely instinctual reactions, all of his jungle-honed senses and strength taking over his movements. He actually held the mahar back! Somehow, with strength far beyond anything human, he held the tusks from his face.

Joshua ran over and jabbed with his crude spear, and when that did nothing, he took up the weapon like a club and slammed it over the mahar's shoulder. The shaft snapped apart with the impact from the blow, but again the mahar didn't even react, didn't even seem to notice.

It was just the creature and Tarzan, locked in a struggle from which only one could emerge. The mahar gave one of its horrid, trumpeting shrieks, wriggled its head back and forth, and forced it down with all its strength.

But still Tarzan held firm, his corded muscles holding the monster at bay.

Then the creature tried a different tactic, locking Tarzan's gaze with its own.

Tarzan felt the waves of hypnosis, the true power of the mahars. A serenity washed over him, a sense of deep, deep calm stealing his strength.

Down came the head; down came the spear-tipped tusks.

"Tarzan!" Joshua yelled, and that familiar voice broke the spell.

Tarzan growled and pushed back powerfully, again holding

the head at bay. He couldn't win this standoff, he realized, for the mahar's great weight was sapping his energy and time was working against him.

Joshua continued to fight the creature; behind him, Jana, too, tried to get in for some strikes, ineffective though they seemed to be.

But it had to be him, Tarzan knew, and it had to be now. He rolled up his left shoulder and pushed out, turning the mahar's head slightly to the side. Then he dropped his shoulder and rolled up the other way, throwing every ounce of strength into the sudden move.

The snap of bone was louder than the snap of Joshua's spear, and suddenly the weight on Tarzan was even greater. But the press was off, the creature quite dead. Tarzan coiled up under it and braced his shoulder against its chest. Then, in a final act of defiance, he heaved the thing away, off the ledge, to plummet into the lava river below.

Tarzan stood and gathered up his bow and arrows, then motioned toward the tunnel. He paused as he regarded Jana; her eyes were wide with disbelief—and with something else.

With awe.

"Slow down!" Paulvitch gasped, trying to keep up with Hadab. The Arab moved like a ghost, silent and smooth, rounding corners in the winding tunnel, leaping cracks in the stone or small rocks in his path with hardly an effort. Behind Hadab, Paulvitch sputtered and huffed, stumbled and even tripped to his knees on more than one occasion.

"Slow down!" he begged.

But Hadab would not slow, and only glanced back to shoot

Paulvitch a glare so threatening that the big man did indeed quiet down. On they ran at full speed—until Hadab came into a chamber with a wide ceiling—high enough for a flying mahar, he knew, and so he did pause and wait for Paulvitch. He wanted the Russian with him if they encountered one of the dangerous monsters, and if they could not defeat it, Hadab wanted fat Paulvitch to serve as the main course while he made his escape.

"We could find the guns," Paulvitch offered.

"We must get out of the tunnels," Hadab replied, his tone offering no opening for debate. Hadab was in control here.

"And then where?" Paulvitch asked.

"And then we chase Rokoff and Mora," Hadab insisted. "And go back through the portal. I have no desire to remain another moment in this wretched place called Pellucidar."

"But if we could get the guns—" Paulvitch started to say, but he was cut short by a noise to the side of the chamber.

A pair of sagoths came into sight on a tier about waist high to the men, both carrying clubs fashioned of metal tubings.

"There are your guns," Hadab sneered, motioning to the primitive humanoids. "The idiots turned them into clubs!"

Paulvitch growled and chewed on his lip, and though he was unarmed, he met the charge of one of the sagoths head on, accepting a smack of the gun barrel across his broad shoulders in exchange for a flying tackle that buried yet another sagoth beneath his great bulk. The pair rolled about on the floor a couple of times, with Paulvitch coming out on top, his hands clasped about the sagoth's neck.

Hadab used more finesse. The second sagoth charged him headlong, skidding to a stop and launching a wide overhand chop, the club diving in diagonally for the side of Hadab's head. Up came the scimitar, the flat of the blade ringing hard against the club, stealing its momentum, and then Hadab altered the flow of his weapon, sliding it down the club barrel, slashing into the unprotected hand of the sagoth. The humanoid howled and dropped the club, and Hadab waded in with a downward slash that opened wide the humanoid's chest.

Still the creature howled, trying to cover up, trying to retreat, but there was no mercy in Hadab. He came forward, cutting another line, and when the sagoth put up its hand to block, he promptly severed a couple of fingers. Only the fact that the humanoid's howls might bring in more enemies caused the wicked man to quickly finish the task, stepping ahead and turning a spin, his scimitar coming straight across at neck level as he completed the pirouette.

The sagoth fell, clutching its gurgling, wheezing neck, trying vainly to hold in its spouting lifeblood.

Hadab looked to Paulvitch, the man's forearms still bulging, though the choked sagoth was no longer moving.

"Come along," Hadab instructed.

Paulvitch dropped the lifeless humanoid to the stone, retrieved one of the gun-barrel clubs and ran off after the Arab.

It was good to be out of the sulfur-smelling tunnels, good to see the sun again—even if that sun was the red-glowing ball of Pellucidar. But even with the welcome sensations that came of being outside, it was difficult for Rokoff to feel relieved, hanging as he was from the storklike legs of the mahar queen.

Mora had come out of the tunnels at full speed, her great

wings carrying her and Rokoff high into the air. She did a quick bank, then a short stoop, finally dropping the man unceremoniously to the sand.

Rokoff rolled to a sitting position and looked up to regard the magnificent, horrifying mahar in her winged form. He didn't know what she meant to do then. Had she rescued him from potential harm in the tunnels, or had she stolen him away to feast on him, to punish him for leading dangerous intruders into her domain?

"Where is it?" she demanded in a voice edged with birdlike shrieks.

"What do you speak of?" Rokoff responded, knowing that to show any weakness or disobedience now would surely mean the end of his life.

"The portal!" Mora crowed. "Your intrusion here has cost me greatly. You have brought weapons that have wounded my sisters, and new enemies for the mahars."

"It is Tarzan," Rokoff tried to explain, "and a man I do not know. I didn't bring them—"

"Silence!" Mora hissed, and she rose up tall and terrible, her winged form outlined by the red glow of Pellucidar's sun behind her. "You opened the portal for them, and with them on the ledge was a female Zorham. You, Rokoff, have brought trouble to the mahars. You can guess the penalty for that!"

Rokoff lifted an arm to shield his face from the horrid creature, though he realized that he could offer little resistance against the power of Mora. He stuttered through the beginnings of a dozen futile arguments, waiting, waiting, for the death blow to fall.

It never came. Finally Rokoff calmed and looked long and hard at Mora.

"Your intrusion into Pellucidar has cost me," she said calmly. "Now you will show me how I can regain that which I have lost."

"Anything."

"The portal," Mora said. "You will take me to the portal, and through the portal, to this world of bounty that you promised to me."

"Follow the wind," Rokoff explained. "The gemstone you wear is linked to the pylon of gold. The wind is the connecting force between them. It ends in a vortex at the spot where Tikka first found us, and there, too, is the portal to my world."

Mora paused and closed her fiery eyes, shifting her head from side to side, feeling the flow of the air. Then, so suddenly that she startled Rokoff and caused him to cry out, she jumped away, snatching the sitting man by the shoulders with her great claws, and off they went, up into the air once more.

Helpless, Rokoff did not know if this was the beginning of an even greater adventure, or an end of the last one he would ever know.

Tarzan fitted another arrow to his bowstring, just in time, for another mahar had come into the chamber, swooping immediately for the ledge. Tarzan leveled the bow and fired, scoring a hit. The mahar did not drop, but it was slowed enough for Tarzan to scramble through the tunnel entrance behind his two friends. A short distance inside, where the tunnel widened somewhat, the three turned back to regard the mahar Tarzan had shot. The mounting volume of the shrieking in the background told them that more of the horrid creatures were entering the slave chamber, and also that the prisoners would not get out alive.

"It cannot get into the tunnel," Jana observed. It was true enough, with its sizable wings, the creature couldn't begin to get through the narrow opening.

"Then run on," Tarzan instructed, and truly it was a difficult command for the compassionate man to utter. The men in the chamber were his enemies, were dangerous for all the world, but it saddened Tarzan to think of their fate. He wanted to go to them, to give them a chance.

But it was impossible, he knew, and so he moved past his companions to take up the lead.

Jana grabbed him insistently, before he could get going, and he turned to look at her, their faces barely inches apart, their hearts pumping from the excitement of the battle and the escape.

"You are right," the Zorham woman said. "The mahars can be fought; they can be defeated." She pointed at Tarzan's bow. "That weapon killed one and hurt another."

"It did, and could again," Tarzan replied. "But you must have the will to fight."

"And the sense to run away," Joshua interjected, reminding them both that they weren't quite finished with this little adventure.

Tarzan nodded to him. "Right now we must stop Rokoff," he agreed. "And Queen Mora. We cannot let this creature get through the portal."

They started away again, exiting the tunnel and running along the steamy ledge, Tarzan leading at a swift pace. He came to the crumbled section where Jana had almost fallen and leaped it easily, then skidded to a stop and wheeled about to help his friends.

Jana was already on her way over, showing no fear at all in springing over the break. She landed lightly, with a couple of quick steps, and again she found herself right up against Tarzan.

"Clear the path!" came Joshua's call, stealing the moment before it ever could begin. The pair moved back a couple of steps, with Tarzan passing Jana, going back toward the ledge. Joshua came right over this time, before his sensibilities could argue. He pitched off balance as he landed, but Tarzan caught him and steadied him, and soon the three were running on.

"Oh, shut up!" Joshua said into one crevice, hearing again the shuffling of some unseen creature. He no longer had his spear, and no longer had the time to even worry about the potentially troublesome thing, so he just put his head down and sprinted past it, working hard to keep up with the others. He wasn't the only one relieved when they came through the last crack and stepped out into the Pellucidar daylight.

Tarzan stood stock-still, sniffing the air, trying to get some gauge on Mora and Rokoff, though he knew well enough where they were heading.

Jana, though, was more animated, glancing around, her expression fast souring.

"I am not surprised that Turro did not wait for us," she explained, responding to Joshua's quizzical look.

There was no time for further talk; Tarzan started off at a dead run.

"Here we go again," Joshua complained, falling in line behind Jana, and finding that the Zorham woman was as hard to keep up with as was his agile friend.

CHAPTER 17

The strange world of Pellucidar whipped past far below Nikolas Rokoff. He saw gigantic animals grazing, their long necks easily lifting their heads to steal the leaves from the tops of tall trees. Far in the distance he spotted a cluster of thatch huts and sheltered caves. And all the while Mora's powerful claws dug painfully into his shoulders.

The undignified trip ended quickly for Rokoff, with Mora swooping low over the spot where he and his companions had battled Tikka. Without the slightest warning the mahar dropped him hard to the ground, his momentum tumbling him along. He managed to roll to a sitting position just as the mahar queen landed beside him. Then Rokoff watched, in sheer incredulity, as the creature transformed once more, becoming again the beautiful raven-haired, tattooed woman.

Mora closed her eyes and focused her thoughts on the feel of the breeze. It was swirling here, and she found it hard to locate its directional source. "Does the wind lead us to the portal?" she asked.

"Maybe," Rokoff stammered, surprised that she had spoken. "Yes," he decided. "I believe that it does."

Mora held up the red gemstone, staring at it, rubbing her fingers delicately against its perfectly cut sides. Then she looked past it, to a pair of trees a short distance away. Their branches, she noted, were moving strangely, in an almost circular pattern, more as if they were caught in a vortex than in a strong breeze. She grabbed Rokoff by the arm and began pulling him in that direction. "I must see this other world you call Russia," she said.

Rokoff knew better than to resist her pull, or even to question her decision, though it seemed to him that they had business to take care of in this world before they even thought of going through the portal. If Mora was underestimating Tarzan, then she was making a tremendous mistake, the Russian now knew.

A few steps on, Rokoff, too, noted the weird movement of the branches, and he remembered falling between those trees on his arrival.

"This must be it," Mora reasoned, reaching the spot directly below the swirl. To confirm her theory, she grabbed Rokoff by the collar and lifted him straight up into the air.

Rokoff protested, but Mora ignored him, lifting him higher, higher. Then, feeling the tug of the grabbing wind, she heaved him upward and let go.

Rokoff continued his ascent for a brief moment, and then he was flying—or falling; he couldn't tell which—along the strange, multicolored, starlit tunnel. He rolled and bounced along, out of control, with nothing to hold on to, and then, suddenly, he came out of the pylon, as if it had regurgitated him, skidding to a stop on his butt on the stone floor of the Temple of the Ancients.

He was up in a second, running for cover behind a pillar, looking back at the pylon all the while, waiting and watching to see if Mora would come through, if the portal would accept her. For the first time Rokoff wondered if bringing the mahar to his world would truly benefit him. Or if he would end up a meal. He had followed events as they had led him, somewhat blindly, he realized now, standing, shaking, in an ancient temple in the middle of a hostile jungle and waiting to be joined by a creature as horrid and purely evil as anything he had ever imagined.

A few more seconds slipped by. Rokoff began to hope that Mora had changed her mind, or that the magical tunnel would not transport a mahar, or would, perhaps, deposit her somewhere else, on some other world.

The thought was fleeting, though, replaced by that nagging lust for power. Once again Rokoff began to imagine the potential of joining forces with Mora and her brutal servants. What gains could he discover through exploitation of their mind-bending powers? His smile was back in full when the mahar queen stepped casually through the pylon, into the room.

"This is Russia?" she asked, her gaze going straight to Rokoff.

"This is Africa," he replied, beaming, all his fear washing away under the lure of visions of power. "One conquest at a time."

———

Tarzan came out of the jungle first, charging into the clearing that surrounded the portal area. He skidded to an abrupt stop, his eyes darting all about, his nose sniffing the air. Mora had passed this way, he knew, and recently. He knew, too, that she was gone now, that her scent spoor ended abruptly and did not lead any farther, and he could guess easily enough what that might mean.

He put the wind at his back, then, and let it guide him to the two swirling trees. There he bent low and studied the tracks, Rokoff's and Mora's, with the mahar in both her winged and humanoid form. All the tracks ended abruptly, right at the base of the trees, and Tarzan tilted his head up.

"Tarzan, wait!" came the call from behind, and he turned to see Jana, and then Joshua, exiting the dense foliage, running full speed to join him.

He stood to greet them, held his hand out to stop Jana. "You'll have to stay here," he explained. "Joshua and I will deal with Mora and Rokoff."

"No," the woman stammered, her expression appearing as if Tarzan had just slapped her across the face. "I'll go with you."

"You can't," Tarzan said. He understood Jana, her fierce pride, her deep desire to fight against Mora, to do the right thing, and, knowing how he would feel if he was in her place, he tried to be as sympathetic as possible. "The world on the other side of the portal is not yours, as this one is not mine. You cannot live there. You cannot even go there for a short time."

"Yet you came here," Jana argued.

"Only out of necessity," Tarzan replied. "I would not

casually visit Pellucidar, nor can I allow you, or any other Zorham, to go to my world."

"You can go," Jana retorted suddenly. "He can," she added, indicating Joshua. "I can also. There's nothing I can't do."

"You must listen to him," Joshua pleaded with her. "Tarzan is right. This is your home, and, unless I miss my guess, you have much to accomplish here."

She was about to argue that point as well, but the last part of Joshua's statement gave Jana pause.

"I know what it is to live in a place where you do not belong," Tarzan said. "You must stay here, with Turro and your people. You must . . ." He paused and considered Jana for a long, long time, then handed her his bow and quiver.

"What?" She balked, taken by complete surprise.

"Take it," Tarzan said to her. "You must teach the other Zorham warriors to use it and to make others like it. They must learn how to defend themselves against the mahars."

"You can help make Pellucidar safe for your people," Joshua added.

"Turro and the others will never listen to me," Jana protested. "Especially not Turro. He thinks I am his woman, and because I am a woman, he thinks I am something inferior."

"We both know better," Tarzan offered.

"Turro will never learn," Jana muttered.

"I think they will listen to you," Tarzan said, his face serious as he moved to stand right in front of her. "You will make them listen." He brought his hand up to gently stroke her soft cheek.

"I know you, Jana of the Zorham," he went on. "I know

your spirit and I know your heart. And so do your people, even Turro, though he tried to deny it with his foolish statements. You take this bow and you lead. They will follow."

"I wish I could stay with you," Jana said, her voice barely a whisper. "If I don't, if I let you go now into that portal, I will never see you again."

"You will," Tarzan said with obvious conviction. He didn't know what logic led his subconscious to that conclusion, but he believed it with all his heart. He would see Jana again; somehow, some way, he would return to Pellucidar. He took her by the shoulders and squared her to him. "You will see me again," he said, "but for now, I must deal with Mora and Rokoff and close the portal. Our two worlds cannot be mixed together."

Tarzan turned and looked up to the swirling branches, but Jana pulled him back around, and before he could ask her anything, she moved right up to him and locked him in a passionate kiss. Their lips lingered together for a long, long time, and then Tarzan pulled away from her, sliding back to arm's length, putting one hand up to gently stroke that beautiful face again.

"You will see me again," he said determinedly, and then he spun away from her and leaped up, intending to grab one of the lower branches.

The vortex caught him instead, lifting him, lifting him, until he disappeared into the portal.

Joshua moved beside Jana. "I never was a good jumper," he remarked with a smirk.

"Then climb," Jana retorted, more harshly than she had intended.

Joshua took no offense. He put his hand on her shoulder.

"Farewell, Jana of the Zorham," he said sincerely. "And lead your people well."

Joshua turned his attention to the tree, and after a brief survey, began the climb.

Rokoff could see the hungry glow in her eyes, the delight of power, and it was infectious, truly intoxicating. Mora kept looking at the pylon, examining every golden brick, then turning back to him and making mewling noises. She was caught by the pylon, Rokoff knew. She was feeling its inner power, basking in the potential, as much as he had when he first came into this place. That was a good sign; as long as Mora remained a prisoner of her own ambitions, Nikolas Rokoff's chances of survival were much greater indeed.

"I much prefer this form to the other," the man said, moving near to her, his dark eyes flashing.

"Both have their advantages," Mora said coolly. She was in charge here; neither of them doubted that. She could play Rokoff any way she wanted. She could make of him an instrument of pleasure, she could make of him a meal, and for some reason that he could not understand, that continued to excite the Russian all the more.

"Yes, of course," he agreed. "But I much prefer this one."

"What is the meaning of this object and these other crystals?" Mora asked with a sly grin. She motioned to the three gems and the six-sided amulet still set in place on the front of the golden pylon.

"I don't know," Rokoff admitted. "You can see the place where the Crimson Eye—" He stopped talking as Mora began fingering the ruby, his words stolen by the sudden glow of the object. The blue stone set in the pylon began to glow, too, even brighter than the red, and Mora, as fascinated by the magnificent gems as Paulvitch had been, reached up her hand to grasp it.

"Perhaps you should not take it out," Rokoff stuttered. "The last time—" The Russian stopped abruptly as the magical gate began to swirl about, and then Tarzan stepped out of it, striding into the room, standing right in front of a startled Mora.

Jana stood before the trees, pondering the vortex that had taken Tarzan from her. She considered disobeying him and going through the portal. Who was he, after all, to tell her that she could not go?

But then she looked at the gift he had given her: the bow and arrows. She had seen this weapon take down a mahar, and even more importantly, it was a weapon that could strike hard from a distance, keeping any warrior out of the range of the mahars' deadly hypnotic powers.

What might that mean to her beleaguered people? she had to wonder. Even Turro might find some heart to fight against the mahars, knowing that he could hit them from a distance, from behind a barricade of rocks and logs, that he could kill them before they used their powers to render him docile.

No, Jana decided, she could not follow Tarzan. Not now. Now was the time for the Zorham. And what that man from another world had given to her, both through his example of courage and with the actual weapon, could dramatically alter the balance of power in Pellucidar. Jana gave a curt salute to the vortex, then started to turn.

Paulvitch grabbed her from behind and wrapped her in a tight bear hug, lifting her right from the ground.

Hadab came running by her then, searching frantically all about. He stopped before the trees, staring up and studying the curiously swirling branches, though he didn't understand their significance. He turned back to the squirming Jana almost immediately.

"Where have they gone?" Hadab demanded.

Jana made no move to answer, offered no sound except her growling protests against Paulvitch.

Hadab calmly walked over and backhanded Jana across the face, raising a welt beneath her eye. "I ask you only one more time," he threatened. "Where did they go?"

"Back to your world," Jana growled.

Hadab turned away from her, moving back to his place at the base of the trees. "But how?" he asked, as much to himself as to Jana. Curious, he took a few more steps, going right under the lower boughs.

Jana saw her chance. She wriggled one arm free and managed to shift the bow to that hand.

"Ho ho!" Paulvitch roared happily, his fears stolen by the excitement of capturing the beautiful woman. "This one has some fight!"

Paulvitch's expression changed dramatically when Jana drove the tip of Tarzan's bow down and to the side, right into his groin. The fat man howled and let go with one hand, clutching at his wounded crotch, and Jana was quick to pull away from him. She turned into a sudden spin, taking up the bow at one end in both hands and smacking it across the fat man's face.

Then she turned, meaning to flee, but kept the presence of mind to pause long enough to scoop up the quiver.

"Get her!" Paulvitch managed to stammer as he went down hard to the ground. "She must tell us where the portal is!"

Hadab was off in a flash, leaping over the prone Russian, following Jana headlong into the jungle.

On she ran for her life, sprinting past trees, leaping stones and brush, and trying desperately to keep a steady hold on both bow and quiver. To lose either would be disastrous, would be to throw away all the possibilities that Tarzan had shown to her.

He caught her off guard, his momentum forcing her to fall back, away from the pylon. Mora kept the presence of mind to hold firm to the blue gem, though, and it went with her, sliding easily out of its deep setting within the pylon. She scrambled away from Tarzan, stumbling over the lowest couple of steps along the staircase that led to the balcony. She caught her balance finally, three steps up, and stood tall, glaring back at the man who opposed her.

Out of the pylon behind Tarzan came Joshua Mugambi. He paused for a moment, considering Mora and Rokoff. "The odds seem a bit more even this time," he remarked, standing tall beside Tarzan.

Rokoff glanced about nervously, looking for an escape route. Mora held her ground.

"You humans are very stupid," she said. "Do you really think that you can defeat Mora, Queen of the Mahars?"

Tarzan's stern expression did not soften; he did not flinch in the least as he came forward a long stride, quickly halving the distance between him and the mahar. "You must return to Pellucidar," he said. "I offer no judgment against you, except to declare that you do not belong in this world and cannot remain here."

Mora's laughter was half an insane bellow and half the excited shriek of a hunting bird. It reached a fevered pitch, and so, too, did the glowing power of the gemstone she clenched in one hand. So bright was the blue radiance that Tarzan could see the shadow of the bones in the hand that clutched it, and Mora's eyes, too, were glowing the same unearthly color.

Tarzan started to advance once more, then, not knowing what to make of the tingling energy he felt all about him, he hesitated.

Twin beams of pure energy shot out from Mora's eyes.

Jana stumbled and tripped over a fallen branch. She was up almost immediately, nervously glancing back to see if the one-eyed man was again hot on her trail.

She was surprised, indeed, when she was grabbed again, roughly by the shoulder, for she thought that she had left Hadab farther back.

Jana twisted and squirmed, pulling away enough to pivot on one foot, then coming back around with a slicing chop aimed for her assailant's throat.

"Jana!" the man cried, blocking the blow with an upraised forearm.

"Turro?" she gasped.

"Why are you following the strangers?" Turro retorted angrily. "They will bring nothing to us but death. Already the mahars are out of their caverns and up in the air, angered by . . ." He straightened and let his accusing glare fall over her. "By what, Jana?" he finished.

Jana let the accusation fall aside like rain sliding off her shoulders. She had not the time nor the inclination to argue with Turro now. He grabbed her again and started to press the point, but a noise from the jungle caught his attention.

On came Hadab, tearing through the brush a short distance away with his scimitar, slashing through plants and maneuvering the deadly weapon expertly, in swift, fluid blows.

"We must run!" Turro cried, easily discerning that he was overmatched by the skilled Arab warrior. He took Jana by the arm and started away.

Jana pulled free of his grasp. "No!" she said so forcefully that Turro straightened, staring at her wide-eyed and slack-jawed.

"Always you cry out for us to run," Jana continued. "No more!" She pulled an arrow from the quiver and set it to the bowstring, as she had seen Tarzan do back in the mahar cave. The fit was far from steady, the arrow dropping off over her leading hand more than once, and Jana grew nervous with the realization that she had no real idea of what she was doing.

And Hadab was getting closer, slashing away at the brush, stalking in confidently, smiling at her pitiful attempts with the unfamiliar weapon.

"Jana, run!" Turro yelled, and he scrambled away a couple of steps.

Jana held her ground and forced her trembling hands to hold steady. She started to pull back on the bowstring, but was surprised by its resistance. Stubborn to the end, Jana gritted her teeth and growled, and pulled with all her strength, bending the bow.

"You will only get one shot," the ever-confident Hadab said. "Can you kill a man? Do you have the heart?"

His last word came out as a stunned gasp as Jana's arrow burrowed deep into his chest. Hadab stood perfectly still for a long moment, staring at the arrow, at his lifeblood staining his shirt about it. The scimitar fell from his hand and he reached up to clench the quivering shaft.

He looked back to Jana in disbelief.

Then he fell dead.

"I run no more," Jana declared grimly.

Paulvitch, who had witnessed the killing from farther back in the jungle, out of sight of the two Zorham, believed her. He turned around and scrambled away, running with all speed for the trees, where he suspected he'd find the portal that would take him, mercifully, back to his own world.

"We must make these," Jana said to Turro, presenting the bow before her. "With them, we can fight the mahars."

"We cannot fight—"

"We can!" Jana interrupted. "I saw it. Tarzan killed one mahar with this weapon and wounded another. Find some courage, Turro," she scolded. "Do not wait like a frightened rabbit for the mahars to come and eat you." Her blue eyes narrowed as she finished. "As they ate our parents."

Turro swallowed hard, surprised by the cruel reminder. For several years he and Jana had waged this verbal battle. On all of the previous occasions, though, Jana's point was moot, her argument had no true bite, for the Zorham possessed no weapons with which they could back up Jana's desire to fight the mahars, even if they had come around to her way of thinking. Now she had such a weapon—a most effective one, Turro had to admit.

"No more running," she said through gritted teeth. She turned her back on Turro and walked away.

Turro waited a while longer, looked from Jana's back to the dead human. It was a tough moment, one that pitted his pride against his hope. Jana wasn't going to listen to him, and maybe, he had to admit, just maybe, she was right.

The Zorham man nodded and followed her.

CHAPTER 18

Like the mongoose dodging a striking snake, Tarzan leaped aside, dipping his shoulder as he went down to the hard floor and rolling right back over to easily regain his footing. Mora's twin beams hit the pylon, spreading harmlessly into waves of rolling blue.

Tarzan ran into the alcove at the right side of the stairs, out of the mahar's line of sight. He went straight to the back wall and leaped high, feet scraping the stone, carrying him to the railing.

Joshua charged out the other way, to the left of the stairs, where Rokoff stood to meet him. The Russian struck what seemed to Joshua to be a ridiculous pose. His feet were spaced well for balance, one in front of the other, but his arms were up stiffly, fists clenched tight and tilted back in toward him. Joshua recognized the boxer's stance, but noticing that Mora was now turning her attention to him, the Waziri would have none of that. He let out a yell, ducked his shoulder, and barreled into Rokoff, bearing both men to the floor.

The blue beams cut across the back of Joshua's leg as he dove, slicing a clean line through the back of his pants, and through several layers of skin, as well. The beams continued on into the stone wall, burrowing deeply.

With Joshua and Rokoff falling out of sight behind that side of the stairs, Mora snapped her glance back the other way, to see Tarzan scrambling up over the low railing to the balcony. Her mystically charged energy beams fired yet again, shattering the stone at Tarzan's heels.

He avoided the blow, though, somersaulting in midair and landing right into a run along the balcony. He hooked his arm on the corner post of the stairs, his headlong momentum spinning him about and sending him down the stairs, bearing down on the mahar. He hit Mora full speed, but, with her incredible, superhuman strength, she didn't give an inch. Her arms wrapped about Tarzan and, with a growl like that of an angry lioness, she tossed him the rest of the way down the stairs, toward the pylon.

Again, only Tarzan's great agility and balance kept him from serious injury, or from hurtling right back through the portal. He rolled over once, then again, down the stairs, coming to his feet at the bottom and cutting a sharp turn back toward the right-hand alcove.

Mora's eyes fired repeatedly, snapping off pieces of stone at Tarzan's heels.

Rokoff managed to squirm away and get back to his feet, squaring off against Joshua once more, and striking the Marcus of Queensbury pose again. Joshua came on, more tentatively, and Rokoff snapped off a couple of quick jabs, straightening the man, staggering him back a couple of steps.

"I assure you that I am an excellent boxer," Rokoff boasted.

"And I used to hunt leopards!" Joshua retorted, and on he came. He started up high, then dipped low, bracing his shoulder against Rokoff's midsection and carrying the man along, slamming him into the wall.

Mora's next blast of blue energy thundered in right above them, knocking them both flat and opening a wide crack along the stone wall.

Tarzan was back up on the balcony by now. He ran to the far wall, moving beside the tunnel that had first brought him to this place. Deep in its recesses he could see the impaled Arab, rotting against the wall.

Tarzan had no intent of running down there, though. He grabbed for the many vines along the wall, testing each one as he pulled it free. Then, finding a suitable one, he carried it along, running to the top of the stairs. He never slowed, leaping high as he took up the vine in both hands, and it swung him in a roundabout arc.

Mora, growling in frustration about her latest miss, turned about and saw him at the last moment. She managed to get her hands up, but could not brace her feet properly, and when Tarzan came crashing in, feet first, her only defense was to go with the momentum, launching herself into a great sidelong leap. She lost her grip on the blue stone in the process, though, and it went flying to the floor at the base of the pylon.

Mora cleared the stairway's railing, touching down at the edge of the alcove. She couldn't possibly halt her momentum, though, and she tumbled on, slamming hard into a pillar, rebounding off it into the wall. Ironically, Mora's own powers now worked against her, for that side of the structure

---

had been weakened by the energy beams that she had shot over Joshua and Rokoff. The heavy pillar toppled over her; a section of the ceiling and the wall followed it down, burying Mora beneath a ton of stone.

Tarzan turned his attention to Joshua and Rokoff, who were up again, the Russian landing another solid jab to Joshua's face. Tarzan started to the side of the stairs, thinking to leap atop Rokoff. He stopped before he even got to the railing, though, for his attention was stolen away as the pile of rubble atop Mora began to shift.

Low, feral growls came from beneath it. One stone slab fell away, then another was shifted to the side. And then Mora, her muscled legs firmly planted under her, began to rise. She no longer appeared human, her face twisted and gray, caught somewhere between her two forms. Her teeth, so white and perfect in humanoid form, now were yellow and elongated, and her mouth widened gruesomely to accommodate the sharp rows. Blobs of drool fell down her chin and matted her black hair to the side of her jowls.

Her growling voice was no longer human, either; it was purely feral, purely savage. With one powerful arm she shoved the pillar up and over. Then, before Tarzan could even register the sudden move, she sprang out, fully twenty feet, turning a complete somersault in midair to reorient her balance, landing in a short run that knocked Tarzan back and to the floor.

Mora was on top of him in a second, her long fingers grasping for his throat.

Tarzan rolled her over and wriggled free enough to stand, but Mora, her strong hands not letting go, came right up with him, thumbs pressing hard, cutting off his air supply.

Now it was Tarzan's turn to find that inner strength, that animalistic surge of power. He hooked Mora's thumbs and pulled hard, growling fiercely.

So was Mora, resisting the pull, pressing inexoribly on.

But Tarzan was up higher on the stairs, and with the favorable angle, he slowly, slowly forced her thumbs from his throat. Then he braced his heels against the stair and drove farther, pushing Mora's arms out and up high.

Mora's head snapped forward, slamming Tarzan in the face, staggering him. He backpedaled wildly, but could not hold his balance and went down hard against the stairs.

Mora lifted her arms high and wide in a victory pose.

But Tarzan wasn't finished. He spread his legs wide and dipped his head between his knees, rolling back toward Mora, back down the stairs. As his legs came over, he put them together and kicked out fiercely, connecting solidly against her belly and throwing her back down to the floor of the chamber.

Tarzan was too dazed to pursue, but he managed to get back to his feet and scramble up the stairs, trying to put some ground between himself and the mahar.

Mora was took quick for that, leaping up and over Tarzan, spinning about in midair to land facing him. She chopped him with an open hand across the chest, then backhanded him as he attempted to grab her. Mora's left hand sliced into Tarzan's side, doubling him over. Her right forearm came straight out, pounding his chest, blowing the breath from his lungs.

He somehow managed to keep his footing, backing desperately down the stairs.

Mora shrieked and charged at him.

Tarzan spun out to the side, his elbow flying high as he came around, smacking Mora on the back of the head as she rushed past him. The jungle lord headed back up the stairs, leaping half of them with a single bound. He heard the growling, though, heard the stubborn pursuit, and knew that he couldn't get away. He turned about to meet Mora's charge.

Rokoff continued his attempt to box against Joshua, but the nimble Waziri kept putting himself inside the blows, kept wrapping himself about Rokoff's snapping arms, stealing the man's power. They went through the dance for more than a minute, punching, grabbing, ducking, twisting, until Joshua finally found some leverage, slipping under Rokoff's lurching right cross and coming up behind the man's shoulder.

"Is this in your precious Queensbury rules?" Joshua asked, and he twisted and shoved with all his strength, slamming Rokoff face first into the stone wall.

The Russian groaned and slumped.

"I didn't think so," Joshua commented answering his own question. He pulled Rokoff back up straight and slammed him into the stone again. Then he turned the dazed man about to face him and drove his forehead hard into Rokoff's nose.

Mora went up the stairs wildly, ducking her head, trying to run Tarzan down.

Tarzan leaped back, but bent his body forward as she came in, putting himself right over her back and preventing any solid contact. Then, wrapping his arms about Mora's torso and holding on with all his strength, he jumped out and rolled right over her, planting his feet on a lower stair and coming up straight in a powerful movement, his strong arms hauling Mora right up over his head.

She thrashed wildly, kicking her feet, slapping with her arms, but Tarzan held on. He took a running stride down the stair and threw her toward the portal, thinking that he was finally done with her.

The mahar queen contorted weirdly, twisting and turning, and landed on her feet right at the portal, facing the opening, throwing her arms up high and wide to brace herself against falling in.

"You cannot defeat me!" she roared, spinning about to meet Tarzan's charge.

He managed to tear the red stone from around her neck, but she hit him again with a rapid series of stunning blows that had him reeling and running.

Mora pushed off to pursue, but Tarzan surprised her, for when he hit the bottom step, he pivoted about and came right back at her, leaping high into a double kick that slammed against Mora's chest and propelled her straight back. This time Mora could not turn quickly enough, could not throw her arms up to brace against the solid parts of the pylon. She thrashed and grabbed frantically, but she was grasping at liquid, and with a final shriek she was gone, back through the winding tunnel, back to Pellucidar.

She changed again as she tumbled along the colorful gate, shoulders widening and sprouting wings, morphing into her more natural mahar form. She came out of the gate sooner than she had hoped, though, and only halfway through her transformation. Her wings weren't yet complete and could not support her, so Mora, Queen of the Mahars, tumbled unceremoniously through the branches of the two trees to land heavily on the ground.

Dazed and hurt, she was in no condition to immediately turn back for another fight, and so she limped away, into the cover of the brush, and tried to concentrate so she could complete her transformation. Then she would go back to Africa, she decided, in all her terrible splendor, in this superior form that the foolish Tarzan could not hope to defeat.

Not so far away, Alexis Paulvitch crouched behind some bushes, trembling with fear. He could not know what was happening on the other side of the gate, but considering Mora's appearance, he guessed that all was not well.

He would try for the gate anyway, he decided, and take his chances in his own world, in a place where he understood the rules. But not right away. Not until wicked Mora was long gone.

Tarzan glanced to the side and saw that his friend finally had Rokoff fully under control. Tarzan went for the blue stone instead, the gem lying on the floor just to the far side of the pylon.

Joshua had Rokoff's arm bent back behind him and he used it to guide the man along, lifting it so that his prisoner squealed with pain whenever the Russian resisted. They came around the bottom corner of the stairs, Joshua dragging the man unmistakably toward the still open portal.

"I never said I was a gentleman," Joshua said in Rokoff's ear. "I don't play by your silly rules."

"Don't be foolish," Rokoff pleaded, guessing Joshua's intent. "I can make you rich and powerful."

"I already have what I need," Joshua replied.

"You're a fool!"

"That, too," Joshua conceded.

Rokoff was right in front of the portal then, his face panic-stricken. Behind him and his captor, Tarzan had recovered the blue stone and turned back toward the pylon—and was surprised indeed to witness his Waziri friend's actions.

"Let me go!" Rokoff begged. "I promise you will never be a slave again."

"I never was."

"Joshua, no!" Tarzan yelled, scrambling toward the pair.

"I can make you a king!" Rokoff cried.

"I already am!" Joshua retorted. And with that he shoved Rokoff forward, into the portal.

Tarzan skidded past Joshua, plunging his hand into the pylon, reaching, straining to grab Rokoff. He felt as though he had something solid, and pulled with all his strength. The muscles on his arm corded with strain; he growled past the pain and tried desperately to hold on.

But whether it was Rokoff he held or not, he would never know, for the solid object became insubstantial and soon Tarzan was holding nothing at all. He pulled his hand from the portal and fell back, dropping an accusing stare over Joshua.

The Waziri shrugged. "Every man has a right to be with the woman he loves," he explained. "They'll be happy together." Joshua gave a dramatic pause, and Tarzan had come to know him well enough to stay patient and let him finish. "Until she gets hungry," Joshua said with a smirk.

"Then it's done," Tarzan agreed, and he lifted the blue

stone into the liquidlike section of the pylon, putting it back into its place. Then he tore the Crimson Eye from the impromptu setting the mahars had given it and replaced it, too.

The wind died away instantly. The swirling liquid center of the pylon shifted to its golden hue and solidified. Then all of the pylon seemed to go quiet. No longer did the obelisk's tingling energy permeate the air, no longer did it thrum with power or glow with its inner light. Now the structure seemed no more than a fabulous pillar of gold, set with a six-sided crystal and four gemstones.

"Then it's done," Joshua agreed.

Paulvitch was at the base of the twin trees when Rokoff tumbled down upon him, sending both men falling to the ground.

"Nikolas!" Paulvitch cried. "What are we to do?"

"Shut up, you idiot," Rokoff retorted. He cradled the arm Joshua had bent, wondering if it was broken, then looked to the portal. If he went right back through the gate, he would have to face Joshua and Tarzan again, something he most certainly did not want to do. But both gemstones were on the other side, and if Tarzan figured out how to replace them, the portal would be closed to him, perhaps forever.

"Help me up," he said to Paulvitch, and when he was standing, still cradling the arm, he motioned for Paulvitch to lead the way. "Up and through the portal you go," the desperate Rokoff improvised. "You throw Tarzan and the other one back through, to Pellucidar, and I will join you in our own world. If we are quick and strong, we will still have the gold pylon and the powerful gems."

Paulvitch nodded eagerly, pleased by the prospect of battling men again, and even more so by the prospect of returning to his own world.

Before he could even start up the tree, though, the wind died away and the branches up above stopped shaking.

"What does this mean?" Paulvitch asked.

"He closed the portal," Rokoff yelled, throwing sand helplessly at the spot where the gate had been. "Damn you, Tarzan!"

"What are we to do?" Paulvitch wailed. "We must get back."

"We cannot!" Rokoff growled at him. For a moment Paulvitch thought that Rokoff would strike him, and for a moment Rokoff considered doing just that. But the man calmed quickly, remembering who he was, finding again the confidence that had carried him through all the desperate situations of his life.

"We cannot get back," Rokoff said more calmly. "We are stranded here, for now at least."

"Here?" Paulvitch groaned.

"Fear not," Rokoff said to him, brimming with confidence. "For we will find a place here, a rightful place for the son of Russia's tsar."

"Indeed," came a strange, resonating voice, a statement that seemed more a thought in the heads of the two men than an actual word. Together they turned and looked up, to see Mora, her transformation to her horrid mahar form complete. She was perched on a branch in a tree across the small clearing.

She shrieked and swooped; Paulvitch screamed and fell to the ground.

———

The humming was gone, the glow was no more. For all appearances, the pylon was a simple structure again, fabulous as it was, and no longer a magical gate. Tarzan and Joshua stood before it, staring at it for a long while.

"I think we should get out of here before this thing does anything else," Joshua remarked.

"Yes, we should go," Tarzan agreed, though he believed his task completed. The portal was closed; there was no further danger here. "Let us leave and speak nothing of this place; let it be unknown to the world. Its power is too great for us to comprehend."

Together Joshua and Tarzan turned for the stairs, only to find a circle of glowing light on the floor before them.

"I was afraid of that," Joshua said dryly.

An image took shape within the circle, a semitransparent likeness of the old man. "Your quest is unfinished," he said to Tarzan, his voice echoing off the stone walls.

"I have returned the stones," Tarzan protested. "The portal is closed and my world is safe."

"For now," the old man answered.

"I don't know what you want of me," Tarzan said to him. "Am I to stand guard here for eternity?"

The old man gave a chuckle. "No, Tarzan, not that."

"Then what?"

"It is what you want for yourself that matters," the old man said.

"You are talking in riddles," Tarzan argued. "What is this quest you speak of?"

"The longing for adventure," the old man replied. "The need to see other worlds and face greater enemies."

"What enemies?" Tarzan demanded.

The old man chuckled again.

"Tell me of my quest," Tarzan said. "How will I know when it is finished?"

Again the laugh. "You will know, Tarzan," the old man said. "You will know." And with that the old man faded from sight, and the circle of light faded behind him. The room grew bright, though, as the pylon suddenly flared to brilliance.

But only for a moment. It, too, went quiet and cold, leaving Joshua and Tarzan alone in the ancient temple.

"I have enjoyed our friendship," Joshua said to Tarzan, "but perhaps it is time for us to take different roads."

Tarzan considered the smile on his friend's face. "Of course," he agreed. "You will have no trouble getting past the temple's serpent guardian."

Joshua blanched and it was Tarzan's turn to laugh.

"Different roads," Joshua said quickly. "But our path does not fork just yet."

Tarzan started up the stairs. "Fear not, my friend," he said. "I have a way with animals."

"I think I liked you better before you learned to tell a joke," Joshua remarked, falling into step behind him.

When he got to the tunnel leading out of the temple, Tarzan motioned for Joshua to lead. And then he turned back to stare at the pylon, to consider the old man's words. What other worlds waited for him? he wondered. What greater enemies? Would his life become a series of challenges, each one more difficult than the previous?

Tarzan smiled and started into the tunnel, ready to accept whatever the fates had in store for him.

EPILOGUE

From his perch on a high branch Tarzan smiled widely as he saw his Waziri friend walk into the clearing below. He hadn't seen Joshua Mugambi for almost two months, though he had heard word, through his Kikuyu friends and the songs of the jungle drums, that the man was doing well.

After their adventure in Pellucidar, Tarzan had accompanied Joshua to his Waziri kinsmen. The mere presence of Tarzan, who was known and respected among all the tribes of the region, had helped Joshua's cause, had helped the Waziri peacefully and rationally solve any potential conflicts of succession.

So it was that Joshua Mugambi, Oxford scholar, was now Chief of the Waziri.

He looked the part, Tarzan thought, peering down at him. Gone were his European clothes and his European gait, Tarzan noted. The man was walking toe-heel now, like a hunter, and not heel-toe. Also gone was that hint of a belly, and all of Joshua's body seemed harder, better balanced and better muscled.

"Could I have expected to find Jean Tarzan anywhere but up a tree?" Joshua asked, his voice still edged with a British accent—though now that accent seemed even more out of place.

Tarzan silently applauded his friend's heightened sensibilities. The Joshua Mugambi who had first gone into the jungle with him would never have spotted him high in the tree.

Tarzan grabbed a vine and swung down, coming to a running stop right before his onetime companion. He looked Joshua up and down, the skirt-loincloth, the loose-fitting and colorful vest, the remnants of the paint he had worn at a recent celebration. "You are Waziri," he said.

"Somebody had to do it," Joshua replied. "Seen any big snakes lately?"

"None as big as the one Joshua Mugambi stared down."

That brought a chuckle from Joshua, and the chief of the Waziri blushed a bit when he recalled the incident, when he remembered just how close he had been to peeing in his pants.

"What news, then?" Tarzan asked, for it was Joshua who had initiated this meeting, sending word to him through the telling beats of the tribal drummers. The call of those drums had been insistent, indicating that this was to be more than a friendly reunion. Also, the location, on the very edge of the jungle, made Tarzan wary.

Joshua shrugged, unsure. "I have been informed by a contact in the city that you are needed there," he replied. "I do not know the reason."

"Achmet Zek?" Tarzan asked.

"I don't think so," Joshua answered, shaking his head. "I

hear that Zek never recovered from the disaster of the Temple of the Ancients. Apparently he had made certain promises to warlords more powerful even than he, and when he could not deliver on those promises . . ."

"He is dead?"

Joshua shrugged once more. "We can only hope," he replied. "Achmet Zek has not been very visible of late; his name is hardly spoken among the people of the city, and when it is, it is no longer whispered with reverence and fear. Even if Zek is alive, I doubt that he has any desire to tangle with Jean Tarzan again anytime soon."

Tarzan looked over his shoulder, across the tall grasses in the direction of the great city. "Then why?" he mumbled, more to himself than to Joshua.

"Let us go and see," Joshua said. "I know where we are wanted, and expected, tomorrow morning. If we move swiftly—and does Tarzan move any other way?—we can get there easily enough."

Tarzan looked at him long and hard. "I can go alone," he offered. "It would not be fitting for a Waziri chief to walk into potential danger that does not affect his tribe."

"But it would not be fitting for a friend to let another go alone," Joshua was quick to reply. "Don't argue with me. I've followed you to worse places."

Tarzan had no answer for that, and so they started off across the grassy fields.

The trek was easy and lighthearted at first, the two catching up on events of the last eight weeks. All casual chatter stopped when they neared the city, though, both of them tuning their senses outward, looking for any hints of danger.

"We appear out of place," Joshua remarked, indicating

both his and Tarzan's lack of clothing. Joshua motioned to a small hut on the farthest outskirts and led Tarzan into the yard, to an old woman tending a small garden.

Joshua winked at Tarzan and held up a pouch of coins. "Privilege of royalty," he said, and after a short discussion with the old woman, the two men walked away from the hut wearing robes more commonly seen in the city.

The streets were loud and boisterous, full of vendors and buyers, all bargaining loudly with the exuberance that no markets anywhere else in the world could match. Tarzan was no fan of cities, and he thought that the entire concept of pricing, of money in general, was a foolish thing, but he did enjoy watching the bargaining sessions, watching the excitement on the faces of those engaged. This was their survival battle, their fight for life and happiness.

He tried not to get distracted, reminding himself that Achmet Zek and his host of guards might be lurking about.

Joshua led the way down to the dock area of the city, to a large warehouse specified in the message he had received. He relaxed visibly when he came in sight of his contact, a tall and square-shouldered man of the Waziri tribe. Joshua didn't know him well, but he was confident that Waziri wouldn't betray Waziri.

"This is Jean Tarzan?" the man asked, coming up to the pair.

Tarzan nodded and extended his hand, but the man just turned and walked away, motioning for them to follow. Tarzan looked to Joshua, as though the snub was the Waziri chieftain's fault, but Joshua only shrugged and followed the man.

"A gift for you, Jean Tarzan," the man said when they had

come to the far end of the warehouse, to a fair-sized crate hidden behind walls of stacked boxes. Both Tarzan and Joshua stared at the crate curiously, for tied about it was the largest red ribbon either of them had ever seen.

Tarzan looked to the messenger, who nodded toward the crate and stepped back.

"Be careful," Joshua cautioned as Tarzan approached.

Tarzan hardly needed the reminder. He took a step, then paused and listened and sniffed the air, then took another quiet step, and again paused and sniffed.

Tarzan relaxed suddenly and looked back to Joshua, offering a wide smile. He walked easily the rest of the way to the crate and quickly pulled away the ribbon, then flipped a latch that let the front side of the container fall away.

The ensuing roar set Joshua back on his heels, but he recovered quickly and dared to move closer to get a better look at the caged cat, a great black leopard.

"The one from Marseilles?" Joshua asked.

Tarzan's smile left no doubt about that.

"For you," the messenger offered, moving over and handing Tarzan an envelope. His job completed, the man gave a curt bow to Tarzan, then to Joshua, then left them with their gift.

"From Paul D'Arnot, I would suppose," Joshua remarked as Tarzan tore open the envelope and unfolded the note.

"No," Tarzan replied, and he was as surprised by that fact as was his friend.

"Well, read it out loud," Joshua scolded after a long minute had slipped past, after a faraway, enchanted look came over Tarzan's face.

" 'Monsieur Tarzan,' " he began, " 'Paul told me of your

fondness for the leopard, and in truth, in looking at it, I, too, could not bear to see it placed in a zoo. Accept it, please, as a reward for rescuing me from that pig, Achmet Zek.' "

"Collette de Coude," Joshua reasoned.

Tarzan nodded.

"And what else does it say?" Joshua asked slyly. "It took you longer than that to read it the first time."

Tarzan only smiled and looked back at the leopard, and that was his mistake, for Joshua's reflexes had sharpened in his months back in the jungle. He moved like a striking snake, his biting hand snatching the note from Tarzan, and then he skittered away. His eyes widened as he considered the rest of the note and he read it out loud, in the mocking voice of a woman obviously swooning. " 'And accept it as a gift from my heart. My dear Monsieur Tarzan, I only wish I could repay you a thousand times for all that you have given to me. My very life, and not just by rescuing me from Achmet Zek. But by showing me that there are grander adventures than those found at the roulette wheel.' "

Joshua eyed Tarzan curiously. "Roulette?" he asked, and then he shook his head, deciding that the game and Tarzan simply did not fit together.

" 'Consider my invitation to Paris open-ended,' " Joshua read on. " 'Any time that you wish to visit, know that you will have a place to stay.' "

"Are you enjoying this?" Tarzan asked dryly.

"Not as much as you should be," Joshua replied. "But why is she inviting just you? I was part of that rescue."

"I have a way with—"

"Animals," Joshua interrupted. "You said you had a way with animals. You never said anything about women!"

Tarzan shrugged.

Joshua turned his attention back to the note, sniffing it deeply, trying to conjure an image of the beautiful Collette as he read the last of it. " 'P.S. As I suspect you will not visit me in Paris, you can expect that I will visit you in your jungle home.' " Joshua gave Tarzan a sly look.

"She will, too," the Waziri said.

Knowing Collette de Coude, that most spirited of women, Tarzan didn't doubt it for a moment. "Come," he bade his friend, "let us see to the transportation of this cage and the release of the leopard."

Late in the afternoon of the very next day, Tarzan and Joshua watched with the deepest satisfaction as the great cat stretched its muscles and disappeared into the jungle flora.

"Will you ever go back to France?" Joshua asked.

Tarzan started to shake his head, but caught himself and shrugged noncommittally instead. "Who can say?" he asked. "You heard the old man. I do not know where the winds of fate will take me."

"I can think of worse places than at the side of Collette de Coude," Joshua remarked.

Tarzan only smiled.

About the Author

A lifelong resident of Massachusetts, BOB SALVATORE began writing shortly after receiving his Bachelor of Science degree in Communications/Media from Fitchburg State College. He penned his first manuscript in 1982, in a spiral notebook, writing by candlelight while listening to Fleetwood Mac's *Tusk* album.

His first break came in 1987 when TSR, publisher of *Dungeons and Dragons*, offered him a contract based on a proposal for the *Forgotten Realms* shared-world setting. Bob's first published novel, *The Crystal Shard*, was released in February of 1988 and climbed to #2 on the Waldenbooks bestseller list.

In 1990 his third book, *The Halfling's Gem*, hit the *New York Times* bestseller list. With a contract for three more TSR books, and with his first novel and its sequel sold to Penguin, Bob quit his day job. He has now produced twenty-one novels, including five hardcovers.

Bob makes his home in central Massachusetts with his wife Diane and their three children. However, when he began the *Tarzan: The Epic Adventures* project, Bob knew he was in a different world indeed. One day, a large box arrived on his front porch, and when he picked it up, it screamed at him—the patented Tarzan jungle yodel ("And I still can't spell it," Salvatore complains). His publisher had sent him some of the new Trendmasters toys for the kids.

"I just hope they find the time to use them," he adds. Between hockey, dekhockey (which even Dad has started playing again), music lessons, Scouts, horseback riding, gymnastics, skiing, and figure skating, the Salvatore clan keeps more than a little busy. Bob also finds time to continue his writing. Currently he's about halfway through his second epic novel for a new series with Del Rey® Books. The first, *The Demon Awakens*, will be released late next spring.

DEL REY® ONLINE!

THE DEL REY INTERNET NEWSLETTER (DRIN)

The DRIN is a monthly electronic publication posted on the Internet, America Online, GEnie, CompuServe, BIX, various BBSs, our Web site, and the Panix gopher. It features:

- hype-free descriptions of new books
- a list of our upcoming books
- special announcements
- a signing/reading/convention-attendance schedule for Del Rey authors
- in-depth essays by sf professionals (authors, artists, designers, salespeople, and others)
- a question-and-answer section
- behind-the-scenes looks at sf publishing
- and much more!

INTERNET INFORMATION SOURCE

Del Rey information is now available on our Web site (http://www.randomhouse.com/delrey/) and on a gopher server—gopher.panix.com—including:

- the current and all back issues of the Del Rey Internet Newsletter
- a description of the DRIN and content summaries of all issues
- sample chapters of current and upcoming books— readable and downloadable for free
- submission requirements
- mail-order information

New DRINs, sample chapters, and other items·are added regularly.

ONLINE EDITORIAL PRESENCE

Many of the Del Rey editors are online—on the Internet, GEnie, CompuServe, America Online, and Delphi. There is a Del Rey topic on GEnie and a Del Rey Folder on America Online.

WHY?

We at Del Rey realize that the networks are the medium of the future. That's where you'll find us promoting our books, socializing with others in the sf field, and—most important—making contact and sharing information with sf readers.

FOR MORE INFORMATION

The official e-mail address for Del Rey Books is
delrey@randomhouse.com